USIA

LILL KNAPP

USIA

TATE PUBLISHING
AND ENTERPRISES, LLC

Published by Tate Publishing & Enterprises, LLC
127 E. Trade Center Terrace | Mustang, Oklahoma 73064 USA
1.888.361.9473 | www.tatepublishing.com

Tate Publishing is committed to excellence in the publishing industry. The company reflects the philosophy established by the founders, based on Psalm 68:11,
"The Lord gave the word and great was the company of those who published it."

Book design copyright © 2015 by Tate Publishing, LLC. All rights reserved.
Cover design by Roland Caballero
Interior design by Mary Jean Archival

Published in the United States of America

ISBN: 978-1-68142-641-9
1. Fiction / Action & Adventure
2. Fiction / Science Fiction / Action & Adventure
15.08.06

1

I DROVE SOUTH on Columbus Avenue, carefully exceeding the speed limit, heading toward the mall. Sunday morning traffic was sparse, so the going was easy. I flew around cars going much slower than me, emergency lights flashing, siren blaring on my way to back up an officer who had somebody running from him. I stopped at the traffic light to turn left into the mall parking lot, paused at the red light to make sure traffic was clear, and raced through the intersection, down the entrance way, and into the lot.

It was a typical Florida day, lots of sunshine, and already the mercury was heading north, promising another scorcher. Those of us wearing bulletproof vests (or what I affectionately called a self-baster) were dreading it again. The truth is, I'd rather die of heat exhaustion than freeze to death any given day, but heat, humidity, and the vest could sometimes make me want to change that opinion. In an age when everyone was concerned about bust size, there was reason to be concerned about personal shrinkage in this thing.

I saw Pete Willard's patrol car on the north side of the building. He was out of the vehicle, gun drawn on the guy. The guy, Cedric Hamm, seemed to be moving in slow motion down the length of a large, white work truck. Hamm was a regular in law enforcement circles. He was one of many who saw the local jail as having a revolving door. He wasn't too tall, but he was pretty stocky. Today he wore black jeans that were halfway down his hips and dragging on the ground, and his T-shirt, which I suspected used to be white, was now probably doing triple duty as night shirt as well as a napkin, judging from the many colors adorning it, as well as how threadbare and wrinkled it was.

Willard, on the other hand, was the poster child for law enforcement. He stayed in great shape. He was tall with dark hair and eyes and what some would call the prerequisite law enforcement mustache. Some of us suspected he pressed his T-shirts, briefs, and socks, and that at the end of a takedown, he would still have ash at the end of his cigarette (if he were to smoke), and not a hair would be out of place. Someone even postulated that perhaps he wasn't human, but more of a prototypical experiment in perfection.

Lest someone be concerned as to why Pete was drawn down on Cedric, the caution was justified. Cedric was known to carry a weapon. Any weapon. He wasn't picky about what he carried, as long as he knew he could hurt somebody with whatever he happened to be carrying. Typically he carried a firearm of some sort. So Cedric was looking down the business end of Pete's .45mm Glock until Pete could be sure of whether or not Cedric was armed.

"Coral Beach, I'm on scene," I said into the microphone. I stopped the car, jumped out, and ran to where Pete and Cedric were. Neither of them saw me; they were so involved in the scene they were playing out. Cedric was totally focused on the gun that was about six feet from his face. Willard had Cedric in his sights; it didn't even seem to register to him that I had arrived. I tackled Hamm from the side, taking him to the ground. Pete holstered his gun and joined me in wrestling Cedric's hands to his back, where we cuffed them.

I'd been out of the squad car for only a few minutes, and yet I was already sweating profusely. I could feel little rivulets of water making their way down my back and between what cleavage I had. My long, brown hair, caught up in a ponytail, was already damp around my face, and my clothing seemed to cling to my figure, which was trim and lean from working out. I took my sunglasses from my blue eyes to mop my damp brow. Pete smiled. True to form, he had barely broken a sweat, while I felt like I had just showered in my uniform.

"Thanks, Jackie," Pete said, toggled the switch to his radio microphone at his shoulder, and said, "One-ten, Coral Beach. Prisoner in custody." Pete and I had been working this zone together for a while. Since we frequently backed each other up, we had become somewhat close, knew what to expect from each other.

"Ten-four, one-ten," came the reply. "Arrest at ten-twenty-one."

Pete and I helped Cedric to his feet. We patted him down for weapons, almost surprised to find none, and put him in the rear of Pete's patrol car.

"What did you have, Cedric?" Pete asked, holding the door open to talk to him.

Full of belligerence, he practically sneered, "I'm not telling you nothing. I got nothing." Pete closed the door and turned to me. "I'll be back in a minute. Idiot here threw something down when I turned the corner and he saw me. Stay with him."

"No problem."

Pete jogged off and returned less than two minutes later with a small brown paper sack that seemed to be about half full. Jim O'Hara arrived at the same time in his sergeant's car.

"What's going on, guys?" he asked, a hint of Brooklyn accent coloring his words.

Pete filled him in, finishing with, "It was great! I'm drawn down on him, telling him to turn around and put his hands on the van, and the next thing, all I see is a brown blur take him down. Took me by total surprise, I was so focused on him."

"So what's in the bag?" O'Hara asked.

Pete opened it up and pulled out a small plastic bag of white powder. "There's got to be about twenty or more like this one in here," he commented.

O'Hara rolled his eyes. "Stupid, stupid, stupid."

I shook my head. "Live by the sword…" I commented.

"You know, I wasn't going to stop him, until he threw it down and ran," Pete said.

"Good job, you two," O'Hara said. "Make sure you tag it and turn it over to property."

"Right, Sarge," Pete said.

The sergeant left. Pete and I chatted for a moment.

"Are you going to the shift party tomorrow night?" he asked.

"I will be there. I'm looking forward to it."

"Are you bringing Learner?"

Jim Learner was a sheriff's deputy I had been dating for the last couple of months. He was nice enough, but he was too jealous of every guy I worked with, arrested, or who happened to look at me twice. He had become too controlling, and it had been getting scary. So when we had been together for lunch two days before, I had dropped the bomb that I didn't want to see him anymore. He was furious and stormed out of the restaurant. He had called a number of times, but I wasn't answering or returning his calls.

"No. We're done," I answered and told him about the lunch date.

"Good. We were all getting concerned for you."

I smiled. "Thanks. You guys are the best."

"Hey. We take care of our own. This isn't just work. This is like family."

"I appreciate you guys."

"Right back at you." He glanced over at his prisoner. "I gotta get this idiot booked. Make sure you write up the assist on this. See you later."

"Coral Beach one-oh-one," squawked my radio.

I toggled the switch. "One-oh-one, CB."

My next call was a car wreck on the bridge that connected Coral Beach to a sort of sister city across the river. I wrote a few tickets throughout the day, ran other calls. After spending time at the station finishing paperwork, I headed for home.

Home was a small house about twenty minutes from work. I kept it warm and comfortable. I tended toward used things as opposed to new. It seemed I preferred other peoples' taste when they grew tired of it, rather than what I could find in new furniture shops.

I went to the mailbox once I got home. Freddy Stone was across the street finishing some pruning on the bushes in front of his home. He was close to retirement from banking and was looking forward to working with his wife full time in the garden when they weren't traveling. He had retirement all sorted out, with no plans to be idle. He was tall and athletic looking in his sixties, certainly not the stodgy, stereotypical banker that comes to mind. I was pretty sure he colored his hair just enough, leaving just a light fringe of gray here and there, making him look that much less than a banker about to retire. He waved and called a hello.

He walked across the street to me, stowing a small hand tool in his back pocket.

"You had some odd visitors today," he commented as he got closer to where I stood at the end of the driveway. He wiped his hands on a rag he'd pulled from a pocket.

"Oh, really?"

"Yeah. Not from the neighborhood. They went up to the door, rang the bell, and looked in the front window. So I went over and talked to them. Normal looking enough, but strange. Said they'd try you later. I called the sheriff, and they sent a car out, but they were gone by the time the patrol car rolled through."

"Thanks, Freddy."

"How was your day?"

"Busy, as usual. Not bad."

I looked around the area, uncomfortable for no apparent reason.

"How's Clair?" I asked.

Freddy's wife volunteered at their church when she wasn't busy with her grandchildren and great-grandchildren. She already had three trips lined up for the two of them when Freddy finally retired. She had been diligent to make sure the trips were planned around birthdays and special events. Clair was tall and lean like her husband. Freddy doted on her, loved giving her beautiful jewelry and other gifts. I couldn't help but admire the love they had for each other after nearly forty years of marriage. I prayed that when I finally met and married, that I would have the same kind of relationship these two had.

"She's fine. She's helping Jess with the grandkids this afternoon. I'll be meeting them at the soccer field a little later."

"Big game?"

"Oh yeah. Tyler is tearing it up this season. He's working hard to get a scholarship to FSU. There are supposed to be a couple of scouts from there. Kid's real excited."

"That's great, Freddy."

Another brief, odd silence. Something felt odd in the neighborhood. I couldn't put my finger on it.

"You know, that's a tough job you have there," Freddy commented.

"No tougher than yours when you tell a potential loan client no."

"Maybe," he half chuckled. "I know I'm just the neighbor, but Claire and I worry about you."

Here it went again. Freddy had to tell me once in a while how he felt. I think he and my parents somehow got a hold of each other, and made a deal that Freddy would talk to me about this at least twice a year. The hope being, of course, that I would leave law enforcement and do something safe and practical. I'm sure the day I decided to do that I'd get hit by a bus—by accident, naturally.

Like many officers, I considered myself well trained. That training was constantly updated, to keep all of us up to date on our state qualifications, as well as to keep us safe on the street. There were constant classes on self-defense, as well as being prepared for the worst, which we all tried not to think about. Backup was not far off, the benefit of working in a municipality that wasn't too huge. I knew county deputies whose backup was significantly further away than mine, typically.

"So do my folks. But they rest assured that I don't take any chances, that I'm well trained, I don't want to get hurt, and backup is usually pretty close. The prayer time I put in keeps a hedge around me, too, Freddy."

"You shouldn't test God so much."

"Hasn't failed me yet," I responded.

"You and Claire have a nice evening, Freddy."

I went inside into my haven from the world: my home, my place to relax and unwind. The four walls where I felt safe, and it was good to be home and I could be myself. It wasn't large, but just big enough for me. Two bedrooms, two bathrooms, which someone else would have called small, was enough for me to keep up with. When I heard about huge homes that people had, I often wondered who cleaned them. Lord knows, on a cop's salary, I'd never be able to have hired help. My home was comfortable and warm. Warm colors on the walls and complimentary furniture that was a kicky blend of contemporary and classic, picked out from Craigslist, yard sales, and consignment shops.

I got changed out of my uniform and into shorts and a T-shirt, put my sweaty, smelly uniform in the laundry, and sat down to go through the mail. There was one bulky manila envelope in with everything else, from a company called Star

Gazers. I'd heard their advertisements on the radio from time to time, usually around holidays. For a nominal price, you could purchase a star. I don't know what you'd do with real estate in the inky blackness of space that you can't even get to conveniently, but some people seem to think it was cool.

I was expecting an advertisement for the company and instead found I had been gifted with a star. I looked over a certificate and star chart, which showed where my star was; it still didn't mean much to me. Looking through the paperwork, I found that Jim Learner, my recent ex, had purchased it for me before we knew we wouldn't be a couple any longer.

The star chart was kind of interesting. I didn't know much about astronomy, but I had spent enough time outside at night watching the stars, which I was pretty familiar with what was up there. This star chart really didn't look like anything I had been looking at all these years. I couldn't find any of the constellations I was familiar with anywhere. There was no notation about hemispheres or anything that I had ever seen on star charts in some of the shops I had visited. I kind of wondered if this was even a legitimate business. Maybe Jim had been swindled out of some good money for something that didn't even exist.

I thought about giving it back to Jim since we were no longer dating, but for some reason, that didn't seem like the right thing to do. There was something about this that held my attention, and I was already feeling an attachment to it.

The odd feeling I'd had outside was with me again. Something was off; I didn't know what was going on, but it was uncomfortable. I took a tour through the house, not knowing what I was looking for, but nothing looked out of place.

I went back to the living room and the mail.

In going over the paperwork included in the packet I found the star had been named after me, "Jackie Laughlin 1107." I took a few minutes at my computer to check the company and the star. Star Gazers had a web site. It was pretty small, just enough to give a bit of background and take someone's money in exchange for something similar to what I had received.

One of the things Jim and I had enjoyed doing was to sit out in chairs in my yard or his in the evening and just gaze at the stars. With enough mosquito repellent, we could do that for quite a while. Watch the tiny light of a jet miles above the earth move slowly across the sky or the brief and speedy arc of a shooting star, as we watched the celestial light show slowly drift by taking more precious moments with them.

The phone distracted me from dwelling on what had been. My best friend, Karen. Karen is the secretary at our church. She keeps me on my toes. She twisted my arm to get me to join the choir for the Christmas production. I still don't know why I had said yes, but it had been a great time. She talks me into a Bible study about once a year. I usually wind up having more fun and getting more out of it than I had anticipated.

"What are you doing tonight?" she asked.

"Not a whole lot. I have to work tomorrow, so I need to keep it simple."

"How about dinner at Applebee's?"

"I can do that. Gotta be home by eight thirty so I can be in bed to be up tomorrow."

"Still running?"

"I keep telling you. I walk. I hate to run. Isn't that why they gave me a gun, anyway?"

I could almost feel her roll her eyes. "Meet me there at six?"

"Sure," I said and hung up.

I sat there for a moment, looking at the star maps and documents. This was definitely curious. I didn't know much about astronomy. This would be a good time to start. Tomorrow I would go shopping for a telescope, a decent one that I could use to try to locate this star. I would check online for sales and then go purchase one. It could be a new hobby, something to relax with. I might even learn something.

There was something in the back of my mind that said I wouldn't find this star.

I got dressed in jeans and a Hawaiian shirt. I tended to overdress for restaurants that tended to be a bit cool for my liking. I took a moment to hang the chart in the hallway, the only place that seemed reasonable to put it. It was out of the way; it was where I could see it, but not readily visible to visitors, for the purpose of avoiding questions, until I could check this out a bit. I would see it a number of times every day this way.

I took care of starting a load of laundry and preparing my uniform for the next day.

—◈—

"I didn't have a chance to talk to you after church on Sunday," Karen said over spinach and artichoke dip. "You seemed kind of wrapped up in what Pastor Tom was talking about."

"I was," I admitted. "It really touched a nerve."

"You want to be a missionary?"

I paused, looking down at the chip I was using to scoop up more of the green goo.

"I don't know," I said slowly. I hadn't thought about it much since I had left church the other morning, but now the feeling came back to me. "I haven't had time to really think about it beyond Sunday morning. But at the time, it seemed like such a cool thing to do." The dip smelled heavenly as I bit into it.

"It's a lot of work."

"I'm sure it is," I responded, patting dip from my lips with a napkin. "The idea of having a simpler life, of talking to people and helping them is very appealing."

"You do that already." Karen nipped into her own chip and dip.

"Not as a missionary."

"Didn't you tell me that you pray with people in the back of your patrol car?"

"It's not the same," I argued.

"You think you have to be in a third-world country to be a missionary? Come on, Jackie. Some of the places you wind up in are worse than some third-world countries. That's your mission field," she finished, pointing at me with a dip-laden chip.

"Tom's sermon just sort of stirred something in me."

"It's supposed to. Just don't think you need to sell off all your belongings and move to Africa next week."

I smiled. "Maybe next month."

She paused, not happy with my response, but being tolerant of the flip answer I'd given her. "What's up with you and Jim?"

The change in conversational direction was so drastic, had it not been the two of us, somebody else might have gotten whiplash.

"I told you. We're done."

"He called me."

I think if they could have, my eyebrows would have shot past my hairline. "What?" I wiped a bit of cheesy stuff from the edge of my mouth again.

"Jim. He called me asking about you. He was real upset that you dumped him and asking if I knew how he could get you back."

I took a deep breath. Shook my head. I told her about the package of stuff from Star Gazers.

"Return it, Jackie."

"I know," I said somewhat reluctantly.

"Wait. You're not thinking about keeping it, are you?"

"I was up until you told me he went to you to try to get me back. I even put it up in the hallway."

"I told you from the start, he's not very stable—"

"Name someone you know who is."

"Very funny. Send the package back."

"I hung it up. I can't send it back damaged, with thumbtack holes in it."

"Why would you keep it, if it's from him, anyway?"

"I don't know. You ever have the feeling you're just supposed to have something?"

"You, who usually make sense, are not making sense right now."

"Yeah, I know," I said quietly.

"You still want him?" She was almost incredulous.

"Lord, no," I said almost too loudly. "He wouldn't be much more than my personal jailor almost."

"Remember that," she said, pointing another chip at me.

"What are you doing Friday night?" I asked.

"Staff get-together," she replied. "We're supposed to do a pizza and game night. I've been looking forward to this for the last week. You should have seen Dave last time when we played catch phrase. Most of them he came up with a song for. Had us rolling on the floor."

"You expect anything less from the worship leader?"

We chatted and ate for the next hour and then went home. I immediately went to the star chart poster. I reached up to remove the tacks but found myself just standing there, looking at it. I couldn't explain my attraction to it. Taken to its basest form, it was no more than black paper with thousands of little white dots on it. And yet something in it had me almost transfixed.

2

MY NAME IS Dolm Corrett. I am the official assistant to our planetary leader, the Lady Constance Minkas. I serve not only as assistant, but as bodyguard and confidante as well. I've been doing this for the last sixty-eight years, according to the Earth calendar. I was trained in our planets' military, first as a warrior, second as an assistant, when it was decided I would take on that responsibility.

Next to a husband, if she had ever had one, I am the closest person to her; I know her moods, her likes and dislikes. I know when she has pushed herself too far as she works, even though she goes to great lengths to hide it, fooling everybody else around her. I have seen the loneliness of leadership she has endured, never marrying or even allowing anybody to get close to her, considering her position far more important than her own desire to have an intimate relationship. I have been at her side and witnessed the horrors of the wars our peoples have fought. I have fought with her when she has come under personal, physical attacks from those who don't care for her and hate the peace and civility she has brought to the different peoples of our planet. I have turned away, as she has wanted me to, when she has cried over things that have been beyond her control, that have devastated others, mourning the loss, the waste, the brokenness.

I have defended this great woman the numerous times she was almost assassinated. I actually took a blast for her, nearly dying in one attempt. She barely left my side as I recuperated, relying on a second assistant for the six Earth months it took for me to fully recover.

All that is about to come to an end—now. Earthers are not as long lived as we, the Usians. She lies now in the bedroom of her home in the capital city of Toowa, her body deteriorating faster than it has in the last several years that her body has started to terrorize itself with its symptoms of aging. Her skin is pale and thin as paper, it seems. Her face, once beautiful, so alive and full of life, is drawn, her cheeks and eyes seeming to have sunken into her bone structure. That hair, dark, long, and which I longed to run my hands through more times than I can think, is still artificially dark, but it has lost its luster and thickness.

I turned, hearing the door to the bedroom open; Omis, the nurse, stood there. She had been caring for Lady Minkas all this time.

"It is time for you to leave," she said quietly.

"I know."

Lady Minkas awoke as I took her hand. It felt dry and cool.

"Dolm. I thought you had gone." Her voice sounded weak and a little hoarse. She looked at me carefully. "You should leave right away, Dolm. I know it's not exactly protocol, but I would like to meet the new leader before I die."

"Yes, ma'am."

I hate leaving her. I can't bear the thought of not being present should she die while I am not here. But I had to leave, to bring back the new leader of our planet.

—◦◦◦—

In the hallway, Terr Domat met me. He looked flustered, but we all tended to look flustered these last months. It is a hard thing to know that the leader so many have worked with and admired so much is about to die. And the installation of a new leader is always a brutal time.

"Terr," I said, in greeting.

"Have you seen the information on the one who received the package?"

"Not yet. What's wrong?"

"It's another female, a protector. I think she is referred to a 'police officer.'"

"That's good. Perhaps she has a strong sense of right and wrong and justice. Perhaps she will be able to bring our planet into further peace," I commented.

"She's not leadership material, Dolm," he complained as we walked together down the corridor. "She has totally kept herself from participating in leadership within her command structure."

"Has she performed well in her duties?"

"Yes, but—"

"Then I say we wait and see what she might bring us in leadership. Lady Constance was not wholly satisfactory to all, and she demonstrated herself to be more of what we needed than any of us anticipated."

"She at least had leadership skills when she arrived."

"True enough. Law enforcement by itself brings with it a certain ability to lead. Let us give her the chance to prove herself."

"You, Dolm, are an optimist."

"Perhaps."

"You have not seen the images. She is soft, has more heart than Lady Constance had."

"She will have to learn."

"We can't afford to go through too many leaders in a short period of time."

"What makes you think she won't be here long?"

"I'm just saying, if she doesn't work out and we need to replace her, the council will be harder than ever to convince that we need outside leadership."

"You are borrowing trouble and an ulcer, my friend. Let's see what she brings when she gets here." I stopped abruptly in the hall. "Now, Terr. I have no more time for you, I am on my way to bring her back here, to her new home."

"I have a bad feeling, Dolm."

"Just don't make anybody's duties more difficult than they need to be, Terr. I have to go now. Perhaps when I return you will have changed your mind."

"Do you think she will feel the same, if she finds out that you are bringing back a human who is not qualified to be her replacement, Dolm?" Terr said bitingly.

I stopped and chose not to react as he hoped I would; this one who had frequently told of how he did not approve of off-worlders ruling our planet would not bait me. There were whole movements of people who thought this way. Of course they had not been here when there was planet-wide fighting, death everywhere, utter chaos. Every ruler we had put in place had failed miserably. There had been too much self-interest, greed, lust, and purposeful division. He was too young to know any of this, despite having been educated about it, history that was kept in front of us to keep us from going back to where we came from.

I knew Lady Minkas well enough to be confident that she would have neither the strength nor the patience to heed what he would say.

"Go, Terr. If you need to cause problems, I can promise you will not be here much longer. The new leader will probably get rid of a lot of old wood that doesn't conform to what she might have in mind. I might not be here much longer for that matter."

And I walked away.

I walked past the many craft lined on the tarmac. My mechanic walked with me. Chasim was tall, heavily built, dark, and intelligent. I had gone hunting with him, knew him to be quite strong.

"You are bringing her back today?"

"Actually, we are."

Chasim stopped and stared. "What? I am not prepared."

"I need you."

"Why?"

"I am not concerned about getting her. I am concerned about returning here. There is much unrest. If Lady Minkas dies while I am gone, there will be much fighting, and I fear for her safety. I may need you to help me get her to where she needs to go."

"I have—"

"Call your family now. We leave in ten minutes."

He looked consternated, confused.

"Chasim. Time is in short supply right now."

"Yes, sir."

3

I AWOKE WITH A start. I was standing in the hallway, in front of the star chart. I wobbled for a moment, got my balance, and then shivered uncontrollably. I was awake at once, and more than a little confused. I had never walked in my sleep before. This was totally odd behavior for me.

I looked around the house to make sure everything was in its place and tried to go back to sleep. After tossing and turning for some time, I got out of bed and made a cup of chamomile tea. Then I sat in the living room and read the latest novel I'd picked up, sipping my tea. When I returned to bed, I read for a short time until my eyes started to lose focus.

The alarm clock was obnoxiously loud, almost had me feeling disoriented. I was exhausted. I thought back to when I woke up looking at the star chart. What was that all about? I hit the snooze button twice then got up and got ready for work.

I had to be in early today. Pastor Tom Darbon was the department chaplain. He and I had started a bimonthly meeting between the morning shifts. Tom had a short message ready for whoever showed up and prayer time for whoever had a need. My part was to send out the e-mail reminders and, if I had an inclination, to bring a baked good to go along with the coffee the officers typically brought in with them. I decided to stop by Dunkin Donuts and pick up a dozen.

So far, we rarely had more than five or six attending; we prayed it would pick up. At least the officers knew we were there. Every now and then, one of them would stop me in the parking lot or wherever they happened to find me, and ask for prayer for something or other.

Since I was running late, I decided a doughnut would have to be my breakfast today.

As I drove into work, I took the time to think about my conversation with my neighbor, strangers trying to see if I was home. I couldn't put a connection between them and the star chart. Maybe there was no connection. There was a part of me that couldn't wait to get home and study it some more.

Traffic was incredibly slow. The Florida Division of Transportation was not making any kinds of friends this morning. Really? Road improvements in the middle of tourist season? Did they really have to show off everyone's tax dollars at work at the most inconvenient period every year? It was inconvenient, yes. But I took the time to organize my day in my head, pray for protection and wisdom, and try to figure out what to do about Jim Learner and the star maps.

The meeting was attended by a grand total of three other officers and Sgt. O'Hara.

"I liked what you had to say Sunday morning," I commented as the other officers were leaving.

"Missionaries?" Tom inquired. He was in his fifties, kind of average in height, had dark hair and eyes, and a full beard and mustache. He was easy to talk to and often rode with the officers, especially the evening shift, on weekends. Tom had gone through the academy and was always prepared. He liked to be in the thick of things with the officers. Tom qualified on the gun range with the officers and was good backup to have around.

"Yes."

"Thinking about it?"

"A bit, but I don't know."

"Pretty good mission field where you work, Jackie."

"I know."

"A lot of people would miss what you contribute on the road."

"What do you mean?"

"I talk to some of the people out there," Tom began. "They know who the good cops are, the ones who care, who take extra time. Think real hard about what you decide to do. There aren't nearly enough officers who give the kind of extra attention that you do."

I was a little surprised. "Thank you."

He smiled and patted my shoulder. "You're welcome. And thank you."

I made it to briefing with a minute or two to spare.

"Jackie," said Sergeant O'Hara, "there's no briefing today. We have calls holding. There's a wreck with injuries in your zone. Two other units are on the way, but they're due to come in."

"I'm outta here," I said and went right out. I got in my car, radioed that I was in service and headed to the scene.

At a little after eight in the morning, the air was already thick and overly warm, gearing up to be another scorcher. People were in shorts and light shirts, flip-flops if they had the day off. If they were the unlucky bunch working during a gorgeous day like this, they were in as little clothing as they could get away with and still look professional for whatever their position was. I passed a hotdog kiosk. The salesperson, a gal with a nice figure who was wearing short shorts and a very small bikini top, already slicked down with sun block over darkly tanned skin. I figured she would do a booming business today.

On the six-lane highway two of the north lanes and the turn lane were all occupied by emergency vehicles, and the two cars that had collided. Ambulance personnel were assessing people in one of the vehicles, and it looked like they were in the process of putting a collar around the passenger's neck in preparation to remove and transport. One officer was collecting witnesses and other information, while the other was directing traffic, which was bottlenecked northbound.

"Here, Jackie," John Mangus handed me two sets of information. "Both drivers. Tan Ford was leaving the lot, the red Honda T-boned him. These are witnesses, all over there." He pointed to three people standing on the sidewalk, watching all the action. "I have two hooks coming for the cars. I'll get the inventories done for you before I head out."

"Thanks." I attached the papers he'd given me to my clipboard and started working the scene, getting further pertinent information, seeing where the vehicles were damaged, taking other notes to complete the report. Once the emergency medical technicians had the guy in the neck brace out of the car, a couple of us pushed one of the cars back into a parking lot, out of traffic, while one of tow tucks worked on getting the other hooked and off the road.

I was always impressed with how quickly we could clean up a wreck off the highway and have everyone moving smoothly again. It was a combined effort of law enforcement, fire and rescue, and the tow companies. Unless there was a fatality, it didn't matter how many vehicles were involved; we always seemed to be able to get things squared away with the road passable in fairly short order. We typically left the area looking like nothing had happened. Glass was cleaned up, pieces of the vehicle removed, and any fluids usually evaporated fairly quickly. Government tax dollar efficiency. Nice for a change.

I had just gotten statements from the witnesses when I turned around to look across the street and just get a look around the area. Two men stood there, looking at me. Pretty normal looking, except there was something out of place about them I couldn't explain. It might have been how interested they were in the wreck and how it was being handled. It might have been the way they were dressed—pretty neatly, but in practically brand-new clothing that they seemed almost uncomfortable in. I was pretty certain if I went over to talk to them, I would find store tags still hanging from the ends of their sleeves, ala Minnie Pearl.

It could have been the way they seemed to focus in on me in particular. They just stared. I nodded to them, acknowledging their presence.

And then I couldn't look away. I tried to look away but couldn't. Something had me locked to their eyes. I could feel things going through my mind that I couldn't verbalize. It almost felt like a searching. I could feel questions as opposed to hearing them, and then my answers given in return; I couldn't help but let my mind reply. I couldn't say what the questions were, though. I was not in control.

My head started to hurt. I felt tears rolling down my cheeks. The report box I held fell to the ground, the metal clattering loudly on the pavement.

"Jackie," Somebody was calling my name. I was pretty sure it was John Mangus. I could hear him, but I couldn't respond. He repeated my name, shook me, and everything stopped.

"Jackie."

I heard the voice, only, I couldn't respond to it. It felt like I was in a deep well, looking up. There was light in the distance above; I just needed to get to it. I felt like I was floating toward it, but it was an effort to navigate myself there. The closer I got to it, the louder I could hear my name being called. I was so tired. Trying to get to the top of the well wasn't getting any easier. It was a struggle all the way. When I was close to the top I could hear a siren and feel movement as if I was in a truck bouncing along. I finally reached the top and felt myself being carried over the top of the well.

"Jackie."

I opened my eyes and saw Jake, one of the EMTs. Jake had been doing this for almost ten years. We had worked more calls together than I could count. I was in the back of an ambulance. He was sitting next to me, all calm, concerned, and relieved that I had come to. I had an IV in my arm. My uniform shirt and vest were off, but I still had on my white T-shirt under the blanket that covered me.

"How're you doing?" he asked.

"My head hurts. Real bad."

"Don't doubt that. You went down hard. Got a good knot on the back of your head. Do you remember what happened?"

I paused. I did remember, but I was concerned about sounding like a nut case. How did I tell someone that I failed a stare down? It was more than that actually. I could still feel the cold tendrils of someone else's thoughts going through my mind. It was an odd feeling, not comfortable at all. In fact, I felt as if I had been violated in some weird way. It was as if someone had taken a part of me by force, but I couldn't put a finger on what was taken. I remembered something about questions, but I couldn't remember what they were.

I had tried to close my mind off to keep whoever it was out, but it was as if someone had been prying open a door. It had been painful. It hurt now remembering.

I swallowed a lump in the back of my throat. I tried to wipe tears that had sprung to my eyes; the IV in the back of my left hand kept me from doing it the way I wanted to. I took a deep breath.

"Hey, it's okay, Jackie. You're okay. Settle down. It's not that important." He put his hand on my shoulder and then rubbed my arm.

I took a moment to compose myself as the ambulance gently bounced along, the siren still wailing, clearing a path for us.

"I was working a car wreck. I'm not sure what happened."

"John said you were kind of staring off into space, and when he tried to shake you out of it, you passed out. Do you have seizures?"

"No. Never." I took a deep breath and held it for a minute, trying to steady my nerves. My head pounded when I started to breathe normally again.

"You're okay."

I nodded and closed my eyes. "The light hurts my eyes. Can you make them stop the siren?"

"We're almost there. We're a minute away. Lotta people worried about you."

"A minute away from where?" As if I didn't know.

"The hospital."

"Can't you just take me home? I just want to go to bed and go to sleep."

"Let's get you checked out first. And make your captain and the others feel better. You scared them, actually all of us, pretty good."

"Sorry."

"Just glad we were there to help."

"How long was I out?"

"Well, you passed out right after the bus left with the guy from the wreck. We got there about three minutes later, got you loaded up, so probably less than ten minutes."

The siren stopped, and I could feel the ambulance backing up to the unloading area to the emergency room. The doors opened, and the gurney I was on was rolled out of the ambulance into the ER. Dr. Mallary was there immediately, walking with me into a room around the corner.

"Hi, Jackie."

"Hi, Doc."

"What happened?"

"I'm told I passed out."

"Have you ever passed out before?"

"No."

"What's the last thing you remember?"

"I was working a wreck on Columbus Avenue. I had just finished talking to the witnesses, and I don't know after that."

"Can I see her?" It was Captain Jones.

"When we get done with her. Give us a few minutes to get her settled."

"We'll call your parents, Jackie," the captain called.

"No!" I called. Bad mistake. That made my head pound harder. I took a deep breath and gripped my head to make it stop. "Please let me do that."

"We can wait then," he called into the room as the door was closed.

The next couple of hours were spent on X-rays, tests, questions, visits from the other officers and brass. I was finally diagnosed with a concussion and encouraged to spend the night for observation. Doctors orders as well as orders from the chief.

The question "what happened" kept being asked. The best I could come up with was that I had slept poorly, hadn't eaten a very good breakfast, was possibly a bit dehydrated, and passed out. To tell anyone that I was mesmerized by some Svengahli-type person would have lead to a bunch of questions I didn't have the answers to. I got the distinct feeling that my story was not entirely believed, but it was the best I could come up with on short notice and under the circumstances. I prayed that I wouldn't be asked again.

There were numerous visits from the people I worked with. I finally had a stretch of time when I could just relax and close my eyes. I was tired and still had the headache, despite the drugs administered earlier. Somebody had heard

I hadn't had lunch and snuck in a sub sandwich, chips and a Coke, the remains of which were on the counter by the sink.

I heard a light tapping on the door and looked up. Jim stood there, one hand in a pocket and a vase of flowers in the other. It was a shame that such a good-looking guy was such a jerk. He was almost six feet tall, had dark hair and blue eyes, and his features were strong. He stayed fit for his job as a sheriff's deputy, and it showed.

"Jim, what are you doing here?"

"Nate called me, told me."

I sighed and did an eye roll. Nate Graham was an officer on another shift who was a close friend of Jim's. I knew instantly that I was probably a pretty frequent topic of conversation for them, especially since I had told Jim I didn't want to see him anymore. There was definitely a brethren thing in law enforcement, but it was also laden with its share of gossip. I was pretty sure that Nate wasn't Jim's only contact regarding what I was doing, who I might be seeing.

To his credit, I could see the concern all over Jim. He stepped into the room and set the flowers on a table across the room from me that already had two other arrangements on it.

"Are you all right?"

"I'm okay," I said.

"What happened?"

"I'm not entirely sure, but it seems I passed out," I said and went on to relate the story I had come up with. Jim didn't look like I had convinced him any more than I had anyone else.

He listened closely and then shook his head a bit.

"What?" I asked.

"I'm sorry this happened," he said in the most concerned tone I'd heard from him the whole time we'd been dating.

"Jim, I'm okay. This isn't your fault."

"Not just this. I mean us. I've been trying to call you, you're not returning my calls—"

"I told you I didn't want to see—"

"I was a jerk, Jackie. Please let me talk."

"Jim, this isn't a good time. I think whatever they gave me is finally starting to take care of the headache, and I'm so tired. I've been poked and needled and X-rayed and everything else, and I really can't—"

"Then just listen. I really care about you—"

"I think I heard her tell you to leave, Jim." Pete Willard stood in the doorway.

"This isn't your business." Jims voice was cold.

"She's not feeling well, Learner. Leave."

Jim turned to me. "Jackie?"

"Please leave, Jim."

"I'll call later."

"No, don't. I'm sorry—"

Jim took a moment to just glare first at Pete, then at me. Then he turned and pushed past Pete. I sighed and looked down at my hands, then back at Pete.

"Thanks."

"Sure. You okay?"

"Yeah. I can't believe him."

"You might have to get a restraining order."

I was about to run my hands through my hair, when I remembered the stuff attached to my hand that temporarily kept me from doing such mundane things.

"You'd think it wouldn't take that for him to get a clue."

"Well, some of us can, and some of us can't."

"Nate Graham told him I was here."

"I'll talk to Nate."

"No, you won't. This isn't about you, and I can fight my own battles. But thanks.

"I guess I won't be making the shift party tonight."

"Nope, you'll be here. I'll drop by after and smuggle a beer in to you."

"Glad you got my back," I said.

He stayed for a short time and was gone.

4

"DOLM, QUICKLY!" CHASIM called urgently.

I went to his side across the small helm. "What's the matter?" I asked.

Chasim had located Jackie Laughlin easily enough in a local hospital. He had been able to access the hospital records and find that she had lost consciousness while working. We both knew there was more to this.

"Did we do a scan upon entering orbit?" I asked.

"Yes. I'll do a larger search. What are the chances that the Ja'Harii got here before us?"

"I don't know, but it's unlike Earthers to lose consciousness like that. If another tried to scan her personally, it would have that effect, and if they did, we will have to move even more quickly than I anticipated."

"Were we not here to bring her back now?"

"Yes, but I was going to wait for an opportune time. We might have to act with a little less discretion than I had hoped.

This just happened this morning. She's spending the night, so we have time to check on her."

I watched as Chasims's fingers raced across the keys and light panels before him. And there on the display was our answer. On the monitor was a Ja'Harii shuttle. That meant the ship was not far behind.

"Oh, gods," I murmured. "They got to her."

"Do you think she is unharmed?"

"There is no way to tell from here."

I contemplated what to do for a few moments. Chasim was faithful not to interrupt my thoughts as I attempted to decide what our course of action should be. We could not risk leaving her unattended by one of us.

"First of all, we need the Klateche here as fast as possible. We may need her firepower, and I don't want to waste time waiting if the Ja'Harii have actually gotten to her.

"Then we need to find out where Jackie Laughlin is. We need to go to her and find out how severely she is injured."

"Their records state it is a concussion."

"We will need to make our own diagnosis and keep a guard on her. If they scanned her mind, there could be more than a concussion. The medical people here are not equipped to handle her injuries if more damage has been done than that. The Ja'Harii will try to take her before we can, and that could jeopardize her safety."

"How could they have found out?"

"There have been Ja'Harii plants on our planet for a long time, my friend. You never know exactly who you might be talking to."

Chasim had been doing a search for her and now had the information, which he relayed to me.

We changed into clothing we had to blend in with the Earthers and left to take a closer look at our future leader.

Within an hour, we had traveled from the ship to the parking lot of the hospital. It was late afternoon, and the lot was full of vehicles. Thankfully, there was nobody around who might require an explanation about our sudden appearance. Our denim pants, shirts, and comfortable sandals seemed to blend in with what most Earthers were wearing. The air was hot, heavy with moisture, and we could smell the toxic fumes of vehicles traveling the highway a short distance from where we were. The noise level was alarming. I thought back to when I had come for our current leader. Of course, we had not been in Florida to do that, but in New York, in a very rural area. The contrast between the noise, the smells, the people, the entire appearance of the area was so impressive, it was hard to believe this was the same planet.

We went immediately into the hospital and to the visitor's desk, where we were given a pass and the room number where she was as well as directions to get there.

Chasim and I stopped outside the room. We took a brief glance into the room to see her sleeping. Seeing her made my heart ache to see Lady Minkas. There was something about this woman that reminded me of our failing leader. They did not look anything alike, but they were both Earthers. I was finding that there was a strength and delicacy in humans. It was probably that combination that Usia recognized as being so essential in what we needed in a leader.

"Scan her, Chasim," I ordered. He removed a small object, about the size of one of their cell phones. He adjusted the instrument and held it just outside the door for less than a minute. A nurse exited a room down the hall, spotted us, and approached us.

"Can I help you, gentlemen?" she asked.

"No, thank you," I replied as Chasim pocketed his tool. "We were checking our pass for the room number and discussing our friend inside."

"Can I help you find the room?"

"Thank you, no," I replied. "We've got it now." We smiled and entered her room as the nurse continued on.

Thankfully, she was asleep, yet starting to become restless, as if waking up.

"Let's go," I said to Chasim, "We have what we came here for."

Once outside in the lot, Chasim checked his diagnostic tool. "She's all right. Her mind is very tired, somewhat bruised. A concussion, and some damage from fighting the mind scan. Nothing permanent. She'll have some pain for a few days, and then she should be fine."

"Good. We can handle that. The Ja'Harii care less about discretion that we do, but they won't take her from here."

I surveyed the lot. It was still loud and warm.

"How far away is the Kletache?"

The Klateche was a galactic battle cruiser. It was equipped with our planet's state of the art weaponry and manned by the best our military had to offer. The ship was the culmination of years of working with all the continents on our planet. It was always a pleasure to step onto that ship and take in the excellence with which it was run. I looked forward to seeing it soon now and hoped it would be here when we were ready to take Jackie Laughlin to her future post.

"It's going to be a while. They will jump as they are able to, but it will still take at least another day, possibly longer."

The waiting would be the hardest part. If the Ja'Harii did anything rashly, we would have to act and take her early. I didn't want to have to do that. When we took her, it needed to be neat and clean, with no loose ends. We owed that much to the ones she would be leaving behind.

5

THE NIGHT WENT fast. I hadn't realized how tired I was. If the nurses had come by to check on me, I didn't remember it. When I awoke the next morning, the headache was still with me. I didn't turn down the ibuprofen when the nurse offered it to me.

I know they try to do what they can with hospital food, but I was not hungry, and the coffee left a lot to be desired. I felt like I might be righteously grumpy if I didn't get a good cup of coffee soon. Someone in the heavens was listening. My dad showed up a short time later with a hot cup of Starbuck's. After a few sips, I felt like I could start to think about what I needed to do.

I had called my parents the night before, after things had settled down a bit. They weren't people to go crazy at not being called right away about their daughter being in the hospital. They were concerned, asked questions, and just grateful they'd gotten the info from me before they heard it on the news. Dad had agreed then to come see me in the morning with the coffee in hand, bless his heart. Mom was leaving town to visit her sister; I insisted she go, that I was all right.

"So when do you get out?" Dad asked after a fatherly hug and kiss.

"I'm told as soon as the doctor does his rounds and can sign the paperwork I can scoot. I'm so ready."

"You could have a wait there, you know."

Doctors never do their rounds when you want them to, especially when you're ready to leave. Some things never change.

Favor smiled on me. The doctor came around about an hour later. He was happy that I was feeling a bit better, had made it through the night without a problem. I could go home.

"Do you want to tell me what really happened?" Dad asked. We were in his truck, headed to my home.

"I told you."

"I know what you told me, but I want the real story now."

I looked at him, a bit startled. "What?"

"I figured once we were away from the hospital, and there was nobody around to explain things you didn't want to explain, you could tell me what really happened."

"Dad, I just passed out. It's just like I said. I don't know why."

He paused a moment. "I love you, and I know you. There's something else going on. When you feel like you're able to, I want you to tell me what went on yesterday."

I was quiet. Never could get anything past my dad. You go shooting with a guy often enough, you get to know each other pretty well. I didn't feel like I could tell anybody that I passed out because of a stare down—at least not yet. Not until I knew what exactly had happened.

Every now and then I could feel a whisper of what had gone on inside my head. It startled me when it happened, took my breath away for an instant. And then it would pass. I didn't want to think or talk about what had happened. It was safer not to for now.

"What's this?" Dad asked.

I went to where he stood in the hallway looking at the star chart.

"It came in the mail the other day," I said. "I think it's from Jim."

He looked at me with a hint of fatherly concern. "I thought you told me you gave him his marching orders."

"I did."

"So send this back."

I paused. "I thought about that. I probably should, but I can't."

"Give it to me. I will."

"No, Dad. That's okay. I really don't want to. If he becomes a problem again, I will."

He walked back into the living room. "You want me to get some dinner for you?"

"No, thanks. I have an idea it's already taken care of."

"Oh? How so?"

I had seen Freddy and his wife Claire come up the walk toward my door carrying what looked like a covered plate of food. Less than half a minute later, he knocked on the door, and I let them in.

He and my dad greeted each other. They had met when I was moving into the house about three years before. Nearly every time Dad stopped by Freddy enjoyed coming over to talk to him. They enjoyed each other's company. I suspected they discussed strategies to talk me into changing careers.

Claire handed me the covered plate of food. "We barbecued last night, this is leftovers. You can warm it up in the microwave."

"Thanks, Claire"

"Our pleasure, dear. How are you? We were so concerned when your father called last night and told us."

I looked at my father, who was deep in conversation with Freddy. I knew they kept in touch. I was sure the conversation last night probably had something to do with stepping up the suggestions to leave the police department. It wasn't like I'd gotten caught in a gunfight or got kayoed in a bar room brawl. I'd like to think it would take a lot more than one instance of passing out to get me to leave my career.

"Thanks, I'm fine. I still have a pretty good headache and I feel a bit woozy yet, but I'm fine."

"Freddy's going to take care of your lawn this weekend. We don't want you doing too much for a while."

"Thanks, Claire." I had placed the plate on a kitchen counter, and now I gave her a hug. "I love having you two for neighbors. You're awesome."

She smiled.

They stayed for a short time, and then all three left. I was relieved to have the house to myself again, take another pill for pain and just watch TV for a while.

I called Karen and told her about the mishap.

"Jackie, I wish you had called, I would have visited you!"

"Sorry. I was exhausted and had a miserable headache. I still have a pretty good chunk of it now, so I'm just resting."

"When do you go back to work?"

"I'll see the doctor the day after tomorrow, and if he thinks I'm good to go, I go back to work then."

"Do you need anything?"

"No," I replied and told her about the meal my neighbors had sent over.

"Want some company?" she asked.

"Thanks, but I don't think I'd be much company. In fact, I'm about ready to go take a nap right now."

"Go ahead and do that. If you need anything, call me, Jackie. I'm only about ten minutes away, so let me know if I can help."

"Thanks, Karen."

I answered the phone a few times and basically took the day to relax and do pretty much nothing. Throughout the day, I felt myself drawn to the star charts. I wasn't sure why. It was interesting to be sure. I spent a bit of time at my computer checking out the star I had been given. It had been named after me—Jacqueline Laughlin. Not in our solar system, according to the computer.

After enjoying what Freddy and Claire had brought over earlier, I fell asleep on the sofa watching a murder mystery. I got up, put things away, made sure the house was locked up, and went to bed.

6

I SAT UP in bed. My head throbbed, and I had to sit still for a minute for it to stop enough to hear above the pain. What had I heard?

Someone was in the house. I didn't hear anything, but I knew someone was in the other part of my home. I quietly opened the gun box at the side of my bed table and removed my .38mm Smith & Wesson. I picked up the phone next to my bed, but there was no dial tone. I remembered leaving my cell phone on the kitchen counter, plugged into the charger. I whispered a mild swear word and got quickly, quietly out of bed. I apologized to God for swearing and then prayed for protection and the cavalry. I moved silently to the wall by the door and waited, trying to look around the corner and listen at the same time. I could barely make out something, but I wasn't sure what it was. It wasn't voices, but I was pretty sure it was movement. Someone was trying to be as quiet as I was. I hugged the wall, moving slowly toward the living room.

My senses were on high alert, more so than I'd ever been before in responding to those calls in progress. This was my home, in the middle of the night and no backup.

I couldn't believe that here I was, in my own home, having to defend it. All the alarm calls I had been on, the home invasion reports I'd taken, burglaries I'd responded to, and now I was on the receiving side of the situation. Which practically begged the statement "why not me." There were enough cops that had dealt with the same thing I was dealing with now, some worse. I didn't want to think about worse right now.

I slowed my breathing as I turned the corner from the bedroom into the hallway to make my way to the living room. Once I got to the living room, I got into a crouch and risked a glance into the room. There were two of them, one taller than the other. They were close to the kitchen area. I took another fast glance and saw they had their backs to me.

I hadn't had to shoot anyone in the line of duty. There was a good chance I would tonight. I took a few seconds to think about that. I was justified in shooting someone I didn't know who was in my home. I would be defending it. I didn't know if they were armed. I was in fear for my life. All those things were in my favor.

I stood up, took another fast glance. They were turning toward where I hid, just beyond where they could see. I mouthed another swear word, crouched. I counted to three in my head, braced against the wall, took aim at the taller one, and fired at the same time that they both brought up their weapons to fire on me. I saw my shot go into the chest of the taller one at the same instant I felt the blow of something hit my left shoulder, throwing me back against the wall behind me. I felt myself slide to the floor. I didn't lose consciousness, but I couldn't move. I was numb all over, except for my shoulder, which felt like I'd been hit with a baseball bat. I willed my other arm to move; it wouldn't. I couldn't make a noise. I heard movement that sounded more fervent now.

I smelled the heat, and a few seconds later, I smelled smoke. My house was being set on fire! I could feel my body reacting to the stress. I was breathing hard now, panicking. I couldn't believe that I shot an intruder only to have the other one torch my house and leave me here to die in the inferno.

The shorter man was by my side. He had carried his partner over, who was not moving, and placed him next to me. He was visibly upset. I was sure it had to do with his partner. If I hadn't killed him, I had at least wounded him pretty badly. I didn't have any satisfaction over that notion.

I made myself slow my breathing to try to think. I still couldn't move, call out, anything.

I watched as the burglar pulled something like a cell phone from his pocket and speak into it. I couldn't hear what he said. What was he doing making a phone call in a house that was about to be burned to the ground? Why wasn't he taking his buddy and getting the heck out of here?

Something was happening. The room was changing. I didn't know what was going on, but I was now more scared than ever.

I think I passed out.

7

I WAS INSTANTLY awake. I was on a floor. My stomach felt like it was being twisted from within. My body ached and had the sensation of pins and needles all over. My head hurt more than it had while I dealt with the concussion the first few hours. I could move now and was on my hands and knees trying to stand up when my stomach lurched and I threw up on the floor in front of me. There's nothing like leaving a calling card that will be remembered, I thought grimly.

I backed away from the puddle of vomit in front of me. The room was small and stark, just a small cot alongside one wall, a small sink and toilet in the corner. The walls were gray. I couldn't see where the dim light that lit the room came from. I was so incredibly scared. Between the pain, the disorientation, my stomach still churning, and the fear, I couldn't keep tears from coming. I half crawled, half walked to the sink, hoping to find a towel or something to wipe my face with. With shaking hands, I turned on the water in the sink, rinsed my face and mouth, and used a towel nearby to wipe my face.

There was a light blanket on the cot. I wrapped myself in it and lay on the cot and rolled up into a ball. I watched as the floor, or something on the floor, absorbed or made my vomit disappear.

I prayed for help of some kind. I didn't know how I'd gotten here, where I was, or who had taken me.

I kept thinking this was a dream, but I couldn't imagine being in this much pain and still be able to sleep. I threw up again on the floor. With nothing in my stomach, it was all acidic and full of bile. I had no strength to get up to go to the sink or the toilet, and I wasn't fast enough. I threw up a few more times before my body had had enough and I fell asleep in self-defense.

I was thrown from the cot—more like dumped out of it onto the floor. My stomach was still upset, my head still throbbed like someone was using it as a boxing fast bag, and my body was still hurting incredibly. There was also a sense of pins and needles all over. I felt even weaker than I had before. The blanket I had was still around me. I attempted to sit up but I could barely do that. I stayed propped up on one elbow on my side. My shoulder throbbed. No wound, just swelling and bruising. I couldn't stop shivering, and I couldn't even look up from the black boots in front of me.

"Get up."

I paused. I was sure he was talking to me, but I couldn't do anything right now. "I can't." I barely whispered.

"Get up!" he ordered and toed me with his boot.

I fell onto my face as I cried out in pain. My nose was bleeding. "I—"

"I said get up!" he yelled.

I struggled to my hands and knees and worked on getting to my feet, trying to keep the blanket around me at the same time. I was still shaking and wasn't sure how long my legs would support me. They felt like spaghetti. I couldn't keep the tears form spilling from my eyes, which made everything hurt worse. I could taste the blood from my nose and wiped it with a corner of the blanket.

I looked at the man in front of me. He was tall and thin. His hair was dark, his skin almost Mediterranean—eyes dark, empty, and scary looking. He wore a dark blue tunic and black pants and boots. Something about him reminded me of Captain Hook from *Peter Pan*.

"You're Jacqueline Laughlin?"

I wasn't sure if it was a statement or a question. "Yes, sir." My voice sounded hoarse. I couldn't keep from wobbling. I was trying so hard to stay standing and couldn't believe I hadn't fallen over yet.

He grabbed the blanket and pulled it away from me, making me fall to the floor again. I was trying so hard to keep tears from spilling from my eyes, but not succeeding very much.

"Get up!" Hook yelled, making my head pound again.

I nodded and slowly pulled myself to my feet again. I wiped at the blood on my face with my hands and then kept my hands to my sides, trying to stand up straight, trying to be without fear, despite wobbling and tears still running down my face. The blood mixed with my tears was now going down my face, to my chin, under my pajama top and down my body. I stood before him, bloody, shaking, and hurting. I couldn't get my thoughts to line up to say anything; I didn't know what to say or do. I was scared out of my mind and yet trying hard not to show the fear. I refused to look away. We kept staring at each other for another minute or more, and then he looked away and nodded. I didn't know anybody else was in the room with us until then.

Another man rushed up to me. He had on a gray tunic, same black pants and boots. He was younger, lighter in coloring with a full beard and mustache. He had some kind of vial that he pressed against my neck for what seemed like a several seconds, and I passed out again.

I was warm. I wasn't in quite as much pain as I had been before. The shivering seemed to be sporadic. I was on the cot, covered with the blanket. I tried to move and found things still hurt quite a lot. My nose throbbed and was stuffy from the bloodying it had gotten earlier. I had to breathe through my mouth, which was now dry.

"Time to get up, Empress."

I tried to respond but could not. I tried opening my eyes, and they chose to oblige. I looked up at the man who had given me the shot or whatever it had been then looked around the room without moving my head. We were alone. He seemed not much happier to see me than the other man had.

"Get up, you need to get dressed."

I nodded and tried to move; I could barely do that.

"Here," he said, offering me his hand. I grabbed it, and he helped me to my feet. I almost fell again, and he helped me steady myself. "I'm Dr. J'neer. Are you feeling any better than you were before?"

"I think so."

"The effects of traveling, especially for the first time, can be pretty severe. The injection I gave you will help you recover a little more quickly, but it will easily be two to three more days before you're feeling substantially better."

"That would be the vomiting and pins and needles and hot and cold and—"

"Yes, all of it. You probably experienced more, since you're recovering from a concussion. That would make it much worse. And then there's the laser blast you took."

He pressed a button next to the sink, and a mirror appeared above the sink. I was a little shocked to see my face. I had very little color, and blood was caked and dried all over my face, going down my front. My hair was a mess, and my nose and eyes were swollen.

He stepped to the other side of the room. I watched as he pressed a series of buttons on a panel, and a closet opened. He took out a jumpsuit and shoes in a camel color, closed the closet and carried them to the cot, where he dropped them.

He took a towel and washcloth from the cabinet under the sink and placed them beside the sink.

"What did you say I was shot with? My shoulder is still pretty sore."

J'Neer came to where I stood. Before I could say or do anything, he yanked my pajama top down enough to see my shoulder. He touched the swelling, making me wince.

"Just from a laser shot. This is pretty standard. It will be about three days before it feels better. Try not to use it too much."

He walked across the room and accessed the door. He turned around and said, "Wash yourself up and get dressed. You need to be ready in ten minutes."

I thought about asking to take a shower, but I figured I was in no position to ask for anything for a while.

"Where am I?" I asked as he turned to leave.

He paused for a second and then looked back at me. There was almost a look of concern on his face, which he quickly hid. "I can't tell you that."

"Can you tell me why I'm here?" I couldn't control my tears as they started again.

"No, I can't."

"What—"

"Don't ask any questions. The less you know right now, the better." His tone was almost consolatory and then became stern again. "Get ready."

And he left.

For what? I thought.

I desperately wanted a cup of coffee and some ibuprofen. That would probably make my head feel a lot better so that I could think clearly.

I looked around the room again. On the other wall was a large map I hadn't seen before. I had been such a mess I could have probably easily missed it earlier. I decided that, as much as I wanted to check it out, I needed to be ready in ten minutes. Since I had no watch or any kind of timepiece in the room, I needed to get myself together first.

I went to the sink and ran the water. There was a pump bottle of soap attached to the wall. I was able to use the soap and warm water to clean my face and body of the blood from my nose. I used toilet paper to blow the gunk from my nose. It bled fresh for a moment before it stopped. I rinsed my nostrils in fresh water, rinsed my mouth, and made a brief assessment in the mirror. I ran my hands through my hair a few times, trying to make it at least look neat.

After using the toilet, I put the jumpsuit on—just a simple suit, zipped up the front. No bra or panties. No socks for the plain shoes.

The pins and needles had stopped, as had the hot and cold sensation, now I just felt like one huge ache. I cupped my hands and drank water from the faucet. It was refreshing, and I could feel the coolness of it spread through my body. I drank for a minute or two, noticing it wasn't affecting my stomach. My stomach had finally quieted down.

Now I was a little hungry. I wondered how much time had passed since I'd first gotten here—wherever here was.

I thought about all the things I'd read and seen and heard about prisoners of war. Was I one now, and if so, who were these people? Was I going to be put to death or tortured or raped? I decided that since they had me get dressed, I might not have to worry about being raped, but then clothing was easily removed.

I tried to figure out how I'd gotten here, and that was another mystery. I tried to go back to the moment I arrived here. I had been defending my home. I had shot an intruder at the same instant that I was shot. I remembered smelling smoke and then waking up to this room, this nightmare.

Visions of the many science fiction/adventure books I had read, shows I had watched came to mind, and I quickly put that out of my mind; that was too bizarre to even consider.

Somebody had to be looking for me. Did my home burn to the ground? They had to know I wasn't in the house. It would have been searched. My parents would have been called.

Oh, Lord, my parents. My poor parents would be beside themselves with worry, as well as the people I worked with. I wondered if I'd ever see any of them again. That scared me even more.

I sat on the cot and just prayed. I had to get centered, focused. All the things going through my head were so overwhelming, confusing and terrifying. I prayed for strength, wisdom, and peace. I closed my eyes, just let the prayer come and willed myself to calm down. I would know what was going on soon enough.

Right now, I didn't know what to do. If I could figure a way out of this, I didn't know where to go. My best bet was to get out of this place and run for help. Anywhere. The thing that kept me sane and just a bit calmer was knowing that no matter what happened, God was still in control, and everything would be all right. It didn't feel like that right now, but I could only hope and believe that there was a way out of this, and He would help me make that happen.

Despite that, I found myself making deals with God. If I got out of this alive, I would spend a year in Africa, the next in China, or wherever He wanted me to go. Heck, as much as I hated the cold, I'd even go to Antarctica for the rest of my life if He would just get me out of here safely and in one piece.

There was no way to say how long it had been since I'd been taken from my home. I didn't know how long I had slept either time. As horrible as I felt, I knew it wouldn't be unusual for someone as physically injured as I was to sleep for a full day or more.

I went over to the map on the wall. It was more of a mural. I studied it for a moment and realized I was looking at the same star map I had received at home. It was just a much larger one, of a much larger area. I was able to find the small area that represented what I had at home.

I wasn't into astronomy, but I could find a couple of things on the map that looked a bit familiar way off on the sides. Then

I found myself trying to make the tiny dots be constellations, and realized they weren't anything at all familiar. I wondered if it really mattered anyway.

The door opened close to me. I turned to the two men who came into the room. They were about the same size, wearing dark gray tunics, same pants, and boots. They had utility belts holding a few things I thought looked familiar. Possible cuff case, some kind of baton, and I wasn't sure, but the other thing with a handle could have been a weapon.

"Come with us, Empress."

"Empress?"

There was a half laugh, and they smiled and looked at each other, seeming to share a private joke.

"I know. The less I know, the better. Or something like that."

"Let's go.

We left the room and walked down corridors that were a decent width. Still the gray color I'd left in the room. No windows, many closed doors to unknown rooms. Eventually into an elevator, where one of them pressed some buttons. I could feel the gentle movement as it first went up and then across. Once we were out of the elevator, we went a short distance down another corridor and into a huge room.

It was the size of an event room. The room was full of people sitting in chairs that were lined up facing the front of the room, where we came in. Where we entered there was a platform set up, about three feet off the floor. Several chairs and a couple of tables were set up on it. Two huge screens were hung on either side of the platform so nobody could miss anything that took place. Hook sat at one of the tables with another man. This new guy was dressed more casually in an unusual, neat suit that seemed to be a cross between a leisure suit of decades ago and a well-tailored suite of today.

"Have the empress sit over there," Hook directed.

I was walked to the other smaller table, where I sat. The two guards sat behind me in chairs provided for them. I looked out at the crowd. All dressed in varying colors and the styles were very different from anything I had ever seen, but very neat, almost modern-conservative.

On the walk here, I had decided to not be a victim. I had a bit of strength now that I was feeling somewhat better, though still very achy. I could think more clearly, but there was still no way to figure out what was going on here. I had been doing a lot of self-talk to feel more confident and able to handle whatever happened, but I was still very confused and felt off-kilter. I was at a disadvantage here, being the captive. Why was I here? Why was I being addressed as 'empress'? Was this another tactic to humiliate me and keep me off balance?

Captain Hook said, "I am Captain Galton D'Nar. I am commander of this ship, the Naringah." He paused. "Tell us about yourself."

"I'm Jacqueline Laughlin. I'm a police officer with the Coral Beach Police Department." My voice was still a bit hoarse.

"You wounded one of my men."

It had to be the man I'd shot in my home. "I was defending myself."

He didn't say anything for a moment and then, "You've never shot anyone before this, have you?"

"No, sir."

He paused again. "Do you know why you're here?"

"No, sir."

He smiled. It wasn't a smile I liked seeing. It was a dangerous smile; it made me concerned about where this conversation was going.

"You don't know who you really are, do you?"

A couple of sarcastic answers came into my head, but I quickly dismissed them. I was hurting enough as it was.

"I don't know what you mean, sir."

"You are the future leader of Usia."

That sent shock waves through my body and mind as my brows climbed my forehead. Where was Usia, how had I been chosen, and what was going on? I was very curious to see where this was going, a bit uneasy as well.

"Uh, sir. There's been a mistake. I don't think I'm the person you're—"

"There's no mistake, Empress," he almost snorted.

I looked out at the crowd. There seemed to be no real sense of what they were thinking. Their faces were empty of emotion. I looked back at D'Nar.

"Captain D'Nar, I'm just a cop. I don't even want to be a sergeant. At least not right now. Now you tell me I've got some position in a place I've never even heard of." I paused. "If you're not happy with this, you take the position or give it to someone else. I have a life to get back to."

That got the crowd to talking, a few even laughed.

"You don't have a choice."

"Begging you pardon, sir, but that's crazy. What do you mean I have no choice?"

"You will become empress or you will be eliminated."

Something in the way he said "eliminated" didn't mean dismissed or disqualified, I could take my seat in the audience and another contestant would take my place. He meant eliminated, as in killed. My mind was racing, trying to get a grip on what I was learning and trying to know how to respond. I thought for a moment about all that had happened, but it wasn't productive. It was as if my world kept tipping degree by degree off center, making everything feel like it was about to go into freefall into a huge, empty abyss.

"Sir, why am I here?"

The man next to D'Nar spoke. "I am Yassok. Sub leader of the Ja'Harii, and I speak for Nereft, our leader. The current empress of Usia is near death. You have been selected to replace her."

Could this get any more insane? I wasn't that kind of leadership material. I had taken the last sergeant's exam, but nothing like that could possibly qualify me for leadership of this degree.

I tried to think of who might have set me up for this, but nothing, nobody, came to mind. I knew of nobody who could possibly put me in this kind of position.

I felt like I was drowning in confusion.

"Sir, I never put my name in the hat, and where on Earth are these places?" I asked. I didn't want to, but I needed to know. I was pretty sure this wasn't some anti-government subversive group, bent on taking America or some other continent hostage. The crowd was conversing and laughing again. I didn't think they were laughing with me. I sure wasn't finding any of this amusing.

"They are not on Earth. They are thousands of light-years from your Earth."

I let that sink in for a few seconds. This was getting worse and worse. I wasn't even on a planet, I realized. Not on a floating battleship in one of the oceans, or any other Earth-type vehicle of any sort.

"What kind of ship is this? The Na—" I started. I couldn't remember exactly what he had called the ship.

"The Naringah is a battle-class star cruiser. Usia and Menaache are both planets."

Through this conversation, I was feeling more and more confused. I had more questions now than I had before. Nothing made sense. They kept looking at me, even the crowd, now silent. What was I supposed to say or do? I was at a total loss for words or anything else.

"I take it you don't care for the Userans?" I managed.

"Usians," I was corrected by Yassok. "And no, not particularly."

"I still don't understand why I'm here, sir. You don't like the Usians. I'm supposed to be their next leader, which I guess you don't care for either. Why am I here, and what do you want me to do?"

"We want to be familiar with the decisions you might make."

I remained quiet. How could I possibly respond to that? I wasn't sure I knew what kind of decisions I'd make a minute from now. I could come up with some trite answers, but I was sure they wouldn't be acceptable.

D'Nar pressed some buttons on a panel on the table. The briefing room from the police department came on the screen. The audio came up. Sergeant O'Hara was conducting the briefing before we all began our shift. There was some discussion of a guy wanted for a series of child abductions, and the reactions to that from all of us in the room who had anything to say about it. I remembered the day clearly. Every shift of officers was on edge, focused on trying to find the perp. Sometimes chasing leads from the public was like chasing smoke. It was frustrating, and we all wondered who was helping this guy, and if someone was getting laughs watching us show up looking for him and finding nothing.

"We can only hope that he has a weapon and points it at one of us so we can take him out," I commented. Most of the officers in the room with me agreed, stating much the same thing.

Then there was another scene. I was in my living room, listening to the evening news. Someone who had broken into an elderly person's home had been shot and killed by police officers after a standoff in the next county. "Thank you for saving the taxpayers' money," I said out loud.

There were three other scenes of me talking with other people or to myself. In each one, my opinion of those who committed crimes against other people was pretty obvious.

I would stand by those statements, too. I had arrested my share of people who demonstrated mans' inhumanity to man, a few of them to the nth degree. Some of them had shown little or no remorse. I knew they would go through the whole process of depositions, trials and appeals, some of them taking years to manipulate the system as it was. Long enough for the public to forget the details and the intense feelings of shock and loss left behind by those who had committed the crimes.

To a large degree, my opinions were no different from most other law enforcement officers. We knew justice was not only blind, but deaf as well. And she might has well have had her hands tied behind her back.

I was shocked. Surprised. Speechless. How could they have gotten this? I looked around to see D'Nar just staring at me, eyes empty and cold.

"How did you get that? Where did you get that? You can't just film people without their consent."

"Your rules don't apply here. That was collected by the two who scanned you three days ago."

"What? Scanned? I don't—"

"You remember the two men who were across the street who held your attention at the scene of that vehicular incident. You fought their scan very well; had you fought it any more, you might have done some permanent damage to your mind, but you lost consciousness before that could happen."

I remembered that. That's what put me in the hospital to start with. I had been home one day when I was taken, which meant I'd been gone for two days. I took a few seconds to process all this.

I took a deep breath and swallowed. "Okay, so I'm a little judgmental. In the five years I've been a cop, I've seen and learned some things—Not a lot of it pleasant—but that's the reality part of my life. That's purely my opinion from what I've learned in my position as a law enforcement officer."

Yassok looked angry. "You would just kill someone for their actions?"

"Maybe not personally, unless I was in a position legally to do so as an officer. But yes."

"Without a questioning of the person accused?"

"It depends on the circumstances."

"Explain what kind of circumstances would lead you to take a life without a questioning."

I paused, trying to choose my words carefully. I wasn't sure that what I would say would make much of a difference. I didn't know what this was all about, but I was fairly certain these people had already made up their minds about whatever was going on and where this was heading.

I took a breath and started, "In the scope of my duties, it is my responsibility to do whatever I can to keep the people around me safe and alive. Toward that end, if someone's life is in danger by someone else, I have the responsibility to do something. If it means having to take the life of the one posing the danger, my department will back me up and support that decision. It's not something I take lightly.

"The other night was the first time I've had to actually fire my weapon at somebody. I have to tell you, I took just a few seconds to make sure in my head that I was doing the right thing. I feel even now that what I did was appropriate, given where I am now.

"As regards some of the statements I made in those"—I tried to come up with the appropriate word—"recordings, those were people who committed horrible acts of violence against people who couldn't defend themselves. They had no remorse and would play the system to benefit themselves.

"I can't be the judge and jury and executioner. I don't want to be. I just know that the system as I've seen it is not very fair, and in a lot of cases not very considerate of the people who have been hurt, some of them even killed. To a large degree, my statements are a result of the reality that I deal with as a law enforcement officer."

The room was too quiet for too long. It was almost painful. I couldn't read the faces; I had no idea if I had scored a couple of points or made things worse.

Yassok nodded to the two guards behind me. They left the room from a door behind them. They returned a moment later with two other guards and two other people. A young girl, about twelve years old, dressed in the same sort of fashion as the crowd. The man was in his thirties. Well dressed, obviously scared about what was going on. I wondered if he was as afraid as I was. I wasn't sure anyone was. I had a very bad feeling about this but continued to stay focused. I could not afford to panic and lose the ability to think clearly. It was difficult enough with the overload of information I had and what had happened since I had been taken from my home.

There was quiet talking from the crowd. D'Nar, Yassok, and the other man just stared at me. My head seemed to be throbbing more and more. My eyes were tired. Fatigue was starting to set in, in just this short time that I had been awake and interrogated. I was beginning to feel nauseous again. I wanted desperately to put my head down and sleep. I was exhausted from this whole interchange and the overload of information I had just been given. I wanted someplace to sit and process what I had been told. On top of all that, it had been two days since I had last eaten and I knew I was weak.

All that was making it more and more difficult to stay alert and attentive to what was going on.

"The child is Nabul," Yassok explained. "Her family was tortured and killed by Reham." The man who had been brought in with her shook his head. "She was made to witness the brutality and then tortured herself. She hasn't spoken since. We conducted our questioning and performed a mind scan. He is guilty. Would you have him killed?"

"What? You're asking me? This is your—"

"We're asking you. Would you have him killed? If you saw him and knew what he had done, would you kill him yourself in your position?"

"I can't. I would have to arrest him and have him go through the whole process in court. Let them decide."

"If you saw him and were able to detain him, would you kill him?"

"Only if he posed an immediate threat. I would have to—"

"But you would have him die, if it was your decision."

"What are you trying to do here?" I asked.

"Answer the question!" D'Nar almost yelled. "Would you kill him if it was in your power to do so, knowing what he has done?"

"I-I don't know! What about evidence?"

"Evidence points to him having committed this act," Yassok stated. "Based on what you have said in the past, you would have him executed. You would have no concern if someone did it for you."

"I'm not God to say who should live or die and why! I do my job."

"But you would be happy to have him gone."

I said nothing. I didn't like where this was going, and I was terrified by what I thought was about to happen next. There was so much going on in my head I couldn't seem to separate one thought from another, focus on one thing.

"Answer me!"

I just stared at them. I couldn't believe this was happening.

"You answer the question or you will be disciplined."

I paused. Where was the cavalry? "Yes, I would," I said firmly.

"I didn't do it!" Reham shouted. "Please! I was with my family! We were celebrating my children's' K'tall! Please lis—"

One of the guards punched him in the side, and he became quiet. Tears of fear streamed down his face. He was in a fight for his life, and I had a feeling it was about to be on the table. It was becoming hard to breathe. My heart was about to beat itself right out of my chest. D'Nar seemed to be enjoying my discomfort with this whole incident. The crowd was murmuring among themselves.

"Kill him," D'Nar said evenly.

"What?" I responded, not believing what he had just told me to do.

"Kill him," D'Nar repeated. He ordered a guard, "Give her a laser. Restrain him to that chair." The guards led Reham whimpering to a chair lifted to the platform by another guard. It was placed between the two tables so everyone had a clear view.

"Stop this!" I shouted, standing up. "This is not my responsibility! You can't do this! You can't make me do this!" One of the guards roughly forced me back in the chair.

"You either take his life, or we will take his and the lives of your family." Yassok looked at D'Nar, obviously startled. This was not in the script apparently.

The screen above the platform suddenly had pictures of my parents as well as my brothers and their families. I was stunned. They had access to my family. They knew who they were, and I had to believe they knew how to get to them. Killing them would not make D'Nar lose any sleep at all. Tears sprang to my eyes, and I blinked several times to keep them from spilling down my face. I could not afford to let him see me tremble. I didn't know how long I could keep this up. If I'd had any color in my face earlier, I was sure it gone by now. The cold cut through me.

"Show me your proof!" I said, stalling for time to think.

"You didn't ask for proof before forming those opinions, you will get no proof now."

"I had information from the other officers and detectives I was working with. We had proof. Show me your proof," I repeated.

I looked at the young girl. "Nabul, talk to me," I said. She stared blankly at me. "Please tell me what happened. Is what they say true? Do you know for a fact that this is the man who killed your family and then hurt you so badly? It could be nobody else but him?"

Her eyes started to pour forth tears, remembering. I waited. I needed to hear it from her. "Nabul, please tell me. Is this the man who did this horrible thing to you and your family?" I couldn't keep my voice from trembling.

She looked at the table of men across from where I sat then looked back at me. I ran my hands through my hair, willing this child to say or do something. The crowd was silent; the room was heavy with what was happening.

Finally, she nodded and then began crying openly. I wanted to pick her up and hold her and comfort her. I couldn't imagine what kind of memories she would have for a lifetime.

"Take her to her mothers' sister," Yassok ordered. One of the guards took her to someone down in the crowd, toward the back.

The air was becoming harder to breathe. I was terrified by what I knew I would be ordered to do next. I couldn't look at the men sitting across from me. The effort to see them, knowing what was next was so heavy in my body, I felt like I couldn't move. I was stunned, shocked.

"Kill him. Give her the laser. And Empress. Any effort to turn that weapon on anybody else in this room will end with your whole family being eliminated."

"Why are you doing this?" I asked. "This is not my responsibility. I'm not the one who should be executing this man! This is between him and your people! You can't make me do this!"

"You will kill him, Empress."

The weight of what I was being ordered to do was heavy. I couldn't move.

The guards lifted me from the chair and escorted me to a spot a couple of yards away from the whimpering man, restrained to the chair. One of them put an odd-looking weapon into my shaking hand. I couldn't hold it still enough. I was an expert shot, but my body was so beaten up by all it had been through, I had no strength to keep it steady.

"Help her steady the weapon," D'Nar ordered.

One of the guards came around behind me and placed his hands over mine to keep the weapon still.

"Kill him!" D'Nar ordered.

There was absolute silence in the room. It seemed nobody was breathing. All waited to see what would happen. My finger was on the trigger. I looked into the eyes of the man I was about to execute. Tears started rolling down my face, obscuring my vision.

"Kill him!"

I took a deep, shuddering breath and pulled the trigger. A beam leaped from the end of the laser, striking Reham in the chest. He screamed, making me jump, then shake even more. He had not died. This was going to be a long process. They were going to make me work to kill him. They would be sure it would be a long, torturous death. I was dealing with exceptionally cold, evil people.

"Kill him! Fire on him until he is dead!" D'Nar yelled above the screaming.

I pulled the trigger again. Reham screamed again, writhing in his seat, begging for me to stop, tears of pain spilling from his eyes, beads of blood seeping from his skin. I slumped against the guard, and he jerked me upright. The screaming was tearing into me. I had the power to stop, but I couldn't. I couldn't risk letting my family be executed.

D'Nar ordered me to shoot again. I was shaking so badly the guard holding me was having a hard time helping me hold the weapon. My legs were like limp rags, and it took all I had to stay upright. I shot him again, and again he screamed. A small trickle of blood ran from his mouth, a moment later from his ears. I had never heard someone in so much pain. The screaming wouldn't stop. Two more times I was ordered to shoot. Each time I fired on that man unable to escape from the weapon. He suddenly stopped screaming. His body went rigid, and he seemed to fight for breath that would no longer come. The blood from his mouth was flowing a little faster. He looked surprised and scared at the same time and then went limp in the chair.

Dr. J'Neer walked to the body, checked for a pulse, and made the announcement. "He's dead."

I passed out in the arms of the guard who had held my hands steady.

8

WE COULD DO nothing—nothing but watch.

Galton D'Nar had been a thorn in the side of Usia for a long time. His allegiance was with whatever world or continent would pay him the most for taking care of things no body else wanted to. Mostly the things he did were not legal, and usually harmful to someone in some way. He could twist words and situations skillfully and was known to be cruel beyond what most on our planet would tolerate. D'Nar was a man constantly in the cross hairs of our legal system, yet unable to be taken in.

There was a lot to be concerned about, knowing he had our empress.

D'Nar had sent us a live feed for us to watch the proceedings, with no chance of being able to trace where the ship was. The techs on our ship were working valiantly to locate her but were having no success. D'Nar had some kind of technology that kept us from being able to find the future empress of Usia. We seemed to be holding our breaths collectively as we watched the scene unfold before us, unable to intervene.

D'Nar seemed to be baiting us to keep us frustrated. Certainly, if that was his goal, he was succeeding. We had been watching since the first few seconds when the screen came to life, seemingly on its own, and the empress had appeared in the cell. It was grueling to see her reactions to traveling and not be able to administer something to lessen the side effects. We were beside ourselves as D'Nar treated her like a common criminal, perhaps worse. We watched as she slept, and we observed the interrogation, and finally the killing of the man accused of murdering a family. As much as we were horrified by what we saw, we were impressed with the strength of Jacqueline Laughlin. We had seen bigger, stronger people collapse more readily than she.

Surely Lady Minkas would be very pleased with the woman who would take her place. She had tremendous courage as she faced these circumstances.

I couldn't guess when D'Nar would be through with her, or what more he would decide to put her through.

"Dolm, she's back in the cell," Chasim announced. I had been busy with making sure Usia was getting the information they were asking for regarding what was going on.

I looked over Chasim's shoulder, at the monitor in front of him. The two guards had dropped her on the cot and were leaving the room. She lay on her side, asleep. The effects of shock and recovering from the traveling as well as the concussion had her completely worn out. She looked as if she had lost some weight over the last couple of days. Her face, though swollen, looked thinner and incredibly pale.

"Can you get a lock on where she is?" I asked.

"D'Nar is very good. He still has us totally locked out, giving us just this. I don't understand this at all. I can't get a reading on where this is coming from. I have a very bad feeling, Dolm, that someone in D'Nar's service is among us on Usia and put some things in place for this very purpose."

I nodded. It would make sense, and it was possible. We found those loyal to other governments from time to time. It was difficult to uncover one, but when we did, it made us realize the depth of the problem.

"What was the battle cruiser's last location? How far away are they now?"

"Another hour," Chasim replied. "They are making faster, riskier jumps than normal to get here. Pray they don't slam into a planet or star."

I heaved a sigh. There was nothing to do but watch and be prepared once they were ready to release her. My biggest concern was that they might not have it in their plans to release her.

I was certain they wouldn't execute her. D'Nar, as far as we knew, took orders from others. He wouldn't do it without being told to. I hoped we weren't being overly optimistic on that count.

D'Nar was a cruel man. The Ja'Harii had sent the one they knew they could use to break her spirit. I wasn't sure he had done that, though he had definitely tried. I wasn't sure I could have stood up to what she had.

We spent the next day taking turns keeping a watch on the empress. She was sleeping again, the sleep of healing. Dr. J'Neer went into the room at one point and administered another injection. I was sure it was another dose of their medication to help in her recovery. At least they were that humane. At the same time, I wondered what else they had planned for her that they wanted her well for.

We were both getting frustrated with the situation. She had now been asleep for almost a full day. A few times she stirred, and then she would be still again.

J'Neer had just administered another dose of medication. A few minutes after he left, D'Nar went into the room. He walked over to the cot, and with the help of one of the guards accompanying him, dumped her onto the floor. She lay on her side as she had the day before, propped up on her elbow, and then got to her feet. Her footing seemed a bit surer. She wasn't shaking as much now. I could see the weariness in her, though, as she stood up straight and tall in front of D'Nar and looked straight ahead. How had she gotten such strength? I wished she could hear us cheering her on.

"You killed a man yesterday," D'Nar stated.

She paused. We could see a slight tremble go through her, remembering. "I didn't have a choice, sir. You threatened the lives of my family."

D'Nar smiled. There was no joy there. "You did well."

"You bastard," she replied quietly. Her voice was hoarse, just above a whisper.

He slapped her across the face, the force throwing her a few feet away to the floor with a cry of pain.

"Get up," D'Nar ordered.

Again, she rose to her feet. There was a red mark across her face from D'Nar's hand. She stood tall, staring straight ahead. We could see tears making their way down her face.

"You're hungry?" he asked.

She paused. "Yes, sir."

"Bring her a meal." He went to a panel on the wall, pressed some buttons and a counter extended from the wall on the other side of the cot. One of the guards got a chair from the closet. A few moments later, the meal was brought into the room, placed on the counter.

We were sure she must be extremely hungry. She had been through a lot in three days, with no food whatsoever. We could even see from here that she was dehydrated. And yet she stood, showing no emotion or any sign of how hungry she must be.

"Do you have questions for me?"

"No, sir."

"Oh, I'm sure you do."

She remained quiet.

"Eat your meal," D'Nar ordered, and he and his men left the room. The empress waited several seconds after they left before she sat down and began eating and drinking, slowly.

And the screen went blank.

"Chasim! What—"

"I have no idea. They have cut us off, and I can't get them back."

"Keep scanning the area looking for their ship."

"I'll use what little we have, but it does not look good. They cut us off."

I knew what they were doing. It was just another of D'Nar's tactics to keep everyone off balance. He knew if he kept her until the current empress died, the risk of an upheaval on Usia would be great. He wanted that upheaval for the purpose of keeping us busy with things that would distract us.

My heart was broken. Our leader would die, and I would be here, maybe on the way back to our world. I would not be there to see my empress depart this life. To hold her hand and comfort her as her life left her body. I closed my eyes and tried not to dwell on it. I was here for this mission. Getting the new leader in place was certainly more important than seeing my beloved empress off. I took a deep breath to clear my mind and tried to concentrate on what needed to be done next.

9

I FINISHED THE meal. It was some kind of soup, a roll, something similar to coffee that was actually pretty good, and exotic fresh fruit I had never seen before that was incredibly sweet and flavorful. I felt a lot better after the meal, but still tired. I was incredibly thirsty and filled the coffee cup with water a couple of times, drinking it quickly.

I couldn't help but wonder what was next in store for me. D'Nar was one scary person. With some food and maybe a little time, perhaps I would have the strength to continue to stand up to him. I knew he was trying to break me. He had succeeded to some degree.

I had killed a man!

The thought came at me with such force it took my breath away. He had committed a horrible crime against a family—one a young girl would never get over. He deserved to die for sure. I had never had to even fire my weapon while on duty, and now I had killed a man. It was to protect my family, yes. But the heaviness in my heart, for taking a life, was so intense.

I couldn't help but dwell on what I had done. It struck me that maybe I wasn't as prepared as I thought I was, as a law enforcement officer. I knew it was possible that I might have to kill somebody in the line of duty. Now I wondered whatever made me think I could actually do that on the job and live with myself. This was harder than I thought it would be. I couldn't help but try to figure out how to justify what I had done, and yet at the same time there was the argument in my head that I didn't need to justify anything. I did what I did to save my family.

I was getting stuck in the events of the day before until I realized I had to do something to get out of here.

The thought came to me that I needed to find or make a weapon. I noticed all I had been given was a spoon to eat my meal. No fork or knife or anything else that could be made into a weapon. Even the plates were a durable plastic. I wondered if I could even use a weapon properly. I still felt so weak. Much of the pain was gone. Now I just felt incredibly weak. I decided I needed to get my strength up before I attempted using a weapon or going into hand-to-hand combat with these people.

I went over the events of the day before. Or whenever it was. I still had no idea what kind of time was passing. Everything that had happened and the things I learned kept going through my head. I tried to take them one at a time.

I had been kidnapped to be the new leader of some planet or someplace. That staggered my imagination. How could someone just do this? How could I possibly have been chosen to lead such a large group? What kind of people did this to someone? How could they even guarantee that I would be a competent leader for them? They didn't know me, my background, my abilities—nothing! How can you just choose someone to be a leader and not know if it's a fit between that person and the people needing to be lead?

And why would another group kidnap me? This was crazy. Wasn't that grounds for war or something like that? And not just kidnap me, but to treat me or anyone as I had been treated was incredible.

Were the Usians even looking for me? Did they know what happened, where I was? Was anybody doing anything to get me out of here?

My family. My friends. People I worked with. I took a deep breath and shoved my hands through my hair. It occurred to me that I might never see them again. I couldn't imagine what my family must be going through, not knowing what had happened to me, where I was, if they'd ever see me again. The pain had to be staggering. I could feel it myself. I suddenly felt incredibly, totally alone. At the mercy of whatever was going on, and the people making all this happen. The weight of all this was overwhelming, and I had to leave those thoughts. I needed to stay focused and do something, but I just didn't know what that something was.

I knew I had to get out of here, but once I got out of this room, where do I go? I was on a spaceship, not in a building.

I couldn't run outside and get help, even if I could subdue whoever came through that door next. Even if I could take someone hostage—there was an interesting thought, the hostage taking a hostage—I was pretty sure D'Nar would have us both killed.

D'Nar. What a piece of work. I hated the thought of having to see him again and just stand there. I couldn't understand the purpose in having me kill that man. The heaviness returned as I thought about what I had done.

I was still so thirsty. I knew I must be pretty dehydrated. I had vomited so much, slept so much, and been without food and water for a few days. I drank more water, trying to quench my thirst.

The door opened, and two guards came in the room. I stood up immediately.

"Dr. J'Neer wants to see you, let's go," said one of them.

I nodded and went with them. A short walk down a couple of corridors, and we were there.

J'Neer stood up from his desk. The room was stark, except for a couple of exam tables and some odd equipment on counters around the room. I stood at attention before him.

"Are you feeling better?" He was all business.

"Yes, sir."

"What happened to your face?" He gently touched the red mark left by D'Nar. I couldn't help but flinch; it was still tender.

"Nothing."

"Get up on one of those tables. I just want to see how you're doing."

I did as I was told. He went over to a cabinet, came back with a white bag of something, and placed it on my face. It was cold.

"Keep that there for a while. It will help the swelling go down. "How much does your nose hurt?" he asked, looking closely at my eyes.

"Quite a bit, sir."

"Doesn't look broken."

He took an instrument from his pocket, flipped a switch, and waved it over my body.

"You're dehydrated. The effects of the traveling are almost gone." He went to a sink and brought back a cup of water. "Drink this."

He rolled up my sleeve as I drank the water.

I watched as J'Neer adjusted an instrument that looked like a large silver syringe.

D'Nar entered the room. He was obviously not happy to see me. He looked around the room and demanded to know what J'Neer was doing with the syringe.

"She's on this ship, she's my responsibility. She's dehydrated and needs fluids now."

"She can drink her fluids, Doctor."

"She needs more than she can drink right now." J'Neer was not afraid of this man. He stood his ground. "You said you need to keep her alive."

"Alive, yes. Healthy, I could care less. Take her back to her room and consult me before you take it upon yourself to treat her again."

"I'm the ship's doctor. I have authority over anyone on this ship before you, as far as their health goes. Get out of my sick bay, D'Nar."

"Captain."

I wasn't sure where the voice came from—only that it was in the room. "The Usians war ship Klateche is two hundred kilometers away."

"On my way," replied the captain. He looked at the doctor. "She's a prisoner of war, not a member of our crew or our people. Don't make me explain anyone's position on this ship, J'Neer."

And they left the room.

J'Neer was about to stick me with the syringe, captain's orders or not, when the whole room shook with such force we both hit the floor. Equipment not secure to the countertops fell and bounced on the floor, a couple of items breaking apart.

I got up and hung onto the table as the ship continued to tremble from whatever had happened.

The doctor got up, looked around, and then at me.

"I'm okay," I said.

"Get on the table, fast."

"But—"

"Just get on the table." He injected my arm incredibly fast. It stung, and I bit my lip. He whispered close to my ear, obviously concerned about being heard. "This isn't just fluids. This will help them locate you and get you off here."

I searched his eyes, questioning.

"I can't explain now. I'll probably die if I'm found out. The less you know, the better for right now."

"You keep telling me that."

"Just—when you get to Usia, be the best leader you can be for that planet. Make it worth while for both of us."

"I don't understand."

"Don't worry about understanding. Right now, understanding is overrated."

I nodded.

He adjusted the syringe and gave himself an injection and explained, "I'm figuring they'll scan our ship. They'll see the two odd-colored blips. No telling who is who, unless they can take the time to do a detailed scan. Hopefully, they'll let me live."

"I'll let them know you helped me. I appreciate what you're doing."

His face darkened. "Just so you know, I'm not on either side. I just can't stomach the idea of selling you to the highest bidder in this quadrant."

"What?" I was stunned.

"Let's go." He grabbed my hand and pulled me out the door as the ship shuddered again. "The captain will sell you if he can. The sex trade out here is very lucrative. Exotics like humans are especially desirable."

I couldn't say anything. My mind was trying to absorb this last piece of information. This nightmare kept getting worse and worse, and I wanted so badly for it to end. As we ran down the corridor, I could feel my strength coming back to me. The fatigue, as well as the pain from my injuries, was lifting. We stopped at an elevator, but J'Neer thought better of it. Before I knew it, we were climbing a ladder between decks. I counted four floors before we stepped onto the floor in the closet like room that went from deck to deck.

"So?" I asked.

"We need to get to the traveling room." J'Neer wiped his hands on the sides of his pants. "I need to go down the hall and make sure it's not occupied. You stay here. I don't know what I'm going to find or what might happen. No matter what, stay here. I'm betting the Usian ship out there will be scanning us, if they aren't already. They will notice the difference in the two life signs they see and realize one has to be you. I'm betting they'll travel us both over, not knowing which of us is you. In the meantime, I need to see if I can get us off the ship if the Usians don't take care of things themselves. Don't go anyplace from here."

10

O UR BATTLE CRUISER, the Klateche, entered orbit, and we docked inside. Within a short time, we were on the bridge and had given a complete account to Captain T'Huur. I was always impressed with the people who operated these ships, as well as the technological wonders that were on board. This one especially, with Captain T'Huur in charge, was the best in the fleet. T'Huur was a well-trained military man. The men on his ship would follow him to the ends of the galaxy if he asked. The relationship he had with them was enviable among other ships captains. We were in the best of hands, and I was confident if anyone could get the empress off the Naringah, it would be this team.

T'Huur had communications try to hail the other ship with no result, but their advanced equipment located the Naringah without much effort.

"Natar," the captain addressed the officer at the weapons console, "open fire on the ship. Take out their weapons, and we need to hamper their life support systems."

"Captain," called one of the engineers, "I've been scanning the ship. I've located two life signs that are significantly different from the rest of the ship's complement."

The captain and I went over to the console where the science officer was busy continuing to gather more information. He pointed to a portion of the ship where we could see a number of blips representing life forms. Two of them were yellow. As he scanned other surrounding areas of the ship, we could see that all other blips were blue.

"I think that's her, sir," said the science officer.

"And the other blip?" the captain asked.

"I don't know, sir, but I think it might be safe to say it could be someone with her, possibly helping her."

"Can we travel them over here?"

"Not at this time. They have some shields still up—"

Natar had been firing at the other ship, and now we were reaping the results. Our ship shook violently, throwing those of us who were not sitting securely at consoles to the floor. We got up and returned to the science officer's station.

Captain T'Huur ordered Natar to continue to fire on the ship, which was taking evasive routes at the same time.

"Natar, what is the status of the Naringah?" the captain asked.

"Weapons are damaged, not inoperable. Working to strike their life support. We've located it and struck it, it's holding. One more strike, and it should be gone. That will give them limited air and operations."

"Keep firing then. Take out their engines as well, Natar."

"Yes sir."

"T'Kir," the captain addressed the science officer, "as soon as we are able, we need to travel those two people. Since we don't know which one is the empress, we need them both here. Let me know as soon as it is happening. I want a medical team to the traveling room to meet her, as well as an armed guard to secure whoever the other individual is."

The battle continued. Our two ships exchanged blasts as I listened in on the conversation between the science officer and the travel room technician. I chose to stay by the science console, intensely aware of how difficult it could be to get the empress off that ship and safely on our way home. One of the blips was remaining stationary, the other on the move down a corridor it seemed.

11

I WAS ALONE in this small closet with the ladder that connected decks. J'Neer had been gone for a few minutes now. The ship was being rocked pretty steadily by fire from the other ship. I hoped I would live through this. I had to wonder how accurate their fire was and if they knew where I was. Were they scanning us and had they located me, as J'Neer had suggested they might? Living and being a leader to this new place was certainly better than dying here from the battle going on.

The battle going on because of me.

The thought came to me that I had two groups of people fighting over me. One wanted me to lead them, and the other—I wasn't sure what the other wanted. D'Nar had some plans that were pretty disturbing, if J'Neer's information was correct.

This time in the closet gave me a lot of time to think and pray. Since I was so scared, I found myself praying more urgently. It seemed more productive than thinking. Prayer lasted long enough to include my family, and then I was back to thinking. Thinking lead to my imagination to places I would have preferred it not go. Like what was being done back on Earth to find me.

I imagined they would be checking my bank account and computer, trying to find out if there was any activity on any of my credit cards. No, my cards and other things should be found in my home. They would be talking to family and friends. Jim Learner would be questioned, especially after the scene at the hospital. They would come up with a list of places to search for me. I wasn't even sure where they would begin to look. Of course, no matter where they looked, they'd never think to go beyond the Earth where they lived. Eventually I'd be an open case that they just looked in on every now and again. They might pass my file onto fresh eyes once in a while. They might remain hopeful that I would just turn up, but in their law-enforcement cynical hearts, they would know I was gone forever. Their words to my family and the public would be laced with some kind of hope, despite what they knew in their gut. I would be one more unsolved case on their shelf that would haunt them just a little more, because I was one of them.

And here I was; on a spaceship being blasted by another spaceship. Waiting for the cavalry. How did this happen? I couldn't figure out how I had gotten mixed up in this. It made no sense at all. I wasn't trained, groomed, or prepared to govern an office of people, let alone a whole planet. How did they set their sights on me? What had qualified me in their eyes? I considered everything that had happened in the last few days I'd been detained here. I thought back to the room I had been in, and I remembered the map on the wall. How it looked so similar to the one I had received in the mail.

The map! The one I had been sent just a few days before. And my neighbor Freddy had commented on someone unusual who seemed to be looking for me. And then I saw the two guys at the car wreck scene where I had passed out. The map that Jim Learner had sent me started all this. I was sure he didn't have a clue about any of what was going on now. Somehow the map was tied into this, I just didn't know how. Somehow, opening that package had initiated an invitation to this party.

Where was J'Neer? It seemed like he'd been gone for almost an hour, even though I knew it had to be only five or ten minutes. Amazing how stress makes your mind seem like time either speeds up or slows down in ways you can't get a hold of. The ship continued to shudder, sometimes violently. A couple of times I nearly went through the hole in the floor that accommodated the ladder. J'Neer had to be doing something to get us out of here. He'd mentioned the traveling room. If some of my symptoms when I first awakened here were from that, I wasn't crazy about going through it again. But if it was my only way off this ship, I was ready to go now, vomiting be damned! But where was he? It seemed he'd been gone way too long. It occurred to me that it could have been found out that he was helping me, in which case I was on my own.

The thought of leaving here and possibly meeting up with D'Nar was scary. I still didn't know the purpose for killing that man. It wasn't my responsibility, but he had threatened my family. I had traded my family's lives for the life of a man who committed a horrendous crime. At the time it seemed like the right thing to do. It still did. But it would haunt me forever. Maybe that's what D'Nar wanted.

I was praying again. It was all I had—pleading with God to spare the two of us. I reminded Him I was willing to go to cold places, if He would just get me out of this. I wondered if J'Neer liked cold temperatures. I'd take him with me.

Where was J'Neer? I was getting very concerned that he had been discovered and arrested. They would be questioning him about where I was, where he had left me, and if I was armed and who he was working for and—

The door opened, and J'Neer stepped in. I gave a grateful sigh.

"I am so glad to see you," I said, relieved.

"Come on. It's just down the hall and the room is empty." He took my hand and led me down the hall into the traveling room. J'Neer went to the console and began running his fingers across the board, checking results on a display and adjusting settings.

The ship shook, and J'Neer said something that I was sure was a swear word in his native language, whatever that was.

"What happened?" I asked.

"That last hit cleared the board. Hope we don't get hit as we're traveling out of here." He reset the board and checked it one more time.

"Let's go, we have thirty seconds."

J'Neer grabbed my hand and led me up to the platform.

The door we had just come through opened, and two guards entered. I think J'Neer used another swear word. He raised his weapon and fired at the guards, dropping them both.

"Stop them!" D'Nar's voice came from the door. He stood there with two other guards. One of them fired off two laser blasts at us, and that was it.

12

I GASPED AND pushed away the cold, wet rag on my face. I fought to wake up and saw that I was fighting J'Neer trying to wake me.

"What in blazes happened?" I asked. I couldn't remember the last few minutes of being awake. I had been standing with J'Neer someplace, and that was it. Maybe it was better that way. My head hurt, and my body felt like it had been zapped with an electrical charge.

I looked around. "Oh, Lord." I groaned. "This has got to be worse than being shot."

"Can you move?"

"I don't want to."

"Is your back very tender?"

"Yes, and the rest of me hurts."

"Me too. It's the effects of the laser blast. Your back's going to hurt for a few days, the rest will start to fade in a few hours."

We were in the cell I had been taken from. Right back where I had started. This was not good. J'Neer got up and pulled me to my feet.

"We need to get out of here," he said.

"I'm sure they've gone above and beyond the call to keep us here," I commented. "D'Nar doesn't strike me as one to forget to lock the barn door the second time."

"What?" Confusion crossed his face, trying to sort out the metaphor.

"Never mind. What do you have in mind to get us out of here?"

"I don't know. Give me a few minutes to think about this."

"We may not have a few minutes."

He nodded, and then I saw the look in his eyes. I knew. He was in as much trouble as me.

"Thank you," I said.

"For...?"

"You tried to get me off here. You're now in the same situation I'm in. Maybe worse."

He nodded. "If we don't get out of here, it will all have been for nothing, now. We've got to have a plan."

We were both quiet, and I realized after a moment that the ship had stopped shaking. Was it possible that one of the ships out in space here had been damaged enough that it was no longer capable of returning fire? I was hoping the Usian ship was the one in good shape and that we would be rescued momentarily.

The door opened, and D'Nar entered with two guards and another man. He was shorter than D'Nar, a little heavier and dressed in clothing a little more conservative than I had seen on anyone so far. It looked expensive. He had the look of someone of wealth and was busy looking me up and down. Thankfully, the outfit I wore was not very figure flattering, and he had to work to really figure out what was under the jumpsuit. My heart was beating faster, and my fear spiked again. I knew what was going on. I looked at J'Neer. He looked as if he had resigned himself to the situation. *Not good*, I thought.

The man with D'Nar fanned the air in front of his face and coughed.

"What is that?" he asked. He stepped closer to me, took a quick sniff of the air close to me, and then backed up, coughing harder and continuing to fan the air in front of him.

"D'Nar, you really need to start taking better care of your merchandise," he commented. "At least a shower and some clean clothes."

"We don't have time for that, Ronnok," D'Nar shot back. "We are under fire. If you want her, bathe and dress her yourself. The deal is that you get rid of her so she won't be found for a very long time, perhaps never. That would be even better."

"Is she good?"

"No idea. We never took the opportunity to join with her."

"Your loss, D'Nar." Ronnok coughed again. "Under all of… that"—he gestured to my jumpsuit and lack of cleanliness—"I think she's probably quite lovely and would be worth joining with at least once."

I looked at J'Neer. I was pretty sure he mouthed the word "sex" to me. I closed my eyes and took a deep, shaky breath.

"I'll take her."

"You need to take her now," D'Nar said. He was in a hurry. "We could be boarded any moment, and I want her out of here. I wouldn't be surprised if they've been able to defeat our shields. They could travel her out any second."

"D'Nar," J'Neer said. "She will be preferable to another that they might select. Wouldn't it be better to let them have this one to lead?"

"Dr. J'Neer, be quiet. Your minutes are numbered."

"Doctor?" the other man said, very obviously interested in J'Neer's title.

"Ship's doctor. I told you he was helping her escape. He will be executed after you leave."

"I need a doctor on my ship. The one I had was killed some time ago. I will give you an additional payment for him."

"That would be fine," D'Nar said. "Take them both. Just keep as tight a guard on him as you do her."

The man took out a devise, spoke some words into it, and the next thing I knew, we were in another room, obviously another ship.

I fell to the floor, violently ill again. Blast the traveler. How could they have all this technology and not be able to get people around any better than this?

The ship shook as if it were coming apart then steadied. I could feel the thrum of engines. Obviously a much smaller ship than we had been on before. J'Neer was kneeling beside me, trying to help.

"Take her to holding, and take the doctor to our medical unit. Keep a guard on him."

13

THE TWO BLIPS had gone down a corridor and into a room. The blips were stationary for only a few minutes, and then they were gone.

"Where are they?" I fought to stay calm enough not to raise my voice.

The science officer's hands were working furiously to pull an answer from the computer, but nothing was happening.

"Is there another ship out there?"

"It's the only answer, but I'm not reading anything. If there is one, it's using an advanced cloak."

"Corrett," called Murr, the communications officer. "Message just came in." He looked at his board and then at me. I could see it in his face and hear it in his voice.

"Lady Minkas has died." He consulted the panel before him again. "Just over an hour ago."

I dropped my head. This couldn't be happening. Our planet was without a leader. There was nobody to fill the gap Lady Minkas had left. The different peoples of our planet needed the wisdom and leadership of another to help bridge gaps and smooth things over enough to at least be civil to one another. Having been Lady Minkas's personal assistant for so many years, I would be called on to make some decisions, knowing how she would have handled things, but this would only be temporary. We needed the new leader now. Later could be disastrous.

I feared for our planet; it was only a matter of time before the continents were at war with each other. It was almost frightening to think we needed an outsider so desperately to keep the peace of our planet, but we had had the system for so long.

With the new empress gone, there was no telling how long we might be without a leader. As long as we knew for a fact that she was still alive, we could take no steps to replace her. The dilemma before us now was trying to locate her and get her to Usia, where she was supposed to be.

I feared for the safety of the future empress. We had not personally dealt with D'Nar in the past, but we had heard of him. None of it was good. He was typically hired by others to do some dirty work or other. He was unpredictable

"I need to return to Usia," I told the captain.

"We can have you on a transport within the hour," he replied.

"That will be fine. Thank you."

We took care of a few details, and I was on my way.

There was a funeral to plan. And then we needed to figure out how to go about locating Jackie Laughlin.

It took three days to get back to Usia. I found myself second-guessing my decision to conduct this last mission the entire three days, when I wasn't quietly grieving the loss of my friend and the leader of my planet.

14

THE GUARDS LIFTED me from the floor and carried me out of the room. A few minutes of travel time through the ship, and I was left in a small cell seemingly in the bowels of the ship. There was the unpleasant smell of machinery, the ozone sort of smell of computers, and something else that was disturbingly close to burning flesh. The smell made me gag, and the nausea I was feeling increased.

The engines were working hard to get us going at top speed, if what I was feeling was any indication. The whole cell seemed to thrum with the labor of whatever powered the ship. It was almost soothing, as I lay there trying to relax and get over the nausea and body aches that kept me from even thinking clearly. I finally fell asleep, curled up in a ball on the cot in the room.

When I awoke, I was so disoriented I fell out of the cot in a panic. I stood up, sore but feeling much better than I had earlier. Again, I had no idea how much time had passed. I took some time to look the room over. There was a toilet in the corner, a small sink, and the cot I had slept in. The door to the room was a force field of some sort that coalesced lightly, resembling Saran Wrap gone bad.

Every time I thought about where I was and the plans this man had for me, I panicked. And then I would pull back from those thoughts and try to come up with a plan. There was nowhere to run, no one to help, and I was relatively certain even a small ship, if I could actually come across one, would be just a bit more difficult to pilot than a bumper car. I couldn't even count on J'Neer now. I was totally on my own. I needed to get out of this room, and if I got thrown off the ship, I was pretty sure that would be better than what this guy had in mind.

It occurred to me that if I was a constant problem to them, they might just send me somewhere else—like a planet. I could handle being on a planet. There would be air and someplace to run.

In theory...

I heard footsteps coming down the corridor outside the cell and flattened myself on the wall next to the door. The two guards peered in then looked to the side. I was just out of sight enough that I couldn't be seen. I held my breath and waited.

"She's hiding, careful going in," one of them said.

I screwed up my courage as I heard the door give a gentle pop, and the force field shut down. The two stepped into the room, immediately looking to the side of the room. The one closest to me spotted me as I launched myself at him.

I slammed my knee into his groin and punched him in the eye. He collapsed with an "oomph." The other guard was on top of me in a second, shouting at me to get down. I fought and kicked out, but he was much bigger than me, and I was quickly pinned to the floor, facedown. I still struggled, not willing to admit defeat

"Settle down," he ordered and slammed my face into the floor. I cried out in pain. My nose, still healing from the last beating, began bleeding profusely.

I stopped struggling. The guard holding me called for medical help. My hands were secured behind me, and I was left on the floor, still facedown, a puddle of blood forming under my face, so I couldn't even rest my face on the floor.

J'Neer came through the door a few minutes later. I could see him try to hide the smile at seeing the guard, but then he saw the pool of red under my face. He started to come to tend to me, when the other guard ordered him to treat the injured guard first. He gave the guard an injection that helped him relax and ease the pain within a few seconds, and then he rushed to my side.

"Take this off her," he ordered, referring to whatever held my wrists.

"We're not doing anything for her," said the injured guard.

"Take this off her right now. I need to treat her, and I can't do that when she's like this. You want to tell Ronnok you didn't follow doctor's orders? Especially when you damaged the goods he wants to sell? If her injuries affect her appearance, Ronnok will blame you two. You want to deal with that?"

The other guard paused briefly and then freed my wrists. J'Neer helped me to my feet and walked me to the cot. I sat, holding my face in my hands. My face hurt so badly, and my nose especially was throbbing. I wouldn't cry in front of these men, but I couldn't keep the tears from going down my face.

I knew now that J'Neer was no longer on my side. He wouldn't flinch when Ronnok sold me to the highest bidder. I was on my own to deal with whatever happened. For now, I needed to get my face fixed. A part of me wondered how many times my nose would have to be injured in the process…

"Let me see your nose." J'Neer took my hands from my face and then was dabbing at the blood coming from my nose. I cried out and pushed his hands away.

"Just leave me alone!" I yelled. J'Neer gave me the cloth, directing me to hold it to my nose.

"I need to get her to the infirmary," J'Neer told the guards. "Her nose is broken. I don't have what I need here to treat her."

"She stays."

"What're your names?" J'Neer demanded.

"L'koe and Waiq," the injured guard answered.

J'Neer took a deep breath. "Fine. She stays here. I'll give Ronnok a full report detailing her injuries. You tell him how she got them in your report. Make sure you include it was your idea not to let her be treated."

The two of them were quiet. I continued to hold the cloth to my nose. Some of the blood was going down the back of my throat, making me gag.

"We go with you and stay with you, then," L'koe stated.

"That's fine. Let's just get her taken care of."

J'Neer took my arm to help me up, but I pulled away from him and got to my feet on my own. I stayed behind him with the two thugs behind me as we left the room.

In the infirmary, I was put on a medical bed. The guards were close by, watching and listening to everything said. J'Neer held a long, thin metal tube in his hand that had a light at one end. "This is a healing laser. Close your eyes. I need to direct it close to your eyes. If the light hits your eyes, you could possibly lose sight in them."

I obediently closed my eyes. I heard the quiet hum and felt the slight warmth of the laser as J'Neer played it over my injured nose and the rest of my face. I could feel the blood slowing and then stopping, as if the arteries were being gently cauterized. The pain was less severe, and I could feel myself starting to relax. Nobody said anything for a long time as the doctor continued to let the laser continue its work on my face. Keeping my eyes closed, the discomfort almost gone, and the quiet of the room, I fell asleep.

"Jackie." It was a whisper.

I mumbled something unintelligible.

"Jackie." Somebody shook me, and I awoke with a start and screamed, the memory of everything one huge overwhelming thought in my head.

"Jackie, stop."

I opened my eyes and looked at Dr. J'Neer. I took a deep breath and let it out slowly.

"Time to go back to your cell."

I sat up quickly and got off the bed before he could tell me not to go so fast and collapsed at his feet on the floor.

"Move slowly. You lost a lot of blood, and you're still recovering. Don't get up fast and don't move too fast. Take your time." He gently helped me to my feet and made me sit up on the bed again. I touched my nose. Just lightly sore. It was still a bit swollen, but it was much better than it had been before the second assault on it.

I nodded.

"Make sure she gets a meal," J'Neer ordered.

"She'll get her meal when everyone else—"

"Then she stays here until I'm satisfied she's getting the care she should get."

J'Neer went to an intercom. The conversation seemed to be with someone in a kitchen. J'Neer placed an order for a meal to be brought to the infirmary. The little I caught of the conversation, the meal was a combination of things I'd never heard of. I was almost touched that he was taking some time to make sure I had what he thought I needed: food and medical treatment before I was sold into a life of perversion. Great. I'd be a healthy concubine. I understood and didn't understand at the same time what he was doing and had to wonder if I would risk my life for someone I didn't know.

I hoped I would be noble enough to do the right thing—whatever that was at the time.

The guards split up. L'koe stayed while Waiq left to tend to his duties, whatever they were.

It wasn't long before another person came through the door with a tray of food. J'Neer took me to the table where it had been placed and encouraged me to eat. It had the resemblance of rice and beans and was very good. I drank the water and asked for more.

When I was done, J'Neer allowed L'koe to take me back to the room. L'koe was concerned enough to call for Waiq. I didn't blame him; I wouldn't trust me either, after what I had done earlier.

Back in the cell, I looked around again. There was nothing to use as a weapon. There was nothing to do. No books, no pencil and paper. Did they use things like that out here?

It still smelled pretty bad. I couldn't see any venting that allowed fresh air. Then again, maybe an air vent would make the smell worse, depending on where the odor was coming from. At least I was somewhat used to it, so that it was no longer making me quite so nauseous.

The temptation was to feel defeated and act on that. There wasn't much to be positive about. The bits and pieces I'd heard told me I could be violated any minute. The fear was palpable. Every time a guard came toward my little cell on his way to somewhere else, I felt myself panicking. I couldn't think past the fear. It was stifling.

It had gone on for most of the day, when something stopped me. I sat down and just prayed. I prayed for a plan. Something to do that would be productive. I couldn't stop praying. That was productive. It wasn't long before I began quietly singing. Some of the songs were from church; some were just fun songs that I remembered. I found myself climbing out of the fear that had me in such a deep pit just a short time before. It didn't change my circumstances, but it cleared my head and gave me something positive to focus on. The guards who passed my room just looked at me a bit curiously before going on about their business.

It was later in the day, I think, that I started examining the walls. Could there be something hidden that could be used? I had no clue what it might be, but it was something to do to pass the time.

I stopped after a while, frustrated. How could I think there might be something on the wall? That was absurd. They would have found it and taken it out of here, whatever it might have been. And then I spotted the camera up in the corner of the room, opposite the door. I was sure it hadn't been there before. I wondered how often they checked it, or if I was constantly being monitored. I couldn't help but think it was a huge waste of manpower to watch one person. I sat down and tried to think of what to do with that. And then the niggling of a plan came into my mind.

I stood under the camera, out of range of the lens. When I got tired of standing, I sat. I was pretty sure nobody was coming to see me. I carefully slipped out of the jumpsuit, making sure I couldn't be seen from the camera. I took the jumpsuit—sleeve cuffs in one hand, pants cuffs in the other—and using it as a loop, tossed it over the camera and pulled. The suit slipped off the front of the housing. I knew I didn't have much time. I threw it over the camera again, trying to secure it more fully toward the mount holding the camera, and then pulled. It held tight. I hung my total weight on it; nothing happened. I jumped and hung onto the suit, trying to jerk the unit out of the wall. It took four strong jumps, but it finally dislodged and fell with me to the floor, leaving wires dangled from the ceiling, like dislocated worms. I dressed quickly and took the heavy piece of equipment to the cot, where I found the control buttons. I started pressing buttons until the quiet whirring stopped, and the light next to the lens went out. I figured it must have some sort of battery backup.

I hefted the camera in my hands for a few seconds and then threw it at the door. It bounced off the clear, shimmering mass and clattered to the floor. Okay, I wasn't going to win any prizes for most creative escape plan, but it was all I had.

"You turkey!" I yelled. I threw it again. Again it bounced off the door and hit the floor. The mount sprang off and the camera sizzled, snapped and popped, smoke came out of it, and then it was quiet. I threw the mount at the door, and an electrical charge from the door enveloped it. It stuck to the door for a few seconds then fell to the floor, smoking and bent out of shape, the heat from the door having made the metal soft and pliable. I began throwing the camera around the room, hitting the walls and ceiling at random. Testing, trying to see if any part of the cell was vulnerable. If I heard somebody coming, I stopped, but I continued as soon as the person was out of sight. The camera hit an area about a foot away from the door, about waist high. A panel I hadn't been able to detect earlier sprang off the wall. The depression in the wall was about six inches square and shallow.

"Well, well," I muttered. There were switches and grooves. I began flipping switches but couldn't figure out what the grooves were for. I hadn't seen anything like it anyplace I'd been so far. I tried putting my fingers in the grooves but then realized if it had anything to do with DNA or fingerprints, it wouldn't respond to me. I stepped back and started throwing the camera at the panel in the wall again. The body of the camera was beginning to loosen and come apart. It only took another few lobs, and it fell apart completely. Cogs, computer chips, a few wires, the lens, but nothing I could use.

The mount had cooled. I picked it up and started using it as a lever to loosen the switches in the panel. I hammered it, which only made the switches recede into the panel.

I sat down on the floor and put my face in my hands. I wasn't sure how much time had passed, but I thought it might have been about an hour, maybe a little more. I was genuinely surprised nobody had come to see what had happened to the camera. Either someone was asleep at the monitors, or it had been put up there to intimidate. Or maybe it didn't work and nobody had the gumption to repair it. I guess initiative is lacking in the stars as much as on Earth sometimes.

I was thirsty, so I went to the sink and cupped my hands to drink water from the faucet. I looked up and had another idea. I took a shoe off, filled it with water, and threw the water at the door. The door snapped and popped loudly, making me jump back out of the way as the power that ran it arced into the room and then out again. The shimmering seemed to have lessened. I filled my shoe again and threw more water at the door. It sizzled and hummed, arced again, but fell back into place, weaker than before. I threw the camera at it, and the camera went through this time, but not without a lot of noise and obvious damage being done to the unit. I filled my shoe a third time, threw it at the door, and this time, it gave a soft pop and everything that controlled the door stopped.

I put my hand through the doorway just to be sure it was really no longer operational. I stepped through and stopped outside the doorway. Now that I was out, I didn't know where to go. Being on the other side of the door was preferable to being stuck in the room, but I had no idea what to do.

This is what I got for not planning things out better.

There had to be a map of the ship somewhere; it would have been nice to have had one of those location maps with a "you are here" star next to where I happened to be, with numbers corresponding to rooms. Not likely…

I heard footsteps coming down the hall and went the opposite direction, after putting my wet shoe back on. I was free! I just didn't know where to go from here. I stepped into a recessed area and hung back in the shadows, waiting. My wet shoe made squishy sounds with every step—so much for stealth.

"Find her!" It was a voice I hadn't heard earlier, and it was angry. Footsteps ran past the area I was in. I waited quietly for a few seconds, listening.

"Hey, you," someone whispered, and I jumped. Behind me was another cell, occupied by an older man. He was short and thin. His head was balding over eyes that squinted, trying to get a better look at me. He wore a dark jumpsuit that looked and smelled like he hadn't had a shower in at least a few weeks.

"You got out," he observed.

"Yeah."

"Are you the empress everyone's excited about?"

"I guess so."

"You either are, or you aren't."

"I am."

"Let me out, I can get us both off this ship."

"Who are you? Why are you locked up?"

"Bezenta. Used to work for Ronnok. Lost a deal for him."

"Must have been a pretty big deal."

"It was. Nearly cost him his fortune. Ronnok only survived by killing the others involved."

"Sweet. I didn't need to hear that."

"Get me out of here."

"I don't know how."

"How'd you get out?"

I told him about using my shoe to throw water on the force field, as well as using the camera.

"Really. That's pretty smart. There's no camera in here."

"I didn't see the one in my cell until I returned from a visit to the doctor's office."

"They have a doctor now?"

"Yes. Apparently new to the crew."

We heard footsteps coming from a distance.

"I gotta go. Try the water trick," I said and started to leave.

"She's down here!" Bezenta yelled.

I looked back at him for an instant, shocked. So much for honor among prisoners.

"Hey, if I can get back in his good graces, I'm going to," Bezenta said.

I took off down the hall, Bezenta's voice directing the guards. I came to a corner and stopped, listening. I heard nothing, so I poked my head around the corner and saw some of Ronnok's men. I ran back in the other direction, saw an elevator-type place, and pressed the button.

The door opened, and Ronnok stood there. I took off back down the hall, his voice trailing after me. I couldn't get away! This was a much smaller ship, and I had no idea where I was or where to go. I took a chance and palmed a door, which opened to my hand. I stepped inside and caught myself before I fell through the space around the ladder that connected the floors. I began climbing as quickly as I could, not stopping even when I heard two guards coming up behind me. At the third ladder set, I stepped onto the floor there. I was out of breath, running on sheer adrenaline. The two guards were not far behind, and looking up, I didn't have too far to go yet. I had to go someplace else. All those cop shows of the person being pursued upward were coming back to mind. It never went well for the one being chased. I opened the door and walked right into two men about to open the door. They were as surprised as I was. I pushed them away and ran down the hall. I heard and felt the laser when it struck my back. I think I screamed as I fell to the floor, losing consciousness.

15

I AWOKE IN another cell. My back hurt like someone had pounded me where I had been hit with the laser. In fact, my whole body hurt so much from the blast that I didn't want to move. It was worse getting hit the second time. Nothing in my body really wanted to cooperate in moving at all. I was content to stay on the floor until the discomfort passed.

I was alone, this time with a guard posted outside the door. There was no sink in this room, just the toilet and the cot. I was pretty sure the camera was in a box mounted up in a corner, unable to be accessed at all. I could feel the thrum of the ships engines. We were still underway to wherever we were going.

And I had no shoes. These guys caught on quickly.

I lay quietly on the floor for almost an hour, just waiting for the pain to subside. I finally felt like I could get up. I wanted to do something. I took my time and was able to finally stand up and wished I hadn't. The room spun around for a few seconds, obviously more effects from the laser blast. Something smelled very bad, and I realized after a few minutes that it was me. Ronnok was right; I was a mess. I hadn't showered in too long. I didn't like smelling me any more. My hair felt horrible, and the jumpsuit was still bloodstained from two assaults on my nose. This was almost worse than being locked up.

The force field did its quiet pop and was no more. I hadn't even heard anybody coming down the hall. I was probably still too messed up from the two laser shots I'd gotten inside of a short time. Two guards came into the cell, never saying a word. One was a female; she had webbed hands, very wide shoes that I guessed housed webbed feet, and I could see something resembling gills on each side of her neck, just below her very short hair.

They secured my hands behind my back with an odd set of cuffs before we left the cell. A few minutes later, we were in a large sitting room. Every few seconds, a woman would walk into the room beyond this one, or one would walk out. They were gorgeous and beautifully dressed. There were subtle differences in their appearances that made it clear that these ladies were not from Earth. It was the color of their skin, or the shape of some of their features, or other unique things that set them apart from human females. As they passed through the room, most of them looked my way. Some of them covered their noses. They all hurried out of this room, eager to get away from me.

A petite woman came from the other room, obviously in charge of whatever this place was. She walked up to us without a word and walked around me twice. I just stood still while the guards stood a short but ready distance from me.

This woman was as lovely as the others coming and going. She wore a floor-length dark-blue gown. The fabric seemed to cling to all the correct contours of her body. Her hair was short, swept back off her face, which was made up to accentuate features that seemed to be pretty close to human, except for her eyes. They were an odd shade of blue surrounded by a ring of purple, and when she blinked, they opened and closed sideways rather than up and down.

"What has Ronnok dragged home now?" she inquired as she finished her second tour around me. She had an accent that I'd never be able to place.

"Courtesy of D'Nar is what we understand," the female guard said.

"It figures. Knowing D'Nar, he probably didn't take care of his toys as a child either," she said quietly.

"Where are you from, honey?" she asked me.

"Earth."

"Ah, a human. I think you're only the second one I've ever met. Humans are not part of the overall population out here. Ronnok probably figures on getting a good price for you."

I looked around. I didn't want to stay here. I didn't care what I smelled like or looked like; I wanted to get away from here. With two guards keeping me company and the other ladies around here, there was little chance of making an escape. I had no idea where to go once I got away from these people anyway. I had to have time to make a plan, maybe make a contact who could help me get away.

She called into the other room, and two other women came out. One of them had features almost chimp-like, yet she was still very attractive.

"Take her back there and get her cleaned up. Put her in something a bit more attractive than that ugly thing. You might as well burn it. Are you hurt anywhere, honey?"

"What do you mean?" I asked.

"Do you have any cuts, bruises, any kind of injuries?"

"Just to my back from a couple of laser blasts."

"Drop the top of that thing."

I hesitated. I didn't want to disrobe in this very public place. Before I could do anything, she unzipped the jumpsuit and then pulled it down over my shoulders, to my waist and wrists. The cuffs kept the top of the suit from going any further. I took a deep breath.

"Turn around," she ordered.

I turned around, facing the two guards. The female wasn't too interested in what was on my chest, but the male wasn't hiding his pleasure at seeing a half-naked woman in front of him.

"What's your name?" the woman asked.

"Jackie."

"Very unusual name. I like it. Well, Jackie, your back has some pretty severe swelling from those blasts. I think Neru and Yass can help make you more comfortable."

She turned me back around. The female guard and the other two women lead me back to what turned out to be a large bathing area. The main room led back into private bathing rooms. The three women with me lead me to a room toward the back. It was a large bathroom. There was a shower stall, a sink and vanity combination, a toilet in a small alcove in the corner, and room in the middle for what I thought might be a massage table. The room was tastefully decorated in blues and greens, and the odd instrumental music that had been playing out in the entry room was played in this room as well.

I stripped down and took a long, hot shower with a shower gel that was fragrant and energizing. It felt good to get clean and smell clean. Once out of the shower, I was told to lie facedown on the table in the middle of the room. A large instrument was lowered from the ceiling and allowed to play over my back. It was a healing laser, much larger than the one J'Neer had used on my broken nose only a short time ago. I could feel a light tingling on my back as it did its work. I was allowed to lie there in the warmth of the room, the comfort of the colors and lighting and the music as well as the soothing fragrance that filled the room, falling asleep within a short time. When I was awoken nearly an hour later, my entire body felt significantly better. The aches and pains were gone. I actually felt fresh and rejuvenated. The little bit of swelling of my face, especially around my nose, was gone.

Once I was done on the table, the ladies put me in a tub of warm water for fifteen minutes. I was told the water had herbs in it to detoxify my body.

The two ladies fixed my hair and gave me a simple gown and underthings as well as a simple pair of shoes. I actually looked good, for a prisoner. I was more frightened than ever that I would be taken to Ronnok for "joining" purposes. Instead, I was taken back to my cell.

I was left in the cell for the rest of the day. Meals were brought to me. I didn't recognize anything on the trays, but whatever it was, was always good and filled me up for a short time.

———∽∾∽———

It was three days later. I had just been returned to my cell after my daily shower and a new gown. Both guards who had taken me to the showers had gone, leaving the guard who stood watch over me. I walked around the cell a couple of times before sitting down. I faced the corner of the room with the guard in my peripheral vision and began to pray and try to remember scriptures to keep me sane.

The boredom was intense. It gave me a lot of time to think, which really was not a good thing. It made my mind go places related to the current situation that I didn't want to dwell on. It was work to try to stay focused on prayer and scriptures, trying to maintain a positive attitude.

"Are you all right?" the guard asked.

He had been taking a shift outside my door for the last two days. His skin was an odd shade of tan with darker spots on his face and arms, probably over most of his body. His eyes were gold, flecked with black. He gave me the creeps as he tried to start some small talk from time to time. If it weren't for the fact that he made me nervous, I would have tried to enlist his help.

I looked up, startled. "What?"

"Are you all right?" He was eyeing me like I was an item on a dessert tray.

"Well, no. I want to get out of here," I said guardedly.

"I could get you out," he said it quietly, his eyes intense.

That statement made me suddenly scared for my safety.

"I think I'm better off where I am."

"You just said you wanted to get out of here. I could get you out."

"What do you want?"

"Let me join with you."

I snorted. "Yeah, I don't think so." I turned away from him, hoping he'd go.

I heard the doorway pop, and when I looked, he was in the cell with me. I got up from the cot and turned to face him as he just stood there for a moment. I looked around for something, anything I could use as a weapon. There was nothing.

"You need to leave."

"You want out of here. I want you. We can help each other." Easy, friendly smile, as if we were in the middle of making some sort of business transaction. I suppose from his perspective, it was.

I considered offering him a handshake and an autograph, but I was pretty sure that wasn't going to cut it.

It was work to keep my composure and not panic. As he approached, I took a breath, and when he was a half step away from me, reaching for me, I slammed my knee into his crotch.

And I cried out in pain as my knee met the equivalent of solid rock. Solid body armor covered him there too, and I had just taken out my knee. The pain brought tears to my eyes, and I couldn't think straight for a second, as I nearly slid to the floor.

A move that should have damaged his chances for a family somewhere in the future, that should have had him permanently singing first soprano in the church choir didn't even make him wince. I had the presence of mind to lean over and removed both shoes. They were only flats, but they were the only thing I had that could even remotely be used as a weapon. I would have given anything right now to have a nice stiletto that I could sink into his skull. He was faster and much stronger than me, and in seconds, he had lifted and pinned me against the wall, trying to kiss me and move the skirt of my dress, while ripping the top of it.

I was swatting him with my shoes, but it was totally ineffective, since I had so little leverage. I started calling loudly for help, but I wasn't expecting a big response, since there weren't a lot of people down here ever. I tried shouting louder, trying a number of different words I hoped would bring help. "Fire," which I thought would bring the whole ship running, wasn't one that worked. The knee was screaming with pain, but I worked to keep it in the back of my head while I dealt with this.

I dropped a shoe and was able to box one of his ears with my hand, making him grunt and stop what he was doing for two seconds. I took that brief time to position myself to box both of his ears at the same time. He screamed so loud, my ears hurt. Blood trickled out of the ear I had struck twice, and tears streamed down his face. He punched the side of my head, stunning me, but I didn't pass out. He threw me on the floor and was on top of me in a second. I wanted to move but couldn't. In seconds, he had ripped the gown off me and had begun removing his own clothing. I heard footsteps coming from the corridor followed by someone yelling something unintelligible. I heard what I thought was an odd weapon blast, and the guard disintegrated in front of me, a few particles of dust settling around the room, all that was left of him.

Several people were in the cell within seconds. Somebody even put a blanket over my nearly naked body. A sort of floating gurney was brought in, accompanied by J'Neer.

J'Neer was next to me, examining the tender bruise on my face. He was talking to me, and then to somebody else, but

I couldn't make out what was being said, and I couldn't say anything. Someone was telling him what had happened as I lost consciousness.

"Jackie?"

I looked up at J'Neer. He touched the side of my face where I had been struck. It hurt, and I pushed his hand away, crying out in pain at the same time.

My knee was on fire, and I tried to move it to make it less painful, but the pain was not subsiding.

"Sorry. The meds I gave you aren't fully effective yet."

I nodded.

"Are you hurt anywhere else?"

"Right knee."

He moved the blanket and saw the swollen knee. "Whoa," he said quietly. "How—" He was shaking his head, seeming unable to figure out what had happened.

"I tried to take out his plans for a family and met body armor."

"Their body armor is pretty amazing."

I gritted my teeth, nodding. "Can you do something to make the pain less? It's really bad." I had tears in my eyes now and pushed them away with my hands.

He took out a small box-shaped thing and waved it over my knee. "Just severely bruised, not broken."

He retrieved another couple tools from a drawer across the room. He set one down on the mat next to me, set the other one he still held, then pressed it against my knee, in a few different places. The pain immediately started to ease. He took the other tool he had set on the mat next to me and set it then started waving it over my knee.

I drifted off to sleep as the pain continued to lessen.

—◆◆◆—

I awoke hearing my name and somebody gently shaking me. J'Neer stood over me.

"How are you doing?" he asked.

I nodded. "Pain seems to be gone."

"Good. Fresh clothing should be here shortly, and you'll be going back to your room."

"Thanks. I can't wait to get home," I said sarcastically.

"Sorry. It's the best I can do."

I nodded. "I know. What's going on?"

"Not a whole lot."

"Where is Ronnok going?"

"I really don't know. I'm just the ship's doctor. They don't tell me much. The only thing I've heard is that he's extremely happy with the opening bids for you."

I closed my eyes and took a deep breath. "Oh man."

"I know."

"J'Neer, there's got to be a way to get me away from here."

He shushed me and pointed to the guard a short distance away.

—◆◆◆—

The next two weeks were pretty much mind-numbing. I stayed in the cell. The guard was always there. When I wasn't praying, I exercised. I did all the floor exercises I knew to do to get in even better shape than I had been in before I was kidnapped. I was allowed a shower daily along with a fresh change of clothing—always a simple gown and shoes, despite my requests for a pants outfit. I figured only guards were allowed that.

I tried to get some information from different people about what was going on; I just wanted to know what plans Ronnok had for me. He didn't confide in anybody, it seemed, so nobody had answers for me. There were only rumors, and they weren't changing. The word still was that I would be auctioned off. No specifics for what purpose, leaving that to my imagination. I tried not to think about it too often or for too long. I had so little information; all I would be doing was worrying about something that might not even be a concern. But it still weighed heavily on my mind, and I prayed constantly that something would happen to help me get out of this situation.

16

THE GUARDS, ONE of them a female, showed up to take me for my daily shower. But instead of going to the rooms I normally visited, I was taken to a different suite of rooms. The large main room was decorated very ornately in reds and purples, with touches of gold and black here and there. The furniture was oversized and overstuffed, the lighting right now, very bright.

The woman who ran the bathing rooms came from what I thought was a bedroom. She was again dressed elegantly. "Very good to see you again, Empress." It was the first time she had called me that. Nobody else had during the time I had been held on this ship. I wasn't comfortable hearing it.

"Please don't call me empress."

"Would you rather I call you by your given name, Jackie?"

"Yes."

"I wish we could be without the guards, but you're still not trusted here. Ronnok would hate to lose you."

"I understand. Who are you? You've never told me your name."

"I don't give my name to any of the girls that Ronnok has plans for. I risk them developing a false sense of security. They think I will do something to keep them from being auctioned off. I can tell you now, though. I'm Jiva. I'm one of Ronnok's wives. You're here for me to prepare to be sold."

I couldn't say anything; I think all the blood left my face.

"You knew that," Jiva stated, almost defensively.

"Jiva, please." My mouth was suddenly very dry. "There must be something I could do for you if you would just—"

"Do not ask again," Jiva said firmly. "There's nothing I can do."

I turned to the guards. "Take me back to my cell."

"It doesn't work that way, Jackie," Jiva said, as if explaining to a child. "You either do as you're told, or Ronnok will hurt you more than you can imagine. He can do that."

"I don't want to—"

"Yes, I know. It's terrible business to be a sold female slave. But once you're there, I'll bet you'll be able to get away, eventually. Or even buy your way out of your position."

"Are you a slave to Ronnok?"

"I'm one of his wives."

One of the guards stepped in, "Get going. We will be there within the next couple of hours. Ronnok wants her ready as soon as possible. He has customers who want to see her on screen before we arrive."

I felt totally defeated. This was where it would end. I would be sold into slavery to be some rich alien's toy. No guarantee of how I would be treated or where I would wind up, even of how long I would live. I was scared out of my skin.

I walked obediently into the room with the shower. Given how I had been a problem for so many, the guard got to be in the room with me as I showered and slipped into a robe.

I sat obediently in the chair in front of a mirror as Jiva applied makeup and styled my hair. She was talented with what she was doing, and as much as I dreaded what was going to happen shortly, seeing the transformation was impressive.

"You know, it might not be as bad as you think," Jiva said.

"Jiva, belonging to someone who purchased me to rape me is about the worst thing I can think of."

"It's not always like that," Jiva argued. "Most times, the man who owns us expects us to have a job in addition to being his wives."

"So you are expected to hold a job too?"

"If we have a skill we can use to help. It's not that way everywhere, though. Ronnok happens to believe that if we can do something to help, we should. Not all owners do."

"Jiva, I don't want to do this. You have to understand, it's not the lifestyle where I come from."

"Well, I think you're making too much out of this. You can't do anything about it, so you might as well get used to the idea right now while you can. When you finally go home with the man who buys you, you'll be in a better frame of mind to accept what comes. Whoever it is will expect you to join with him. Some of them are better than others."

I paused. "I can't imagine anyone purchasing someone else."

"You said it's not done where you come from?"

"It happens, but it's not legal, and it's not common."

"Well, just remember you're not there anymore. You're out here, and this is your life now."

Something in that last statement made me do a mental double take. This was my life now. What a horrible thought. This was going to be my gauge for normal—life as usual. How was I going to do this?

"Listen, Jackie. Once you get wherever you wind up, you might be able to buy your freedom, escape, or you might even end up enjoying whoever takes you home. You're wasting a lot of energy on something you're not even sure about."

Jiva was giving me a few minutes to do nothing before I got into the gown she had for me.

"You know, there are some men out here who you might like," she said.

"I'm sure there are," I said sarcastically.

"Well, who's to say you couldn't wind up with one of them?"

I shook my head. "Jiva, I'm sorry, but I don't think I can make you understand how I feel about this."

She had me wear a dress that was extremely form-fitting, no sleeves, and more cleavage than I had ever worn in my life. The bottom of the gown clung to my curves. Jiva pinned my hair up and put a pair of dangly earrings on me, as well as a collection of decorative bangles on both wrists. Four-inch heels completed the outfit. I stood up, trying to balance on the heels.

I looked at myself in the mirror. I couldn't remember ever looking as good as I did now, and I couldn't believe it was all for the purpose at hand. The chance of ever being found felt entirely out of reach. I felt totally numb, as if I was standing at the edge of a cliff, about to be pushed off.

"You are beautiful!" gushed Jiva. "Ronnok will be pleased. He'll get a huge price for you."

The air had suddenly become hard to breathe. I felt lightheaded. I was not ready for this.

"Wait a minute, just a minute," Jiva said. "Sit down, Empress."

I did as I was told. I'm not sure I could have come up with an idea of what to do on my own.

She looked at the guards. "Give her a moment. She's going to faint if you take her now."

Jiva went to a small kitchenette area of the room and came back a moment later. She set down what looked like tea and a small sandwich in front of me.

"Eat a bit. It will help you get through this."

I sipped the tea and took a small bite of the sandwich. It had an odd flavor and didn't sit well in my stomach. I wasn't sure if it was nerves or the sandwich, but I wasn't feeling well. Jiva encouraged me to eat a little more.

"I can't. It doesn't taste right, and if I eat anything, it's not going to stay down."

"It's fresh, nothing wrong with it."

I drank a little more tea but couldn't touch the sandwich. My stomach was slowly feeling worse.

Jiva told the guards I could go now, and they started to pull my hands behind me.

"Don't do that," Jiva said. "She's too unsteady on her feet right now. Just keep your eyes on her."

I allowed myself to be led out of the suite to the elevator. I tried to keep my breathing steady. I wanted desperately to run, but there was no place to run. In these shoes, there was no way I could run and not break an ankle. The way my stomach was feeling, I was sure that running wasn't a good option anyway.

It was a short walk to the communications deck, where Ronnok was already in conversation with about seven men on as many screens in front of him. He turned when I walked into the room with the guards. The faces on the screens were obviously able to see me as well. Eyes grew large, appreciating what they saw in front of them. I never felt more self-conscious in my life.

"Twelve thousand," one of the men on the screens called out.

"Twelve fifty," responded another.

They were bidding on me. I think the color left my face as I realized I was on the block. Numbers were called out for the next few minutes, going higher and higher. When the bidding slowed, Ronnok moved me closer to the screens. It had the desired effect. I didn't know where to look, what to do. I felt naked, vulnerable. There was no way to prepare for something like this. I would have been ecstatic if the ship had blown to bits with me in it right then. Ronnok turned me around slowly at one point for the benefit of his clients. The bidding escalated a bit more.

"Smile," Ronnok whispered in my ear.

I shook my head no. Now I was feeling nauseous. The small snack Jiva had given me before leaving her rooms felt like it was eating a hole in my gut. I was sure some of the nausea was from stress and some from the food. I didn't normally have a weak constitution, but my body seemed to have reached its limit with the current situation I was in.

"Please let me go back to my cell," I whispered.

Ronnok smiled at his clientele then glared at me. "You will do as I say. You are making me a wealthier man. Nobody in this quadrant has an Earther female."

"I...I'm not feeling well." My stomach cramped up, making me bend over to try to ease the pain. Ronnok grabbed my hair and straightened me up. The bidding got busy again.

I locked eyes with Ronnok, hating him more than anything else in the world right then. And then I threw up all over him. He said something in his home language that I was pretty sure was a collection of swear words and threw me to the floor. Three of Ronnok's clients disappeared. Four remained, bidding even more. Ronnok removed the duster he was wearing over his suit, which I hadn't vomited on. The bidding stopped after a moment. I was on the floor. My stomach had stopped being upset, but now I felt weak. When I looked up, there were only two men bidding on me.

Ronnok had the two guards in the room lift me to my feet. He went behind me and opened the gown I was wearing, forcing it down to my hips, taking me down to the ornate bra and panties I wore. Bidding went crazy between the last two men for almost a minute.

The smell in the room was horrible from the vomit on the floor. Someone came in and removed it faster than I could watch. That was followed by something sprayed into the room that made the air smell tremendously better.

The bidding was still going on. The number was over two hundred thousand mitas, whatever that was. I could tell it was starting to slow down when Ronnok made me turn around slowly again, making the bidding pick up once more between the last two men. After a moment, it slowed and stopped. Nothing happened or was said for a few seconds.

"Sold to Kanir Op'untu for 216,000 mitas!" Ronnok almost yelled gleefully.

One screen was still occupied. I half expected to see a leering grin from a man who had just won a prize. Instead it was a man in his forties. His dark hair was full, slightly graying at his temples. Scarring traveled down the left side of his face, disappearing into a full beard and mustache. Dark eyes were somewhat brooding, assessing what was in front of him on his side of the screen. He was handsome in a rugged way. I couldn't read what was in the eyes, except they seemed to draw me in. I couldn't look away for a moment.

"I will see you within the hour," Kanir said, looking now at Ronnok. His voice was deep and soft. In another circumstance, I would have loved listening to it. The two men exchanged some information, and the screen went blank.

"Get her out of here!" Ronnok roared. I could see the fury in his eyes. "If I wasn't getting paid so well for you, I would have you beaten within an inch of your life," he said between clenched teeth.

The guards lifted me up and led me back to my cell. It wasn't long before they showed up with Jiva. She had a fresh slinky gown in hand and helped me get dressed. This one was navy blue with a halter top, floor length, and slit up nearly to my hips on both sides.

"I heard you're going to Kanir," she said, plainly excited. "It won't be nearly as bad as you think. He'll take such good care of you! You won't want to leave him. The Matakians are considered the gentlemen of the galaxy."

"Jiva, you don't get it. I don't want this."

"I know, dear. But you'll get used to it."

"Please help me get out of here now," I whispered. "Jiva, I'm glad this works for you. This isn't for me. What do you want from me that I could give you to get me out of here right now?" I could feel the panic rising inside me and couldn't control it.

"Ronnok would kill me!" She laughed. "Men rule out here, Jackie. It works for us. At least you're getting Kanir. You could be going to D'Pok. He passes his women around to different men at whim. Anybody's whim, actually. He's a pig. But I've heard Kanir is practically celibate."

As if I could count on that… I sighed.

Jiva left with the guards. I really needed the cavalry to show up right now. I sat on the cot for a few minutes and then started to wander around the cell. The fear was overwhelming. I was about to be handed over as a piece of property for whatever purposes he wanted. I couldn't even let my mind think about what was going to happen over the next period of time, and yet my mind kept going to those places.

The guards appeared at the door.

"Please don't make me go," I whispered.

They took me by my arms and lead me out. In a few short minutes, we arrived in a small meeting room. He stood there, tall, dark, and ruggedly handsome—add intimidating, scary. His eyes were again assessing me. He nodded to the guards who released me. His eyes held mine, seeming to peer into my soul.

"She's even lovelier in person, don't you think?" Ronnok said. "Do you want a room to enjoy her here before you leave, or do you wish to go back to your ship?"

I stiffened, trying to hide the panic I felt.

He paused, almost smiled. I got the impression this man was tolerating Ronnok. "Thank you, Ronnok. I will take her with me to my ship. If we are done here, I'm ready to go now."

"Of course."

17

THE USIAN COUNCIL is made up of nine individuals representing the nine continents of our planet. According to Lady Minkas, they are no different from any politician from Earth. They are elected and serve a term of five years. Lady Minkas made it mandatory that they not serve more than two terms, and election seasons are extremely brief.

Our leader didn't want politics to invade people's lives, as she believed it had on her planet. She was very concerned that those in charge never forget that they served, not the other way around. The few times one of the council members crossed a line all found out very quickly that she tolerated no misdeeds.

Most of the people of Usia loved Lady Minkas because of her stand on many different issues. They felt cared for and appreciated the opportunity to earn what they needed.

Of course, there were those who preferred to be served and attempted to twist those edicts Lady Minkas had set in place. When they realized that they would not succeed or be tolerated, they were allowed to leave rather than stay and stir up the masses for their benefit.

The council sat at their desks, not pleased. I'd had to tell them that my mission to Earth to bring back Jackie Laughlin had been unsuccessful.

"This should have been seen to significantly earlier, Corrett," Bahan Nyast said. He was the councilman of Minsar, directly to the east of where the council met here on continent Cestra. He was likely the least patient of the bunch of them. It benefited his continent in that he got things done quickly, but it also made him difficult to deal with when he was on a tangent.

"I understand that, sir. I was operating under orders from Lady Minkas at the time. She and I both believed she would still be with us by the time I returned, and we certainly never foresaw the taking of the new empress."

"Wasn't the package delivered in a timely manner?" Nyast asked.

"It was, sir. However, the Earthers misplaced it. We sent a team to locate it and send it on its way. Once it was placed in the program, it was another week before a friend of Jackie Laughlin, who gave it to her as a gift, claimed it. We estimate it took nearly another three months more than we anticipated to have it claimed."

"We need to get the empress here as soon as possible," council member Anishuq said.

"That is understood, councilman. Toward that end, I have secured the services of some who can help us with that."

"Explain that to us, Corrett." Nyast was growing less patient.

I paused. I knew that what I was about to share might not be appreciated by a good many of the council, but there had been no choice.

"We know that Galton D'Nar has her. We have no idea where she is, what he intends for her. We were not able to follow him when his ship left the planet.

"Lady Minkas had some contacts who were mercenaries. She insisted that we should maintain a working relationship with them for—well, just such an occasion. I've contacted a couple of them, and they have passed the information onto others in their organization. Right now, there's nothing left for us to do but wait."

"Mercenaries?" Nyast spat out the word as he turned a shade of red.

"Yes, sir. They have ways and means of getting the job done that far exceed what we can do." I refused to let his anger intimidate me.

"And what do we do until that time?" Nyast was on the edge of losing his temper.

I paused. "If you will look at the notes on your screens, you will see that Lady Minkas left her assistant to replace her under these exact circumstances. It's temporary, until we can replace the former leader and is expected to take no more than six months. If she has not been located and brought to Usia in six month's time, the procedure to acquire another leader is repeated."

The council members were all busy looking at the screens on their desks, checking what Lady Minkas had left for us. If the council wanted to argue the points before them, it would be a long night. The pride some of the council walked in could prohibit them from letting someone lead whom they considered less than themselves. I would be the target of a lot of abuse. I knew I could handle it for the short time it would take to get Jackie Laughlin back or find a new leader.

In all actuality, it should have come as no surprise to them. Lady Minkas had gone over all this long ago. I suppose the ones who had not forgotten were the more recent additions to the council who hadn't taken the time to read through much of the documentation given them when they first joined the group.

Nyast and two of the other council had pinched faces that clearly expressed how they felt about what was before them.

"It seems," Nyast began, "that we are bound to conform to this piece of legislation Lady Minkas left for us."

Council member Jinkeh cleared his throat before speaking. "I believe we are well lead until the issue of a permanent leader is resolved."

"I thank you, councilman," I said. "I will do my best."

"We are sure you will."

"There is another issue that needs some attention," I said.

"And that would be?" Nyast said.

"Who is responsible for what has happened to Jackie Laughlin."

"You said D'Nar has her. He's with that subversive group."

"The point is," Sergat said, "the information of who our new leader would be was not to leave this council, or Lady Minkas."

The quiet was thick as they all absorbed this.

"I don't think any of us here truly believe that this was a random kidnapping." I stated, "D'Nar reaps no benefit from taking her. I believe he is working for someone."

"And you believe it was a council member?" Sergat asked.

"Nobody outside this room was to know," Nyast offered.

"What about Lady Minkas?" Sergat asked. "She had been very ill. Could she have spoken it to someone without realizing?"

Again, a heavy silence filled the room for a few seconds. Nyast predictably responded first. "Are you saying someone from this council made this happen?"

"I have no idea," I responded. "I've done some research. D'Nar gains nothing from this, except perhaps some monetary reward from whoever he's working for. He had whatever he needed to send a feed to our ship to let us see her as they confined her and dealt with her."

"How badly was she treated?"

"She reacted badly to the traveler, and D'Nar was less than a good host. He had her kill someone accused of a horrendous crime against a family."

"Why would he do that?" Kenbar, representative of Junth, asked. She was one of the two female representatives. Of the nine of them, she was the one I preferred to deal with. She was always fair and concerned about all nine continents as a whole.

"I'm not sure. I think it was an effort to break her and see how far he could manipulate her. The safety of her family was in the balance, which finally made her take his life."

"I don't suppose these mercenaries gave you a time frame in which they believe they can deliver her to us," Nyast said.

"There is no guarantee. I told them we were operating in a time frame of six months. They have given it top priority, all due to the relationship that Lady Minkas was able to forge between us."

"How do you propose finding out who leaked the information?" Kenbar asked.

I took a deep breath. "I have discussed this with security," I began, "and they recommend starting with you, the council, as the information was not given past this room. You will each be investigated to—"

"This is completely unacceptable!" Nyast was out of his chair.

"If you have nothing to hide, why are you concerned?" Kenbar asked.

"To serve, we must go through many tests and applications that bare our soul. Once here—"

"Once here," Kenbar interjected firmly, "we must maintain accountability. I have nothing to hide. If nobody else here does, there should be no problem answering some questions."

"Thank you, Madame Kenbar," I said.

"So who do you propose should head this investigation?" Sergat asked.

"I will turn it over to security and make sure that they assign it to an investigator who can best carry this out."

There was quiet all around the room again.

"I think it is time that we let Corrett take some time to make some adjustments to his schedule to accommodate his new temporary position," Kenbar stated.

The rest of the council agreed. Nyast and two others who tended to side with him did not look pleased, but I dismissed myself and left the chambers. I was surprised the meeting with them went as smoothly as it had, yet I was concerned about the future. The next several months could be very long indeed.

18

WE WERE ON Kanir's ship. It was a floating office building moored in space with the ability to travel wherever its owner wanted to take it. The corridors and offices we passed looked like any other office building I had ever visited on Earth. He took me directly to a suite of rooms. Kanir's living quarters were a decorator's dream. Everything was plain and utilitarian. There was no color, no personality. The furniture looked as if it had been born here and was close to dying here. Kanir seemed to not notice. Had to be a guy thing. Who knew that so many men across the galaxy were clueless about personalizing a space?

"Sit," Kanir said simply. I sat on a sofa, trying hard to keep my composure. I didn't know what to expect, and I didn't know what to do. My stomach was doing flip-flops, and I'm sure my blood pressure, normally in better-than-average shape, was about ready to ring the bell.

Kanir went to a counter area in a corner of the room, where he poured two glasses of some kind of liquid. He brought them back to where I sat and placed them on a table in front of the sofa, taking a seat not too far from me. I looked around for somewhere to go, to run. Nothing. I had seen him order someone to stand guard outside the room as we entered, and now I felt totally intimidated, scared. I was working hard to keep a strong, stoic veneer, not let the fear show.

"Tell me about yourself," he said.

I paused. "What do you want to know?"

His right eyebrow shot up, and he almost smiled. I wanted him to be the lecherous moron I was expecting so I could hate him. He wasn't what I was expecting, but nothing I had been through since I was taken from my home on Earth was what I expected. Why should this be any different?

"I understand you were a warrior on your planet."

"I am a law enforcement officer."

He nodded. "Protector of the people. How do you feel about where you are?"

"I don't want to be here. I want to go back to Earth, home."

"I can't do that. You're mine now."

"I'm not a thing you can own," I said firmly.

"Of course you're not. Tell me how you came into Ronnok's possession."

I paused. I hadn't told anyone about how this had all taken place. Why would he even be interested? "I was home recovering from a concussion. D'Nar's men had done something to me, locked me in a mind scan—I think it's called. I passed out and hit the street and hit my head pretty hard. So I was home recuperating. The little bit I remember, two men were in my home in the middle of the night. I shot one of them. The next thing I knew, I was on D'Nar's ship."

"Were you treated well?"

"No. I reacted badly to the traveler, and D'Nar was not exactly host of the month." I told him about some of the things that had happened on the ship.

His face darkened almost imperceptibly. "I'm sorry, although I'm not surprised." He motioned to a tray of food that had been brought into the room. "You may eat, if you'd like."

"I'm not hungry, thank you." My stomach was still upset.

He nodded. "I can't stay here for long. I have a business to get back to. You will stay here."

"So this is my cage?"

Both eyebrows went up. He almost smiled again.

"What about the planet I'm supposed to lead?"

"Let them find another."

"Won't they find out where I am? Try to get me back?"

"Space is large, mostly void. Usia is a long way from here. They will likely never even hear of where you went." There was no sign of arrogance in the statement. He was simply stating a fact.

Kanir took my hand, kissed it, and released it. His eyes were intense, never leaving mine, searching. I was getting lost in his eyes, feeling myself fall into them, almost into his arms. I straightened up, cleared my throat, and stood up. Kanir was obviously disappointed.

"I will give you time to adjust. But I must tell you, I will eventually grow impatient."

"How many wives do you have?" The change in topic would have given a lesser being a severe case of whiplash.

He paused. Someone else asked the same question might have seemed startled. I wondered if anything could rattle this man. "I had three others. Why?"

"If you had three wives, why do you need me? It sounds like you prefer to be single."

He was assessing me again. "It's not a matter of needing, so much as it is of being able to have you."

"Where are they?"

"My former wives?"

"Yes. Where are they?"

"They are no longer part of my life." He paused. "Are you jealous?"

"No, not at all. I would like to meet them."

"My other wives were of convenience for the sake of diplomacy with other leaders of galactic industry. I saw them from time to time, but there was no real love between any of us. The relationships were never consummated. Over time, they were all released from those arrangements."

"I'd like to meet them."

"I don't think so. I've heard you've tried to get others to help you escape." He paused a moment, looked around the room and then back at me. "You will accompany me on business matters when it is appropriate. I want my associates to know you, and I want you to know them. I will assign a guard to you and this room at all times."

I was almost proud of myself for the reputation I had already made for myself on that account, but it didn't help me much.

"So I'm a trophy."

The smile grew bigger, not quite full size. The eyes were as intense as ever. "I would like to think that you will be more than that to me over time."

"Kanir." I took a deep breath, sighed. "I don't want to be part of your new harem. I want to get back to Earth. If I can't do that, at least let me go to Usia to do what I was brought here to do."

"I admire your dedication. I don't have a harem. I don't want one. My experience has been that having one wife at a time is as much as I can handle."

Kanir seemed thoughtful for a moment. "I have to leave. I will return later." He looked around the room for a few seconds then back at me. "We will be—I think your word for it would be—married tomorrow."

I was stunned. "What?" I stammered. "A marriage of diplomacy with who, Earth? Usia?"

"Neither. You will be my wife."

"I don't want to be your wife. I don't want you for my husband. I don't want to get married."

He was assessing me again. There was no smile. His eyes just seemed to draw me to him. He nodded, turned, and left.

———

I cruised the rooms, getting a feel for where I was. For a prison or a cage, it wasn't too bad, but there was no way I was going to stay here. The second I had a chance to bolt, I would. I didn't know where I would go, what I would do, but I would figure it out. I just needed to get to a shuttle. It couldn't be that hard to pilot one of those things.

A short time later, someone knocked quietly on the door. A husband and wife, Mada and Sheeb, Kanir's private tailor and seamstress, came into the room. They set about taking measurements. Conversation was limited to discussion about color and style. It was pretty much the two of them asking me what I thought about what I wanted in the gown as well as other clothing. I couldn't get them to understand that I had no interest in being part of what they were trying to do.

"You must have something to say about this," Sheeb said

"I don't want to marry anyone. I don't even want to be here. I would much prefer to get off this ship and as far away from here as possible, with directions to home."

"I'm sorry, Jackie. We can't help you with that," she said quietly.

"I know."

I spent the next several hours trying to figure a way out of this. I couldn't find a weapon in the rooms. I checked closets, drawers, and other storage places. I didn't care if I was being nosy. It would probably be the only way I might find something to help me, but there was nothing. The door was locked from the outside, preventing me from going anywhere. The guard Kanir had posted was still out there when the tailor and seamstress had entered and left the room. Escaping was going to take some creative thinking.

There was a computer in the corner. I tried to access it, but it was too foreign to me. It didn't help that I wasn't very computer literate. I found a devise similar to an electronic reader, and after some experimentation, I was able to access it. The downside was that everything on it was in a different language, and I couldn't find any way to switch things to English.

Kanir and the evening meal arrived at the same time. He had a single flower that almost resembled a rose. When he handed it to me, he held my hand in his as I inhaled its intoxicating fragrance.

"Thank you." I tried to remove my hand from his, but he held firm.

"You're welcome." His eyes held mine.

I tried to step back, but he still held fast.

I swallowed hard. "Please let me go."

He lifted my hand to his lips and kissed it softly, never releasing my eyes from his.

While he ate, I mostly picked at my food. I had no appetite but knew I needed to keep my strength up to try to take some action, preferably before the next morning.

We had been sitting on the sofa quietly talking. I decided to be bold and ask about the scar on his face.

"I was in the Inonya wars."

"So you were a soldier once upon a time? On another planet?"

"A planet my world went to war over trading disputes and political leading. I led a large battalion onto Inonya. We were taking a city on their major continent, Mykapic. We were trying to do it with as little firepower as possible. We were ambushed. I lost thirty men and took a blast to the face from one of their more incendiary weapons. I could have had this cleaned up, but it is a reminder to me of the preciousness of the lives lost that day."

I was mildly surprised at the rawness in his voice.

Kanir paused only a few seconds and then said, "Tell me about Earth."

"I can't tell you about the whole thing, but I can tell you about the small area where I live.

"I live in the United States. In the state of Florida, in a small city called Coral Beach. It's warm all year long. During the winter months, when it's freezing up north, it gets chilly. I'm pretty sensitive to the cold, so I usually need a jacket. I get laughed at a lot for that. It rains a lot during the summer. We get a few tornados and sometimes get caught in the path of a stray hurricane or two. The storms are probably my favorite weather."

"Storms?"

"Yes. They are just incredible. They're dramatic and loud. The lightning and thunder are so loud and frequent, it sometimes sounds like the Earth is being pulled apart. I love watching the storms come in off the Gulf of Mexico. It's nature's entertainment at its best.

"I even enjoy working in the storms, as long as they aren't too severe. There's something energizing about being out in the middle of it. My dad—" I stopped. I had only been gone for a few weeks, and I missed my home, my friends, and my family. The lump in my throat kept me silent. I didn't want to become a bawling mess right here in front of this man. I took a deep breath and held it.

"Jackie?" I wasn't sure, but he sounded a bit concerned.

I shook my head, took a deep breath, and held it for a moment. I blinked away tears. Minutes seemed to go by quietly. At one point, Kanir put his hand over mine, but I pulled away. He let me get my head together.

Finally, he said, "I hope I can show you some sights that will compare with what you had on your Earth... Tell me about what you did as a protector."

I paused until I was sure I had my voice under control. "I'm in patrol. I work with the public, write a lot of reports, make arrests, write tickets, settle arguments sometimes. It can be dangerous in different circumstances."

"Such as?"

"Domestic disturbances. Couples fighting. Alarm calls, burglaries, robberies, there's no telling what might happen."

"But you enjoyed it."

"Yes."

"Why?"

I thought it might sound corny, but it was the truth. "Sometimes I feel like I make a difference."

He nodded. We talked for a long time, the conversation going in many different directions. Neither of us brought up the subject of the wedding the next morning. Kanir was easy to talk to, and I found myself relaxing just a little bit with him. It had been so long since I had been able to let my guard down even the least little bit. It felt as though I had been under assault for so long, it was as if I didn't know how to behave without a threat at hand. And I wasn't sure how I felt about being so comfortable with him.

Asking him about what he did out in the final frontier, I found out Kanir was the CEO of his own company, which built spacecraft, most of it for planetary governments. It was successfully spread out across a large portion of the quadrant we were in currently. He was concerned that what left his plants were quality vessels that served the needs of his clients. The ships produced ranged from small shuttles to ships that would dwarf an aircraft carrier. Kanir employed thousands of people. He was very concerned that those who worked for him were compensated properly and grew in their positions.

Except for the fact that he was happy to have me miserable here, it kept becoming more difficult to find something to dislike him for.

He was interested in what I had to say and was eager to answer questions that I had about him. I was surprised to find that a couple of hours had passed, and I was feeling tired after the long day and all that had gone on. The stress of the "auction" for my purchase was catching up to me.

"You're tired," he said some time later.

I was terrified he would expect me to sleep with him. More stress. I tried to hide my exhaustion, but it felt like my eyes were spinning in my head from the weariness. "No, I'm fine."

Almost the smile again. "Jackie. Go get ready for bed. You are exhausted."

He seemed to sense what I was thinking as I tried to come up with excuses for being sleepy. How long could I stay awake and not have to deal with what I was sure he was expecting?

"I will sleep out here tonight, probably on this couch."

I paused for a moment, surprised and relieved. How long would I be able to dodge what I thought might be inevitable. I went to the bedroom, closed the door, and got ready for bed. I found a closet with a few things hanging in there. I didn't want to think about who had worn them. I found a tunic that I was sure belonged to Kanir. It worked as a nightshirt.

I slept less than half the night. I tossed and turned, got up, and walked around the room a few times. There was no clock to see what time it was or how long I slept or was awake.

The next morning, I awoke to Kanir peeking in from the door. He just stared at me for a few moments, admiring his new possession. Which I was. And then he left.

I stretched and slipped into a large purple robe I found in the closet. I tried looking around the rooms for something to help me get out of here. I didn't know what it would be. I just kept an open mind and hoped something would occur to me. When I couldn't find anything still, I sat down and prayed. I prayed for continued protection and a way out of this mess. I had my eyes closed, occasionally adding something in my conversation. All at once, I felt someone in the room with me. I opened my eyes to see Kanir just inside the door, watching me.

"What were you doing?" he asked.

I hesitated for just a second. "Praying."

"To whom?"

"God."

"Really? Tell me about your God." His tone was curious.

"How long were you watching me just now?" I asked.

"A few minutes."

"So you heard me ask for direction, protection, guidance, wisdom. A way to get home."

He nodded. "Yes. A tall list."

"Well, I believe he can deliver on all of those."

"I suppose we'll find out," Kanir said. "But I can tell you that you're not leaving."

Kanir thought about all this for a moment and asked, "What if none of the things you prayed for happen?"

I paused. "Sometimes the answer is no."

I could sense the wheels turning in Kanir's head, processing what I had just said. "You believe in a God who might not answer your prayers? That almost sounds counterproductive.

Why would you put your trust in that?" He seemed to be careful not to make fun of what I said.

I chose my words carefully and spoke quietly. "I've seen Him do things in my life that I know are from Him. And I know that if my prayers aren't answered the way I would like them to be, it's because He has a better plan." I paused, thinking, and then added, "And right now, He's all I have."

Neither of us said anything for a moment.

"What about you?" I finally asked quietly.

"What?" He seemed almost startled. I think he had been lost in thought over this conversation.

"Do you pray? Believe in someone bigger than you?"

"I've heard of others who do. I've never had that for myself. I've done everything on my own. I haven't"—he paused, searching for a word—"needed to pray or rely on someone or something."

Kanir seemed uncomfortable for a moment and then told me to come have breakfast with him. It was without a doubt the best meal I'd had since I had been out here. Maybe because I hadn't eaten much the evening before, and I was pretty hungry. There were fruits I hadn't seen before, breads and spreads. There was even something almost like bacon that accompanied some eggs.

Once breakfast was done, Kanir excused himself, told me he would be back within the next hour, and left.

Mada and Sheeb came to the rooms a short time later, carrying a gown with them as well as a few other outfits.

Sheeb took the other clothing into the bedroom and hung them in the closet, returning with just what I was expected to wear for the occasion I was dreading.

"What do you think, Jackie?" Sheeb asked, showing off what he and his wife had assembled in what I considered to be record time.

It was almost floor length, off white, satiny. Off the shoulders, curve hugging. Beaded at the right places, daring neckline. It was breathtaking. Matching shoes.

"It's lovely, but I'm not wearing it."

Mada's smile faded. "Jackie, why not?"

"I can't marry him. I don't know him, I don't love him. I don't want to marry him!"

Mada shushed me, almost fearful. "Jackie, don't say that. He's a good man. Will not hurt you. You will grow to love him."

"Mada, Sheeb, help me to get out of—"

The door opened, and Kanir was there. He took in the scene before him; I was still in the tunic and robe. Mada and Sheeb stood next to me with the gown. I knew he had heard what I said, and I really didn't care.

"I'm sorry, sir," Sheeb said. "She's not cooperating."

"I'm sure." He paused, eyes still never leaving me, "You two may leave."

Mada held up the dress. "Leave that," Kanir said. Mada draped it carefully over the back of the sofa, and they left.

"Get dressed," he said simply.

"No."

The only reaction was that his right eyebrow shot up. He did a shrug. "As you wish."

I took a deep breath. I wasn't sure if I'd won a battle or not. I went to the bedroom, willing myself not to freak out. I wasn't about to change until I knew what was going on. I was praying I'd find jeans and a T-shirt, but I hadn't seen anything in any of the closets even vaguely resembling what I wanted. A few minutes later I heard voices in the other room, but didn't dare go out again. I didn't need half the ship knowing what I looked like first thing in the morning and later exchanging comments on my night wear.

"Jackie," Kanir called quietly.

"Yes?"

"Come out here."

"I'm not dressed."

A second later, Kanir was in the room. He took my hand. "Come with me."

"Who's out there?"

"Tolf, captain of my ship, as well as my friend."

"Let me get dressed first, please."

"You had your chance."

"Why do I need to meet him now?"

"He's here to marry us."

"I'm not leaving this room!"

"That's fine." He pulled me to the doorway. "Tolf, in here, please."

Tolf came into the room. He was about the same age as Kanir, lighter in coloring and a bit taller than Kanir. He carried a piece of electronic equipment with him.

"Please, my friend, marry us," Kanir said.

"No!" I said. "Please, I don't want this!"

It was the first time I'd seen something close to anger in Kanir's eyes. "You will be silent," he ordered quietly.

It wasn't a threat, but I knew instinctively to be quiet. Without a word from me, Tolf married us. Kanir kept his arm around my waist, keeping me from going anywhere. It was all of about two minutes, and it was done. I wasn't expected to say anything at all; I wasn't even asked. Brief ceremonies out here, to be sure. Kanir eyed me when the ceremony was over. I could see him having an inner debate as to whether or not to kiss me. He opted to kiss my forehead.

"I will have it posted, Kanir," Tolf said as they shared a hug of congratulations, and he left. Kanir saw him out and then came back into the bedroom.

Kanir looked very pleased with himself. "I would ask where you would like us to go to spend our first couple of weeks alone as a married couple, but I know what you would say."

I didn't reply. I was angry. I didn't know what to say. The comfort I thought I had experienced around Kanir the night before was gone. My life was not my own, never would be as long as I was with him. I had no control over my life, and I didn't think I would for some time yet. The possibility of never getting out of here was overwhelming.

"I will be back shortly. I expect you to be dressed and ready to accompany me as I conduct business," Kanir said, kissed my cheek, and left.

19

I DIDN'T KNOW what to do. I could feel myself starting to panic. There was no place to run, nobody to help me. I was trapped. From what I had just experienced, I knew I had better be dressed, or he would take me through the ship, on whatever business he had, decked out in what I wore now. I didn't need the lack of appropriate dress to be the center of gossip around whatever water coolers that might be on this ship.

I didn't know what to think about this man. He was intent on keeping me here, and I was afraid of what would happen tonight, our wedding night. I was sure he would expect his bride to sleep with him. I had been away from home for some weeks now, and all of it had been a nightmare. Everything was so far out of my control and constantly changing. I was constantly in defense mode to deal with those changes. Things kept getting worse.

Jiva had said Kanir's reputation was that of a man who was gracious; the Matakian men were supposed to be the gentlemen of the galaxy. I wasn't so sure about that. I saw a man who was arrogant and didn't care what I wanted or needed. Of course, purchasing me had made me his. I got showered and slipped into a simple dress Mada had dropped off and was waiting for him when he returned over an hour later.

"Much better," he commented on seeing me in the dress, which, according to some of the styles I had been seeing on the different ships I had been on, was pretty much business attire. It was just above the knee, very contemporary according to Earth standards, in a royal purple. I had found a pair of black heels and brushed my hair out, letting it curl and fall naturally around my shoulders.

Kanir took me to his office to start with. His secretary Nava had a small office outside of Kanir's office. She seemed warm and happy to see her boss and me. When we went into the office, it was quite different from Nava's space. Where her area was well lit, bright, and showed some of her personality, Kanir's office was almost a blank slate. The lack of style and personalization in his rooms had been carried over into his office. It was a fair size but needed a paint job. There was enough space for his desk and a credenza as well as a sitting area furnished with pieces that had seen better days. There was a large window that looked out to space that kept me transfixed for a short time. Other than a name plaque on his desk, there was nothing that personalized the room.

"You need some help here," I commented.

"Really. What do you mean?" Kanir asked.

I told him what I thought of his office as well as his rooms.

"I'm glad you said that. You may get started on it right away."

"I'm not a decorator."

"Give me your ideas."

"Kanir, I—"

"We need to find things for you to do. This would be a good start. Tell me what would be good in here."

I paused. "What's your favorite color?"

"I like green. Dark green."

"You could paint the room or some part of it a dark green, throw in some neutrals, and do something with the floor."

Kanir nodded. "I like that. I will put you with the ship's supply office. You may order what you like."

I was a bit confused. I wasn't sure this was what I wanted to do. I had gone from law enforcement officer to planetary leader to prisoner to decorator in what might be considered record time.

"Do you do a lot of business in here?"

"From time to time, but mostly I'm here taking care of business on my own, with Nava helping me when I need her."

"I noticed you made sure her desk and area are nice, and you've allowed her to personalize it a bit."

"It's important to me to take care of those who work for me. If they are happy, they work better, and I get more business, I get more done. It's one of the key reasons my business has thrived for so long."

"Don't you think you're important to take care of?"

"That's why you are here."

That shut me down. It took me a moment to collect my thoughts. Someone else might have considered the remark a compliment. I didn't want to be here and didn't know how to respond. No matter what I said, it would probably be the wrong thing. I finally chose not to say anything at all.

Kanir had finished gathering some things from his desk. He went to the door, calling for me to accompany him.

"Where are we going?" I asked.

"I have a meeting with several of my suppliers, as well as several of my engineers. I'd like you to be there."

"Kanir, I know nothing about what you do. I would be lost."

"You need to know what goes on. You are my wife. I expect you to have some knowledge of what goes on in my business."

The argument was on the tip of my tongue. It would be futile. As far as he was concerned, I was bought and paid for. The next best thing to a mail-ordered bride. Unwilling, but that didn't seem to matter to Kanir. Entering the meeting room, I was immediately overly self-conscious. There were five men and women seated around an oval table. None of them were human—big surprise. All of them took me in with curiosity. I was definitely Kanir's trophy. Kanir introduced me but carefully left out where I was from. He took a seat at the head of the table and had me sit to his left.

I stayed quiet as the meeting got underway. I listened to what was going on, trying to make sense of the terms and diagrams and other things that were discussed at length. Kanir was in his element discussing changes, new procedures, and integrating parts that were being discontinued or upgraded. I decided it probably wasn't much different from what CEO's discussed around tables with similar people on Earth as they discussed the building of airplanes and space shuttles and probably most any vehicle.

Once the meeting was over, Kanir took me to a dining room apparently for those in key positions within Kanir's organization. Tolf was there, already at a table. We sat with him.

"So, Jackie. I'd say you look a lot better now than when I saw you last." His smile reflected the tease in his voice.

"I decided that if I'm going to set trends, they'd better be to the benefit of the business."

"I think the outfit you had on earlier would have benefited me," Kanir said. There was the half smile, almost warm, trying to tease. I ignored the remark, ignored him.

A robot came to take our order, which Kanir took care of. It turned out I had ordered something pretty close to a club sandwich and chips.

The two men took the first few minutes to discuss some business, when a woman came into the dining room and had a seat with us. Tolf quickly introduced her to me as his wife, Shala. She was nearly as tall as Tolf, with long, red hair and huge brown eyes. She was dressed conservatively in something loose that closely resembled denim.

"It's good to meet you, Jackie," she said, helping herself to some water from the pitcher on the table.

"Thank you, Shala. Nice to meet you too."

"It came as quite a surprise to us when Kanir said he was marrying so suddenly. I hope you like it here."

I looked at Kanir. "I'm sure Tolf told you I was not very cooperative."

"Give it time."

The meal went by quickly as we talked and ate. It seemed fairly easy to relax with these people, and I actually found myself enjoying the time with them. All too soon, lunch was over and Tolf had to get back to some work he needed to finish. Shala, who worked in the ship's gardens, was due to be back at her post as well.

Kanir took the next couple of hours to show me around the ship. He took his time, obviously enjoying being with me. Almost everywhere we went on the ship, he made introductions, always sidestepping where I was from. I was impressed that he knew the names of easily 95 percent of the people he had working for him. He even knew some of the details of some of their lives, asking about circumstances some of them were going through. Those we met were genuinely pleased to see their boss. Kanir's quiet enthusiasm over what he had built and accomplished was genuine.

I kept thinking that it would be so easy just to give in to what was going on and let this be my life. Kanir was a very attractive man by any standards. He had a thriving business, and I would want for nothing. The little bit I had learned about him so far lead me to believe that he was basically a good man. I imagined that if I gave him my heart, as he was clearly hoping, he would gladly give me anything my heart desired, with the exception of going home.

Kanir returned me to our rooms then left for a while. I had a guard posted outside the door, clearly to keep me where he wanted me.

That evening, Kanir arrived at the same time dinner was brought in. He had another fragrant flower. Over dinner, he asked me a few questions from time to time, and I answered them as briefly as possible. I was trying to keep my distance; maybe he would get tired of this and let me go. Again, he slept on the couch that night. There couldn't be too many men who would be willing to call the couch their bed. I didn't understand it, but I wasn't going to look at this gift too closely.

At least this cage was better appointed than the ones I had been in before this. There was a large portal through which I could view the stars and planets we passed. One of the crew came and gave me some brief instruction to use the computer. It took both voice commands and had a keyboard. There was quite a bit I didn't have access to, such as communication outside of where I was, but there were a lot of other things I could occupy my time with. I could bring up literature, which I spent a lot of time reading, as well as news in different parts of the galaxy. I was even able to find the Bible, which I took a long time reading and then meditating on. I missed having mine and was happy to have access to even this one on the computer.

The beings casting the news were pretty interesting. One was downright scary. None of the networks back home would have ever considered a woman with three eyes, each of which blinked at different times, hair the color of the Partridge Family bus and the body of a stick bug.

I ordered paint for the rooms as well as Kanir's office. It would be several days before it would arrive, leaving me plenty of time to accompany Kanir as he tended to his daily business.

The routine was pretty easy. When I got up, Kanir was on his way out to do whatever it was he did first thing in the morning. By the time he got back, I was showered and dressed and ready for breakfast. I took some time in my Bible and prayer. After the meal, we left for whatever business he had scheduled for the day.

I kept looking for a way to get out of the rooms and make an escape. I still didn't know where I would go, but I was pretty confident I could get on a shuttle and get off the ship. I'd figure out where to go once I had that accomplished. As we toured the ship, I made it a point to remember where everything was, especially the shuttle bays.

20

I HAD BEEN on this ship for almost a week when I tried to escape. The young girl who was bringing in our meal had just entered the room and had moved quickly to the table across the room. The door was still open. Since I was not officially a prisoner, but the CEO's wife, security had become a bit lax in the way they looked after me within that short time. I had not been a threat to anyone, and they had let their guard down. I took that second to blast through the door, push the guard down, and take off down the hall at a full run.

I thought I heard Kanir's voice as he came from the other direction. He sounded angry. I had to get away now. I wasn't sure what would happen if I was caught.

I heard feet running after me once the guard figured out what had happened, as well as somebody yelling something about stopping. My feet flying down the hallways, I passed doors on each side of the corridor, not knowing what was behind any of them, and trying to find an open door I could slip into. An alarm was sounding so loudly around me, I was almost convinced it was sounding my location at every turn I made.

I turned a corner, found an open door, and stepped in, closing the door after me. I heard the footsteps pass the room, going down the corridor. I was in a meeting room. I looked around, panting, trying to find somewhere to hide. There was a door across the room, on the other side of a large meeting table. I ran around the table to it, opened the door, and stepped in, closing the door behind me. It was full of different kinds of supplies—first-aid stuff, napkins and silverware, electronic office supplies, other things I couldn't identify. There were also a few uniforms hanging in a corner.

I stripped off the skirt and blouse I wore and slipped into a pair of pants and a shirt, both a bit large, but probably passable. I pulled my hair back into a ponytail and prayed the flats I wore on my feet were close enough to what passed for the uniform of the day. I was pretty sure the pants were long enough it wouldn't be an issue.

It seemed safe to just sit and think about what I needed to do. I needed to get to a shuttle. I wasn't sure if I could pilot one, but I was willing to give it a shot. If I had enough time to study the control panel and make what I would hope would be logical choices in trying to fly the thing, I just might be able to get off this ship. Of course, I had to figure out where to go once I got out of this vessel.

Why couldn't some part of this be easier? I just wanted to get home. I wanted to get back to my life. I had no idea how to get back to Earth on my own, and I was very sure there were no signs pointing out the way to get to the third planet from the sun in the part of the galaxy I came from. There was nobody on my side to help me figure this out.

I thought about what I had said to Kanir a week ago: God was all I had. It was never truer than right now. I prayed He would show me what to do, where to go.

The alarm was still sounding. I was sure they had some kind of surveillance something or other that could be used to find me. I had to get out and get far from here, find some way off the ship. I left the closet and went to the door to the corridor and put my ear to the door to listen. I couldn't hear anything. I took a chance and opened the door, stepped back into the room, flattening myself to the wall. Nobody went past the room. I slowly stuck my head out the door. Nobody was around, but the alarm continued to wail away.

I stepped out into the corridor and started walking as if I knew where I was going. Within a few seconds, I was passing others in the corridors. I even tried to be on the lookout for me; I had to blend in. A moment later, the alarm stopped, but red and blue lights on the walls flashed brightly, a replacement to the noise.

I was going down a corridor, looking for clues to the shuttle bay. I had just passed a ranking security officer, when I heard him say, "Stop right there!"

I stopped and stood at attention, trying not to sweat.

The officer walked back to where I had stopped and stepped in front of me, studying me. I remained looking straight ahead, hoping he couldn't sense my panic.

"Where's your name tag, officer?"

"I was getting dressed when I heard the alarm, sir. I thought looking for her was more important than putting my name tag on."

He looked me over for another moment. I prayed my footwear was hidden well, that I looked like "one of the guys" enough that he would just let me go. Even though I was human, I still blended in.

"What's your name, officer?" he demanded.

I'd had enough time to think about a name and rank while I had been in the storage closet, just in case. Without missing a beat, I responded, "Officer Rinba Awah, sir."

He paused, still studying me. "You one of Chah's men?"

"Yes, sir." Whoever that was…

"How long have you been serving?"

"Two months, sir." My mouth was suddenly dry.

"As soon as she's recovered, get that tag and see me in my office."

"Yes, sir." I looked at his name tag. "Jerptah." If I could find a ship's directory, I might look him up, if I couldn't find my way off the ship. He might be interesting to work with. Was I getting cocky?

I went down several corridors, finally came to an elevator. I stepped inside and ordered it to take me to the shuttle room.

A moment later, the doors opened to another corridor. Across from the elevator was a closed bay door, as well as another regular door, both of which had writing on them that I had seen often enough to know this was the shuttle bay. I couldn't open the regular door at first. I opened a panel next to it and began punching in random codes. After a minute, the door finally slid open, and I walked into an immense hangar.

There were two shuttles, the size of large step trucks. I walked around them, trying to figure out how to get in. I finally found what looked like a side door, with a panel next to it, just below eye level. I opened the panel, and after pressing several buttons, the door whooshed open. I stepped inside, figured out how to close the door, and looked to the front of the vessel. As I walked to it, my hopes started to fade.

I was in over my head. I didn't have a clue as to how to operate this thing. The panel made my head spin—buttons, switches, faders, dials, and other things. I didn't know what to do first. I sat down, looking at the panel. I felt defeated and frustrated. I didn't know what to do, and nothing was coming to me. I pressed a couple of buttons, pushed a fader; nothing happened. Thankfully, none of them was an eject button. There was no "start" button, nothing obvious that indicated how to get this ship off the floor.

The door I had entered opened, and two guards ran in, guns drawn. I knew they wouldn't shoot to kill. I was concerned about going through anything that would hurt a lot, but if it got me out of here, I was willing to deal with the pain.

"Stand up, ma'am," the taller one ordered.

I did as I was told. I was shaking from fear, adrenaline, and frustration.

"Please just let me go," I said, trying with all my might to keep my voice from cracking. "Tell him you were too late, I got away."

"Can't do that. Let's go."

They had me turn around and placed restraints on my wrists.

Kanir was waiting for me in a meeting room down the hall from our rooms. He looked angry. I was scared of what he would do to me. I was told he was gracious and gentle, but I was sure he wouldn't take my escape attempt quietly.

The guard and the girl I had escaped from were there, seated across the table from where I stood. She looked down, concerned for her future. He looked straight ahead, ready for whatever might happen.

Kanir motioned me to a chair. "Sit down," he ordered.

I did as I was told, my wrists hurting. He noticed my discomfort and had one of the guards remove the restraint.

"What were you thinking? That you could actually leave this ship?" he finally asked. His voice was quiet, but the anger was palpable.

"That was my intent."

"You are my wife. You belong to me—"

"I don't belong to anyone!" I said firmly, trying to keep my voice from shaking. "I don't want to be here. I was forced into this…this marriage." I spat the word out. "I don't want to be here. I don't want to be with you. I don't belong here. I don't even belong out here in space. I just want to go home! I want my life back!"

I could feel the tears starting to spill and couldn't stop them. I used my hands to push them away.

Kanir watched me for a few minutes, eyes dark and unreadable.

"I can't do that," he said quietly.

It took a few minutes for me to gain control. The tears had slowed, but I felt exhausted now. I had been running and hiding and trying to get away for almost two hours. I wanted to sleep. I wanted to punch something, or throw something. I was still waiting to find out how he would punish me.

"I need you to listen to me," he said quietly, firmly. I nodded, looking at him. His voice was controlled. "I cannot have you behaving like this. I am not going to punish these two, although I could. They were foolish not to be on their guard. We all know you don't want to be here. None of us can afford not be on our guard around you. What I am going to do is this: these two will not be punished as long as you never attempt this again. The second you try to escape again, they will both be executed. Do I make myself perfectly clear, Jackie?"

The girl looked absolutely panic-stricken. The guard had no reaction at all.

I nodded numbly. This was almost worse than a beating. Two people I didn't even know were now pulled into this craziness because of me. I would have their lives in my hands every time I considered trying to leave. I felt deflated and powerless.

"Answer me," he ordered. "I need to know that you will not try this again."

"Yes, sir."

"Do not call me sir. I am your husband."

I nodded.

I looked at the two people sitting across the table from me. "I…I'm sorry," I said softly. "You will not have to worry about your safety, or your lives. I won't do this again."

He had the guard and young girl leave and had the other guards step outside the room.

"What are you going to do to me?" I asked.

"What do you mean?"

"Aren't you going to punish me?"

"No. It's just been taken care of." Kanir walked me back to our rooms with the guards as our escort, one in front one behind us. He kissed my forehead and left.

When he returned to our rooms for dinner later that day, it was as if nothing had happened.

21

THE NEXT MORNING, we were right back to our routine. The only difference was that the guard and whoever brought in breakfast were a whole lot more on their game. No chances were taken.

Kanir made sure I only had contact with others as long as he was with me. I understood what he was doing. I knew that he wanted me to be entirely reliant on him so that he could, over time, manipulate me gently to be and do what he wanted. I knew it was manipulation to break me down to be his wife, as he wanted me. He was never unkind. He was incredibly considerate, making sure I had whatever I asked for that he could provide. It was pretty obvious he was in this one for the duration, however long it would be. It didn't seem to bother him that I felt just as strongly about not being his wife.

One evening over dinner, I asked if there was a gym or fitness room.

"Of course. Would you like to exercise there with me?"

"Yes, I would."

"The room is very well equipped. Nerrett is our expert on the subject of staying fit and can put a plan together for you, I'm sure."

Nerrett was a tall, bald, blue-skinned man with a toned and muscled physique. Kind of a cross between a Smurf and Mr. Clean. He put a schedule together for me, and within a couple of days, I was running and working out on machines I had never seen before, but which helped me tone up, gain strength, and give me something to do that I considered constructive. I knew I needed to be fit for the day I might be able to do something to fly this coop.

I was desperate for jeans and shirts that were comfortable. I spent some time with Mada and Sheeb, did a bit of research to show them what I wanted, and a few days later, I had several pairs of custom-fitted jeans and some shirts. Kanir wasn't sure what he thought of them at first, but I wasn't concerned about that. It wasn't long before I was seeing others similarly dressed. All by myself, I had started a fad for jeans and camp shirts.

We began having dinner with some of the different people Kanir had business with as well as friends. Tolf and Shala were frequent dinner partners in their rooms or ours. It wasn't unusual to have dinner on another ship with dignitaries Kanir had contact with. He was pleased to be able to show me off to those we visited, never giving away where I was from. I did my part to play the role of his gracious wife.

As time went on, the battle to keep up the barrier between us became more and more difficult. The stress was crazy and exhausting. A part of me wanted to just let all this go, declare defeat, and be Kanir's wife. The louder side of me insisted the battle wasn't over. We worked as partners when there was some part of the business for me to offer a contribution, but there was still no physical contact beyond the hand kiss he gave me when he brought me a flower each evening.

I tried to come up with a way to leave, but I knew it was hopeless. As long as the guard and the girl's lives were in the balance, there was nothing I could do. I had pretty much resigned myself to where I was, yet at the same time, it was hard not to consider how to get away from here.

Between activities and work, we stayed busy. People no longer gave me much of a second glance; they were used to seeing me around with Kanir. We were with so many different people in different circumstances, with different requests for what they wanted in the ships being ordered, that there wasn't a chance to be bored. It was constantly interesting, constantly changing.

The rooms and his offices had been transformed from blank slates to spaces that were warm, peaceful, and inviting. I could tell that Kanir enjoyed the transformation of the rooms. He seemed more relaxed and always seemed to take a look around, as if mystified by what had been done.

I was spending time every morning before breakfast in prayer and study, keeping my faith up and continuing to seek guidance. Occasionally, Kanir joined me. He usually wanted me to read to him what I happened to be studying from the Bible that particular day. He asked questions once in a while and just listened as I prayed.

When I asked him why he was doing this, he replied, "I've noticed that when we do this together, it makes our day more pleasant. We see things we might have missed or taken for granted, and we get a lot more done." He paused and added, "And I'm getting to know you and what is important to you."

"It's only been a couple times."

He nodded. "I know. I've been reading this Bible of yours."

"Really." I was genuinely surprised and uneasy.

"Yes."

"How far have you gotten?"

"I have almost completed the first part."

"So you've read Genesis?"

"Yes, all the way through to"—he consulted his own electronic reader—"Zechariah."

I blinked a couple of times. "You read the whole Old Testament in two weeks?" I was impressed, maybe a little concerned. Very peeved that I couldn't read quite that fast.

"Yes. It was very confusing. It's a collection of stories, poems, and other things. A lot of it is not in order. Some of it is very hard, impossible to understand. A bit of it is repetitive." He shook his head. "I don't understand your attraction to this book."

I didn't know what to say at first. I think he had taken speed-reading to a new level, for sure. And of course, I was concerned about anything he might have read that mentioned how a wife should treat her husband. That would lead to conversations I wasn't ready to navigate.

"Well, the Old Testament is a difficult place to start," I offered. "I think if you keep a lot of it in mind as you read the New Testament, it might come together for you a bit. And I would suggest starting with the book of John."

Breakfast and the need to get to the office put off any more discussion until the next morning. I spent the rest of the day praying for wisdom. I knew there were going to be questions, many of them I wasn't sure if I could answer adequately. I knew I had to keep it simple.

The next few mornings were interesting. Kanir had questions I did my best to answer, and those I couldn't, I had to admit I didn't know as we took time to study together. I was intimidated by how quickly he was reading through the New Testament. I asked him to take it more slowly and give himself time to absorb what he was reading and understand it better. He seemed to be doing that, which was a great relief.

What we were doing seemed to bring more peace to what was still a relationship that felt strained. Kanir seemed to be more on a fact-finding mission, than anything else, which was fine. I couldn't figure out how much of it was going to his heart, as compared to what he was learning. It probably wasn't that important. If he was going to accept God into his heart, it would happen when he was ready. I wasn't sure how I felt about any of this, since I was still keeping my distance from him on other fronts.

If there was an upside to this whole mess, it was that I seemed to be safe. I no longer was in constant fear for my life or safety. I wasn't being prepared to be sold or attacked or anything else. Life, a bit confusing and crazy, was settling down.

A few weeks later, we were in his office. Kanir was going over some details he thought I could handle. He had ordered a snack, which was delivered. It looked, smelled, and tasted like the spinach artichoke dip I enjoyed when I was on Earth. I had actually gotten in touch with our chef, as I called him, and told him what I wanted. After a number of experiments, he had come up with this concoction, which both Kanir and I enjoyed a couple times a week.

I was loading up my third chip with some of the green goo when I got a sudden strong whiff of the dip, making me stop with the chip midway to my mouth.

It is amazing what the sense of smell can do. It can transform a mood in less than a split second. I could remember being on Earth when I could tell when the seasons changed just by how the air smelled outside. The sense of smell can also bring forth past memories, no matter how trivial or how long ago with incredible clarity.

Like now.

I was instantly transported back to the last time I had enjoyed this snack on Earth. I had been with Karen in a restaurant. We were talking about a lot of things, mission trips being only one subject we had touched on.

I was stunned that I may have been brought out here for a particular purpose. Was this a mission field God had sent me to? I couldn't wrap my mind around it. The idea was absurd. Why not someplace on Earth? Why did I have to be taken out here? It was hard to breathe for a moment, and I could feel all the blood leave my face.

Kanir had been talking to me about one of his more difficult vendors. His voice was suddenly distant, and I couldn't understand what he was saying. He was asking me a question. I think it had something to do with how to differ our approach with this particular person.

"What is it, Jackie?" Kanir could see that something had startled me.

I put the chip down slowly. "I need a break," I said hoarsely and left quickly. The guard followed me to our rooms, stayed outside the door while I went in.

I went into the bedroom. The lights came up as I entered, and I shut them off. I sat in the dark in the corner of the bedroom with my knees pulled up to my chest.

I couldn't get away from the conversation I'd had with Karen at Applebee's over the spinach artichoke dip. Missionary work. Hard work. The tug to go…to serve…was it really possible that I was sent out here to do that?

It couldn't be. The idea was absurd. Crazy. I wasn't capable of doing what that required. I wasn't trained. There were arguments going through my head about why this possibly couldn't be why I was here. Behind that conversation going on in my head that begged the question "Why me?" was a tape loop that kept repeating, "Why not me? Why not you?"

I thought about what was going on. I had thought missionary work would be interesting. I had felt a pull. I had joked about it. Now I was doing it. Doing it crudely, I thought, but doing it, nonetheless.

I remembered someone saying, "Those God calls, He prepares." I didn't feel at all prepared for this. I didn't want to be here. I didn't want to be married to this man. I didn't want to go through the hell I had gone through the first few weeks I had been out here. I couldn't believe this could possibly be God's will for my life.

And what about what was happening to my family and friends back on Earth? This certainly wasn't to their benefit.

I sat for over an hour in the corner, my knees pulled up to my chest, thinking, praying, and sometimes crying.

"Jackie?" Kanir knocked on the door, trying to open it. "Are you all right?"

I cleared my throat and tried to make my voice as normal as I could. "I'm fine."

"May I come in?"

I thought it was interesting that he could have defeated the lock and come into the room with no problem. It was one of many ways in which Kanir defined being a gentleman, which made being here just bit easier.

"I need more time."

"Do you need anything?"

"No. Thank you," I called back. "I'm all right, really."

I waited for him to follow that up with another request for something that he thought he'd be able to do to feel like he was doing something to help. Heck, I didn't even know what I needed right now to get past this. I just knew I wasn't ready to face anybody right now. None of these people understood what I was going through.

What was I supposed to do now? I got up and started walking around the room, still trying to work my way through what was going on in my life.

I was so angry with God for doing this. I ranted and raved quietly. I wasn't going to Africa. I wasn't going to China. I wasn't even going back into the city streets where I worked anymore, the place others had tried to tell me was my own personal mission field. This was where I had been sent. There was no time to get used to the idea, no time to prepare, no time to say good-bye to family and friends. This was it.

I think I was more startled, stunned, than anything else. Occasionally I brushed away a tear. I didn't want to be here! I didn't sign up for this, any of this! I didn't want to be married to Kanir; I didn't want to even be his companion or work partner or whatever we seemed to be. It was as if someone had played a big joke on me and I had suddenly gotten the punch line, only to find out the whole joke was on me.

I felt helpless and hopeless. I was never going back home. I knew deep down inside, I was never going to see Earth or my family ever again. More tears.

How could I have been chosen? Why me? I wasn't qualified, prepared, ready, and I had no desire to be out here. How could He have chosen me to do this?

I wanted to feel my dad's arms around me giving me the hug I so desperately needed right now. To have him tell me everything would be all right. That's just what he did, and I needed to hear him tell me he would help me fix it. Make it better. Make it go away. Chase away the bad guys.

I couldn't breathe. My nose and face were so congested from crying, I couldn't breathe through my nose. I hated when that happened. I made my way to the bathroom and splashed cold water on my face, blowing my nose some more.

Back in the bedroom, I sat in the corner of the room again, feeling deflated, defeated, lost, confused, angry, scared out of my mind, lonely. Alone.

I didn't say or think anything for a long time. I just sat there. I don't know much time passed. I had poured my heart and soul out to God and now I just sat quietly. I wasn't sure what to do. Every now and then a few more tears came.

And then I felt warmth slowly envelope me, a knowing that I was not alone. I was okay. I was safe. I allowed the warmth to cover me and smooth over all the emotions I had let go of the past couple of hours. I knew it was Jesus, letting me know he had everything under control.

I just wanted to rest in this blanket of warmth. It felt so safe and secure. I felt protected, loved, cherished. I would have been fine spending the rest of my life right in that corner, wrapped in the love that enveloped me.

Thoughts came. I was all right. I was right where He needed me. This was my home. Kanir was my husband. I needed to let him be my husband. This was just the beginning. I was here for His purpose.

More tears came—maybe tears of surrender. Knowing this was it. Finalization of a decision made for me. Acceptance.

There was more. All encouraging. All letting me know He was with me. I didn't have to be afraid of where I was or who I was with.

I didn't have to fight anymore. I didn't have to run or try to get away or try to get home. This was home. I was where I was supposed to be. I was loved. I wasn't alone; Jesus was there. There was such relief, such peace. I was going to be all right.

Kanir. He was my husband. How could I do this part of it? Why did I have to do this part of it? I didn't want to be his wife. The idea of having to share a bed with him was out of the question. So far we were like roommates who happened to be business partners. I had a hard time going further than that. There was silence as I considered that. Just silence.

And then I argued that this was all too much at once. Why couldn't I take all of what was going on in small steps, one thing at a time, over a long period of time. How could I do this, especially this last part? And then all I could hear was "Trust Me."

"Then give me what I need to do this," I said out loud.

"I have," came the response. It was like someone had whispered to me.

I could hold out for a long time against anybody else but the Almighty. I knew I had to do this part of it. I didn't understand it. I had hung onto being anything but Kanir's wife for so long, I wasn't sure if I could actually do it now. But minute by minute, the aloofness, the distance, everything else I had put between the two of us started to melt away. I started to see Kanir in a different light. God had made him, and for this time—and for me. More overwhelming thoughts and feelings followed.

I let the thoughts wash through me and over me, comforting me, quieting me. I was so tired and exhausted, emotionally drained. I felt myself drifting off to sleep in the corner of the room.

———◦◦◦———

I was being lifted. I jumped, and Kanir almost dropped me.

"You're all right," he whispered, adjusting me in his arms.

I nodded and put my arms around his neck. He stopped still for a moment and held me tighter. I hung on to him, feeling the strength in his arms. I couldn't believe how good he smelled. I hadn't noticed it before. Actually I had, I just hadn't bothered to care. His beard, which I had never really touched before, felt bristly and warm against my face. His breath warmed my hair. I thought about what had been shared with me in the darkness and just clung to my husband. I hadn't wanted to call him that before. Now it felt right. I knew it was right.

After a moment, he put me in the bed and pulled the covers up over me. He kissed my hair and left the room. I fell back asleep.

The crying and emotional upheaval left me with a headache and feeling horrible when I got up the next morning. I got showered and dressed in my gym clothes, which only helped a little. I didn't feel like going to the gym, but it was our routine.

Kanir was looking out the portal, enjoying a cup of coffee when I stepped out in the living area. He was dressed casually.

"Good morning," I said a bit cautiously.

He nodded. "Good morning." He paused and took a sip of coffee. "You don't look well."

"Bad headache," I said, pouring a cup of coffee.

"There is a remedy in the bathroom. Come." He led the way back into the bathroom and poured a liquid into a small cup for me. It was pretty nasty, but within minutes, I could feel the pain starting to ebb away.

"Get changed into something comfortable," Kanir said, "We're not going in today. I want you to rest. I think the stress of the last several weeks might have been too much for you. We got a lot of work done. I was able to accomplish more than normal, I believe because you were there to help. We're going to rest today." He paused and looked at me closely. "And I want to know what happened to you yesterday."

I changed quickly, and we sat down to eat. We had been praying a blessing over meals the last week, and Kanir looked at me now, waiting for me to pray. I reached over and took his hand, resting both of ours on the table between us. He looked at me curiously. I had never reached for him before; I had purposefully pulled away from any physical contact he tried to have with me. This was new for both of us. As strange as it felt, this first time, it also felt very natural.

"You pray," I said quietly.

An eyebrow threatened to hit the ceiling. He lost just a bit of color. I could see his mind working to remember what I had prayed at previous meals, and he repeated some form of it that was really pretty good. I squeezed his hand, and he gave me the half smile that I suddenly found very charming. He looked at our hands on the table for a few seconds and then looked at me. Kanir slowly lifted my hand and kissed it then released it.

We finished breakfast, talking quietly, and then took our coffee to the sofa in the living area. Kanir set his on the table in front of us and just looked at me for almost a moment, making me feel uncomfortable.

"Something has changed," he commented.

I nodded. It was amazing what a change in perspective could do in a short time. I suppose it has a lot to do with being willing to change and accept the new perspective. Everything seemed different, more peaceful. There was no question that Kanir was an attractive man, but he looked even more so to me now.

"Are you going to tell me?"

"I can't tell you everything," I began slowly. "I don't think I need to, at least not now. Maybe in the future—"

"Jackie, you're babbling."

I think I almost laughed. That made me stop and think. It had been ages since I had laughed. I had been so busy fighting and protecting myself and everything else since I had been taken, that short burst of laughter, the smile—it felt so good.

"I'm sorry." I looked out the portal at planets and stars in the distance. He wanted to know about the day before. "Yesterday, that snack we were eating prompted a memory. A lot of things happened. I needed to be alone. I needed to pray through what was going on in my head and my heart and my spirit."

"I could hear you sobbing. You had me worried, but I didn't know what to do."

"I'm sorry."

"Stop apologizing."

"I'm s—" I stopped myself. "Um…I don't know how to tell you what happened and not confuse you or make it sound strange or weird." I was babbling again.

I paused. I felt vulnerable and scared. I was taking this conversation to a place I never thought I would have to. I had been praying about it all morning as I showered and as we ate, and I still was having trouble reconciling the entire thing in my head.

I made myself speak quietly and slowly. "I prayed. A lot. I poured my heart out to God. I was very angry with him. I guess a lot of things in my mind kind of came to a head. I've been gone from my home now for almost two months. I've thought the whole time that I would get back there that I would find a way or I would make a way. Somehow. You know I haven't wanted to be here. With you or anybody else for that matter. I don't know why I was chosen to be here. I don't know why I had to go through that nightmare with D'Nar and then Ronnok. I…I got a revelation, I guess. Something clicked. And I knew without a doubt that I'm not going home to Earth. Ever." I brushed away a tear and tried to stop my voice from breaking. Kanir stayed where he was, watching and listening.

I took a few breaths, trying to contain the tears. "What I got out of it is that this is my home now. I'm where I'm supposed to be." I took a couple more deep breaths and made myself look directly at him. "And you are my husband."

Kanir nodded, still looking at me. I could see stress starting to melt off him. His face softened; the set of his mouth relaxed. His whole body seemed to do a silent sigh. It made me realize he had been as stressed as I had been and how that had affected Kanir. I was struck by how patient he had been, the grace he had extended to me. It was humbling, to say the least.

"Kanir, I don't know you," I confessed. "The short time we've been together, I've figured out a few things about you, but I don't know you. And I don't think you know me."

"We will take care of that as we go along," he said simply. From somebody else, it would have sounded trite, blasé. Not from this man. He was on many levels the most sincere, real person I had met. Ever. There were no attitudes to get around, no weird perceptions. Kanir was Kanir.

Kanir moved closer to me on the couch. He seemed a bit tentative, making sure that I wouldn't jump up and move to another part of the room, which had been what I had done a lot of over the time we had been together.

I nodded. "I know I haven't been even much of a friend to you this whole time. But I can't just suddenly be your wife. I want to be." I paused, trying to organize what I needed to say.

"On Earth, when two people want to get to know each other, they date. They go out together. To dinner, maybe a movie, they spend time together. They meet each other's families, spend time with friends, making sure this is the person they want to spend their life with. I need to know you before we"—I paused—"join."

Kanir seemed to consider this for a short time. "How long do you need us to date?"

I pondered this for a moment before I answered, "I don't know. I promise not to take it beyond what is reasonable. I just need that time."

Kanir nodded. He reached over to tentatively touch my face gently. I didn't pull away. It actually felt sweet, and I turned my face into the warmth of his palm. "May I kiss you?"

I smiled. I hadn't expected him to ask me. "Yes."

Kanir moved closer to me. His lips brushed mine, and then he looked at me, considering. He kissed me again, pulling me into his arms for a long, sweet kiss. I could feel him holding back, not wanting this contact to go beyond where he knew I would be comfortable.

I leaned against him, almost content for the first time since I had been taken. After some time to study and pray, we spent the rest of the morning and the afternoon together, carefully avoiding talking about the business. The last weeks, I had only seen the business side of this man. It was a treat to see the personal side of him. Kanir either held my hand or had his arm around me most of the day. It took a short time to get used to, but then it was so natural. I wanted to be held and Kanir seemed to be happy with the new arrangement. We walked through the corridors and the gardens, talking or sometimes saying nothing, watching as we passed stars and planets.

The conversation went in so many directions: family, career, friends, places we had lived, and visited. Dreams we had, some of which we shared. We touched on ideals and values and things that were important to us.

The peace that surrounded us was hugely different, certainly much preferred to the coolness and stress that had ruled the atmosphere around us.

Kanir and I had dinner with Tolf and his wife. We had had meals with them before, but this time was much better, without the stress that seemed to accompany Kanir and me wherever we went.

"So what's going on?" Shala asked. We were in a corner of the living room, while Kanir and Tolf talked by the portal. Dinner had been cleared away.

"What do you mean?" I asked.

"You're a different person. There's none of the—almost hostility you had before."

I smiled. I had been smiling almost all day. It felt good. I just didn't quite know how to put it into words. Finally I just said, "I had an attitude adjustment."

"Kanir looks so relaxed. Whatever you did, don't stop."

I nodded. "I don't think that will be a problem."

"Tolf was pretty concerned last night. They had a meeting last night, and Kanir was asking him about what to do about a distraught woman."

I laughed. "Well, it's a long story. Some day I might be able to tell you about it."

Shala really wanted to know, but I didn't feel comfortable sharing unless she had some idea of what had been happening the last several weeks.

There was a peace in our rooms that made sleep a lot easier that night. Kanir was still on the couch, but I didn't think it would be for long.

The changes in the way we were relating to each other brought with it more contentment between us. Work, which we were able to do well together, was even easier to get through. The whole atmosphere in the offices had changed with our relationship. It was amazing.

As I now allowed myself to see this man in this new light, I had an even clearer picture of who he was. I saw the man who walked in integrity. He thought beyond himself. He truly cared about the people around him. He cared about me, not as a possession, but as his partner and companion, as well as his wife.

22

A FEW DAYS later, Kanir announced we were going off ship for the next couple of days. We had docked at one of the construction sites. I went to the window of our rooms and looked out. The sight was impressive—a sort of halo of equipment that kept stationary a huge ship under construction. Small shuttles went here and there around the structure. There were even a few people in space suits along the immense ship, some of them working alongside robots.

My heart almost skipped a beat when I looked below the massive production and saw the planet. It almost resembled Earth, but I quickly realized it wasn't. The landmasses were all wrong. Even though it wasn't my home, I was ready to visit it. I was hoping it would be similar. I was anxious to put my feet on soil again, feel the warmth of the sun and a cool breeze.

"Where are we?" I asked.

"My home world, Matakia. I want to show it to you."

I was more than a little surprised. I hadn't been planet-side anywhere and wondered if this was how everyone got by. I was excited by the prospect of getting off the ship and spending some time on terra firma.

"What about the ship?" I asked, looking at the huge structure outside the window.

"I'm here to do business planet side. The ship is in no condition for us to look at just yet. It will be months before we can do that. And we're going to spend time with my family."

His family. Gulp. Meet the parents. I felt my blood pressure go up a bit. Who wouldn't be a bit concerned about meeting the parents? Too many of them believed there was nobody in the universe worthy of their child, no matter that said child was a successful adult.

Despite my concerns, I was already excited about meeting these people he had told me about. I had seen pictures, and I was anxious to meet them.

I dressed in a pair of jeans, a camp shirt, and comfortable shoes. Like everything else here, there was a twist of contemporary that was signature to these parts. Kanir gave me a pair of sunglasses as we left in the shuttle.

I couldn't take my eyes off the front window, watching as we approached the planet. It was odd to think that this planet that looked so familiar in color was not Earth. It was midmorning in the area of Matakia where we were headed. We cruised over cities and forests, finally landing on the roof of one of the largest buildings in a city.

The noise of the city struck me at first. Earth cities were loud—car engines, horns honking, the occasional emergency vehicle. Here, there was just quiet. An occasional shuttle sped quietly by from a great distance, but other than that, it was quiet.

Kanir told me we were on the building his company owned. We left the shuttle and took an elevator down a couple of floors. It opened into a suite of spacious offices, the largest one being Kanir's. His office was quietly elegant. Overstuffed furniture near one huge window was a conversation area. His desk was modest in size but beautifully crafted. Various pieces of office equipment foreign to me were on the desk and credenza behind it. Tables and his desk were all in dark wood. Paintings on the walls were handsome touches along with a few pieces of sculpture on the shelves and side tables. This was a huge difference from what I had first seen of his offices and rooms on the ship.

I stood looking out the huge window that offered a view of the city that kept me transfixed. Steel and glass, some wood thrown in here and there, made up the scene before me. My guard stood behind me, ever vigilant as Kanir did some work at his desk.

A woman, well dressed, came in—his secretary, Anuyush. I broke away from the window long enough for us to greet each other. I walked around the room, checking out the decorative pieces and other things while they worked on gathering material for a meeting Kanir had to attend. The shuttles going past fascinated me. There were obviously some docking stations, for lack of a better term, where they entered and exited the buildings. Most of the stations were close to the tops of the buildings. Some of the shuttles were pretty large, some fairly small. To that degree, it wasn't much different than watching traffic on Earth—the huge SUVs and the sports cars and every other size vehicle in between.

The office door whooshed open, and a man and woman came into the room.

Kanir looked up. "Hello, you two," he said, almost smiling. He came to where I stood, grabbed my arm, and we walked together to the couple at the door. "Jackie, this is my sister Doshah and her husband Remon." There were hugs all around.

I noticed quickly how introductions here and how Kanir responded to his family differed significantly from how business associates and others were handled. He was more at ease with keeping his arm around me and giving me a quick kiss in front of his family. When we were with others, everything was business. I liked the difference in how he handled the two situations and was happy to see this lighter side of him.

Doshah was gorgeous, dark, like her brother, slim, and elegant. Her husband was barely lighter in coloring and rugged-looking. They were a striking couple together.

"Kanir, she is lovely," Remon said, holding my hand.

Kanir was beaming. He was containing his excitement, but I could feel it. I'd never seen him like this; it was a stark contrast to the stoic front he kept up in the offices on the ship and our rooms.

"You will have beautiful babies," Doshah added.

I tried to keep smiling, hiding my shock at the remark. Children? For whatever reason, I hadn't thought that far yet. I sent up a silent prayer, probably more of a surface to God missile asking for memos to be sent more frequently.

Doshah was looking intently at me and then at Kanir. It was making me feel uncomfortable. "Is something wrong?" I finally asked.

Doshah looked at her brother. "Kanir, you have been married for over a month, but you have not yet joined?" Her voice was quiet, but there was no mistaking the question. I couldn't figure out how she knew, at the same time thinking the remark was a bit rude.

"Don't embarrass Jackie," Kanir replied, offering no explanation.

"Mother will not be pleased."

"Hopefully, Mother will be interested in more than our joining."

His sister gave him an odd look. She returned her polite smile to me as she seemed to decide to leave the topic alone. I recognized the look; I had four brothers, and I knew she would have something to say to him later whether it was her business or not. Siblings were siblings the universe over.

Kanir smiled. "Jackie, I have two meetings to attend, and I should be done by lunchtime." He had his arm around my waist, holding me close. "Doshah and Remon are going to take you around, show you the area, do a bit of shopping."

"That would be great," I said.

We made plans to meet for lunch and spend the afternoon together before going to his parents' home for dinner. It was all much as things would have been done on Earth, almost no difference at all.

Kanir pulled me close to him and kissed me. When he finally released me, I stepped back, surprised and a bit dizzy. Kanir's eyes were dark, and I was very happy that we were not alone. It was the most passionate kiss he had given me yet, taking me totally by surprise.

His sister laughed. "Kanir, if you leave her breathless, she won't be able to shop."

Apparently having the guard accompany us wasn't unusual. Neither Doshah nor Remon commented on having an escort for the day.

Kanir gave me one last hug as well as something used for spending, and we left. It was a gorgeous day to spend outside in the open-air markets, experiencing the sights and sounds of the city. It was rich and diverse in many ways. There were a number of people from different places, judging by appearances, dress, and language. We went down one street to vendors selling a wide selection of different kinds of food, and down another street where clothing of all styles, colors, and textures was being sold. There were a couple of entertainment venues here and there, mostly musicians playing instruments I had never seen before. The smells of the different foods that were being prepared kept all three of us feeling hungry. We discussed where we wanted to go for lunch several times as we passed different restaurants. It was hard to come to a final decision; it all smelled and looked so good.

"You make my brother very happy," Doshah said as we sorted through scarves at a booth.

"Do you think so?" I asked.

"It's been a while since I've seen him this settled and content."

"What do you mean?"

"He's been chased by the most beautiful, wealthiest women, but he wasn't interested in any of them. He married purely for business purposes but paid them no attention. They finally asked for their independence, which he granted them. He never brought them home for us to meet. We were all surprised when he let us know he was bringing a wife home. Our mother cried for joy, to not have to worry about him so much anymore. You seem good together."

"Moms are the same everywhere, aren't they?" I said.

"How did you happen to be out here?"

"It's a very long, confusing story," I said, hoping I had dodged that discussion until Kanir was around. We hadn't really come up with a story. It seemed he didn't want to reveal the details of how we came to meet with anybody.

"Maybe someday you'll share it with us."

"We would have to make sure Kanir is there, to be fair."

I noticed pretty quickly that all the Matakians were dark in coloring, like people from the Mediterranean. All eyes were brown or variations of the color, and hair was black or dark brown. In the midst of all the dark skin, there was no missing me. I would have to work not to be noticed with my fair skin, blue eyes, and brown hair. I was one of the aliens here, and it was obvious, given all the people who looked me over carefully or did double takes. I didn't see anybody who resembled me. There were plenty of other people from different planets just by looking at the diverse beings around us—just nobody else from Earth that I could see.

Kanir met us for lunch at an outdoor bistro. The food was wonderful, even though I couldn't identify it. Most of what I was seeing was very much like Earth with a twist here and there. I found that I didn't mind the twists so much.

The afternoon was spent walking through the market for a while longer, through a park and then through some shops. I managed to collect a few things to take back to the ship for our rooms and offices. Kanir seemed to enjoy watching me search and collect.

"I see you've managed to loosen his money from his fingers," Doshah said, loud enough for Kanir to hear.

"Actually, did you ever see his rooms and offices on the ship?" I asked.

"Yes," Doshah said, looking at her brother. "Please tell me you did something about that before you brought her to your home," she said to Kanir, obviously appalled.

"It's all taken care of," Kanir said. "I let Jackie put the colors and furniture in there that she wanted. It just so happens that I'm very pleased with the results."

Doshah was impressed. "Very good, Kanir," she said and then asked for details. Doshah must have been a lot for Kanir to keep up with when they were younger.

Our last stop was a jewelry shop.

"Hello, Kanir," said the owner, a gorgeous Matakian woman. She approached him quickly with her arms out in greeting. He took her hands and kissed her cheek, sidestepping the hug she seemed almost intent on giving him. She was very obviously happy to see Kanir, and I was sure there was some kind of history between them. I watched for just a second and then looked away as she seemed to silently settle into the idea that Kanir was not there for her.

"Juvka, good to see you again," Kanir said, "This is my wife, Jackie."

Juvka smiled and asked what she could do for us.

"We are looking for a special ring."

My ears perked up. Ring? I hadn't even thought about a ring. I wondered what they had that might be like a diamond.

Juvka took us to a display case that took my breath away. Diamonds would have paled in the presence of these stones. They sparkled, sitting in their settings, and some seemed to coalesce through different colors.

"Oh my," Doshah said. "Juvka, where did you get these?"

"Down, my love," Remon said.

"She can look," I defended.

"Doshah doesn't know how to just look!" Remon teased his wife.

I looked at Kanir. "These are incredible."

"Choose one." The half smile was there. He was enjoying this.

I was speechless. "What—"

"We won't find better in the city. Choose the one you want."

Juvka and Doshah were great helping me. Kanir watched and approved the one I chose. It wasn't the largest stone, but the setting was beautiful.

Kanir paid for the ring, took it from the box, and placed it on my finger. He kissed my hand and then my mouth. Doshah dabbed at tears in the corners of her eyes, and Juvka looked just a bit disappointed that it wasn't her.

I spent a good portion of the rest of the afternoon looking at the ring on my hand. How do you not feel giddy when things like this happen?

—◦◦◦—

We were in a horse-drawn carriage, taking a tour of the city. I called them horses. They looked very similar to a horse, yet larger than any I had ever seen on Earth. Their hair was longer than I was familiar with and covered their bodies, while their heads were scaly. It was late in the afternoon, and the sun was starting to set. One of the four moons was barely visible in the distance, a dark gray disc in the sky. Colorful clouds morphed the sky into an interesting painting of colors and shapes that we could barely take our eyes off of. It changed often, making the ride around the city even more relaxing. It was like watching an art show in motion, between the sky and the attractions we passed.

I was pleasantly tired. It had been a good day. Everything just seemed so natural. Doshah and Remon sat across from us, whispering quietly, smiling and kissing.

"What are you thinking?" Kanir asked.

"This has been an amazing day," I commented

He tipped my chin up with his fingers and kissed me. I was getting lost in the kiss. I was feeling dizzy again. My mind was going places I didn't want it to. It was almost as if I could feel Kanir becoming part of me, but I couldn't figure out where that was coming from. His kisses before this had never affected me like this, but they hadn't been quite as enduring either. I had kissed boyfriends before but had never been left feeling like I did now. I had conflicting feelings going on in my head; I wanted this to stop, and I didn't want this to stop.

When he finally released me, I leaned into him, feeling breathless and a bit woozy.

"We'll have to tell Mother that you two want an early bedtime tonight," Remon commented.

His parents' home was comfortable and elegant. Smells of dinner cooking wafted through open windows as we arrived, welcoming us when we stepped out of the small shuttle.

Kanir turned me to him before we walked from the shuttle. The guard had been sent back to the ship. He would be recalled tomorrow if Kanir felt he was needed.

"My mother is likely to have a lot of questions," he said quietly.

"Trust me, Doshah has a lot too."

"She said something?"

"I sort of danced around some of her questions. You're okay."

"You mean we're okay."

I considered that for a moment. "I suppose so."

Kanir almost smiled.

"What?" I asked.

"I don't think I've enjoyed being with my sister as much as I have today. She can be very opinionated. The two of you together are a good combination," he commented.

Something came to my mind from a conversation in his office. "What was your sister talking about back in your office? How does she know we haven't joined?"

He almost smiled again, and his right eyebrow went up. "I'll have to tell you later. We need to get inside. Mother is expecting us."

"It can't be that confusing. Come on. What...how can she tell?"

Kanir took a deep breath, looking at the sky for a moment before answering. "When a couple is married and they join, they develop a hrova. It's sort of a...an aura, I suppose. Most other people on our planet can see the hrova. In a way, it shows that you belong to another and are to be treated with respect, left alone by others who might find you desirable. We haven't joined. We don't have a hrova. Yet."

I blinked, listening to this. "You mean I would have one, even though I'm not Matakian?"

"Probably. We'll just have to find out." He smiled, almost teasingly.

Although Kanir's parents were sweet, there was a distinct coolness in the way they treated me. His mother was obviously disappointed. She had something else in mind for her son, not the simple woman in front of her who was neither from her planet nor from a family of wealth or stature. At least, that was what I was sensing from her. His father seemed a bit less reserved.

I suppose I understood in some way. All parents want the best for their kids. They likely have an image or expectation of who they'd like to see them settle down with, the person who will be a new member of the family. I wasn't of this world, had no wealth, and no prestigious position from anywhere. I hoped it wouldn't take too long for them to realize that, despite who I wasn't in their eyes, I loved Kanir and wanted to be not just a part of his life, but a major factor that contributed to the success he experienced personally and professionally. His business was also mine, so my interest in seeing that continue to grow and develop was not in his best interests only, but mine as well.

I figured his mother was in her late sixties. She was tall and thin with dark hair shot through with touches of gray, just a beautiful woman. His father was taller than Kanir, a bit on the stocky side. Dark, graying hair and eyes that assessed me as much as his wife did.

Now she took her time looking at us, studying the space around us, and I knew what she was looking for. I looked to Kanir, smiled, and shrugged.

"Shimra, don't embarrass them," Kanir's father said quietly.

"Kanir," she said quietly, ignoring her husband. Kanir came to her as she held me at arms length. "She is lovely. I will have beautiful grandchildren" was all she said.

I hoped the conversation would go other directions besides this one. This was the second time in one day that someone commented on babies. Yes, I supposed I eventually wanted a few; I just wasn't focused on it right now. I wasn't sure I wanted anybody else focused on it on my behalf.

Kanir kissed the top of his mother's head. "You think so?" he asked, watching my expression.

"Shimra, don't embarrass her," his father said.

Dinner was incredible. Again, foods I didn't recognize but found to be incredibly delicious. Kanir's family was quick to tease him in front of me, tell me tidbits about him they seemed to think would help me understand him. Through it all, his dark eyes continued to almost smile, and a few times he even laughed quietly at what was shared, ever reserved.

I helped in the kitchen afterward, as Kanir, his father, and Remon sat in the other room talking about their businesses and other things.

Conversation in the kitchen seemed to revolve uncomfortably around me. I was the eldest son's wife and the women with me were curious about Kanir and me as a couple.

I answered their questions as best I could without revealing too much. How had Kanir and I met? What were our plans? Because we'd only been together for a month, it was easy enough to say that we were still in the planning stages of our relationship. I knew they wanted to ask more questions about me and my background, but there was something that kept them from that subject. The coolness from his mother continued. Not being able to give her all the answers she wanted certainly didn't help.

I was beginning to rethink this whole part of the dating ritual. Maybe we didn't really need to do the family part of it.

But here we were…

When the last of the kitchen was put away, we joined the men in the living room. I sat next to Kanir as discussion went through what was going on locally, catching Kanir up on things that were of interest to him. Not knowing anything about what they discussed, I listened, but there wasn't much I could contribute. Not too long after, I found myself starting to nod off.

"Mother, I think I need to put my bride to bed," Kanir said.

"Of course, Kanir. Take the guest room. The large bed is in there, ready for you two."

All at once, I was wide awake with the idea of one bed, one room. I was just a bit concerned. Kanir was already standing and pulled me to my feet into his arms. He kissed the top of my head. We said our good nights to everyone and went to the second floor and into the bedroom.

"What are we going to do?" I asked.

"What do you mean?"

"There's only one bed."

"Good observation." There was no sign of a smile, and yet, I could tell he was enjoying my concern.

"What...where are you going to sleep?"

"With you. You're my wife."

I took a few seconds to consider this. "Okay. You stay on your side of the bed, and I'll stay on mine."

He nodded.

I gathered some toiletries and went into the bathroom to get ready for bed. I hadn't expected to be spending the night in a bed with this man. I was stalling for time. I looked at the ring on my finger and shook my head. What was I doing here? I could have stayed on the ship and not gotten in this situation. I wasn't ready for this part of our relationship. Or was I?

Kanir had been a gentleman for most of the time we had been together. There was the whole incident of me trying to leave on one of the shuttles, which now had two lives in the balance if I tried to take off again, but that wasn't going to happen. If there was such thing as a perfect husband, this man was it.

I thought about the evening, what a good time it had been, how wonderful his family was. This was the ultimate situation I would have loved to have had on Earth.

Being here with his family made me ache for my own. Even though I knew I was supposed to be where I was, it didn't make the pain any less. The hole in my heart that was the shape of my family was still massively empty. Yeah, this was my home now, this was my life, but oh, what I would do to have time with my family. It suddenly occurred to me that I had never been given the chance to say good-bye to them. I wondered how much of a difference that would have made. To have gotten some sage advice from my parents before I left. To feel my brothers' arms around me one last time before I left, never to return.

For what seemed like the millionth time, I wondered how my friends and family and co-workers were doing. What they were doing. How they were handling losing me, and what a horrible feeling it must be not to know what had happened to me. I took a deep breath and told myself not to cry again. It helped nothing. It was an effort to push the angst out of my head and leave it alone. Tears were not going to help at all.

Okay, enough stalling, I thought. Time to put on the big girl panties and just do whatever needed to be done.

Kanir was studying something on a handheld piece of office equipment I had seen in his office. He was sitting in a chair across the room with a glass of what I thought was something like brandy or wine next to him. He looked up. "Can I get you anything?"

"No, thank you. I'm fine."

"You made my mother very happy tonight," he commented, putting his work aside.

"I think she'll be even happier when she knows we've joined." I said.

Eyebrows shot up to his hairline as I felt my face go red, realizing what I had just said. What had I just said? Kanir was my husband. I knew he loved me, and I knew I loved him, but enough to join with him now? I was still so conflicted.

"I…I didn't mean that we—"

Eyebrows slid back into place. Kanir was expressionless. Warmth slipped into his eyes. "Jackie. Not until you're comfortable."

I paused, looking at this man. He got up and walked over to me, pulling me into his arms.

"I love you, Jackie," Kanir said quietly. "You no longer have your family or anything that was supposed to be for you. I don't want to force you into anything else you're not ready for." He was looking so intently into my eyes, I couldn't breathe. "I have you with me. I know the rest—our joining—will happen soon. I'm all right with waiting."

I nodded. I couldn't say anything. I felt amazingly protected and cared for. He was putting me before what he wanted. All at once, I clearly realized just how much he loved me. I couldn't look away from his face.

Kanir looked away first and encouraged me to get some rest.

I slipped into the bed. Kanir was already in his nightwear. He turned off the light in the room and came into bed with me. He kissed my head as I was drifting off to sleep. "Good night, my love," he whispered.

"Good night, Kanir."

23

I FINISHED SIPPING the horrible-tasting liquid, rested my head against the back of my chair, and allowed myself some time for the pain in my head to subside.

The problems I was handling were things our former leaders had dealt with. I could only hope that I was doing an acceptable job. Our former leaders were so much more capable than I would ever be. Lady Minkas, for example, had brought our planet to a place of peace that was amazing. She just knew what to do, what to say, to get enemies to talk to each other. Many times they became friends; sometimes those friendships lasted lifetimes, others for brief spans of time, until sensitive personalities faced dilemmas that required more cooperation.

Cooperation. A word Lady Minkas used a lot. Along with concession. And no one would ever forget compromise.

I was using those words a lot in helping continents and nations sort out slights and accusations.

Nyast was talking, sometimes too fast, to investigators. He had been accused of trying to change borders between three of the nations on the continent he governed. Unfortunately for him, there was enough evidence stacked against him, that he had reason to be concerned for himself. Nyast had the three of them understandably angry with him. They were working hard to keep the peace among their people. Nyast's only defense was that he was trying to make the populations equal among the land areas. It was a gamble, and not one that worked well. He was at risk of at least losing his position, at most, his life.

Because of this, Investigator Tarr was taking a closer look at Nyast regarding the Jackie Laughlin incident. Nyast was unaware that he was being looked at again, and everything in his background was being gone through with extreme care and in great depth.

Councilman Kenbar had uncovered a large group of activists on the continent Junth, who were against our method of obtaining a leader. They threatened the safety of her family when they realized she had incriminating evidence that was turned over to authorities. Shortly after, an attempt was made on her life as she was leaving her office. She and her family now had constant protection as protectors, and others worked to find those guilty of these actions. Those responsible were in hiding, and with the number of people not keen on our leadership practices seeming to grow constantly, they likely had many helping them evade capture.

Two assistants to two separate individuals on the council were being investigated for fairly large thefts of funds that were to benefit a particular organization that worked with those needing assistance.

There were numerous other small situations I was trying to deal with. Some of them needed my attention daily, others seemed to do better if I let them work themselves out and simply checked in on them every few days. I was, of course, available to those who needed my counsel regarding any of these things.

As I navigated all this, I marveled at how leaders I had worked with in the past had stood up so well to the stress involved in dealing with all the problems that presented themselves. I realized they had taken it in stride, did what they could, and went on. I helped where I could, was often a sounding board.

My sounding board these days, while I worked on just getting through, was Mahorjah Tarr. Through checking in almost daily as to what was being done to find the people responsible, we had become not just coworkers, but friends. He was a confidante I could depend on when I needed somebody else to give some perspective to a challenging situation.

Finding Jackie Laughlin was still top priority, with still no success in sight. The men I had employed to find her were keeping us updated, but there were as yet no solid leads on where she was or who had given out information about our new leader.

I looked forward to having her found and brought to Usia to take her place as our leader. I was ready to hand over the running of our planet to her.

I was already considering assigning a new assistant to Jackie Laughlin, knowing it would likely be time for me to think about the next stage of my life. I had served a long time and was ready to hand over my former duties to new people who were ready to serve in that capacity.

I took a deep breath and opened a new piece of mail that had come across on my planner.

24

I AWOKE WITH Kanir snuggled into me, his arm around me. It wasn't a bad place to be really. I slipped out of bed, put together my clothing and toiletries, and went to get ready for the day. When I returned, Kanir was awake, sitting in the same chair as the previous night. He had a cup of something that smelled like very good coffee.

"You slept well?" Kanir asked.

"Yes, and you?"

Again, almost a smile, "Never better. Probably my best night's sleep in weeks."

I didn't doubt that, since he was still sleeping on the couch back on the ship. He could have brought in a bed, could have taken another room, something else all together, and yet he still chose to sleep on the couch. I didn't even try to understand it.

I put my things away, and we went down for breakfast. His father had left for work already. His mother had prepared a simple breakfast that we all enjoyed as we planned the day. Kanir had to work during the morning. I would spend that time with Doshah and Remon again. Kanir and his parents would join us for dinner at a restaurant they were all familiar with.

It was another gorgeous day. The sky was an incredible blue with an occasional cloud that passed through. The sun, yellow/white in the distance, warmed us again. I was impressed that so much of what I was seeing was so similar to Earth. It was amazing in some ways. Comforting in others. It was a darn sight better than being on the ship. I was getting as much sunshine and fresh air as I could, knowing we would be back on the ship in another day or two.

Kanir dressed and left for his office a short time later, while Doshah, Remon, and I took some time to go to a local zoo.

The zoo was set into the backdrop of the forest surrounding the city. It was huge, with hundreds of birds and animals on display. The settings for the animals were lush and large, giving us the chance to see the animals of this planet in something close to their natural habitats. Again, the animals were similar to those on Earth, but with a twist. The tigers were larger. The zebras were more of a gray and white with stripes that looked just wrong, somehow. The peacock had tail feathers only half the size of what I remembered from Earth, but its body was beautifully painted. I remembered going to zoos on Earth and being amazed by animals I hadn't heard of or seen before. This was more of the same.

The conversation was light. Every now and then, I got the impression Remon or Doshah wanted to ask more but were polite enough, knowing they wanted Kanir to be present when they could ask for more information. In the meantime, there was still a warmth and connection that was growing between the three of us.

We had just left a display of monkeys and other primates when we heard a commotion coming from the elephant display. It almost sounded like people screaming in terror. The law enforcement officer still living in me drew me toward whatever seemed to be going on, and we started that direction. I lead the way.

Remon grabbed both of our arms and pulled us back as we got closer. "It sounds like one of the animals got loose," he said.

Something in my head said to go forward and see what could be done to help.

Like I had been a zookeeper in a previous life or something? I just knew I had to do something.

A second later, several dozen people rushed past us. Following them was something that resembled an elephant. The twist was that he was much larger than any elephant I had ever seen, and his trunk looked more like an extra long fire hose in size. He was a distance away from the last people leaving the display where he had been and was closing the distance between himself and a young mother pushing an air stroller and pulling a toddler along by the hand. The terror in their eyes was stark. The children were screaming. The giant animal was bearing down on them. The mother fell, bringing the toddler down with her.

I had to do something. I couldn't just let this family be attacked. I left Doshah and Remon and went to the mother. I heard Doshah and Remon call something to me about returning to where they were, but I was already committed to what I was doing. I pulled the toddler to his feet as his mother stood up. She looked at me, grabbed her son's hand, and continued to run. I had taken two steps when the long, thin trunk of the elephant grabbed my waist, locking my right arm to my side. He was lifting me higher into the air. When he trumpeted, his trunk tightened around me, hurting my arm and sides. This close to him, his voice was deafening. He wrapped me into his trunk, making me dizzy and disoriented. Breathing was an effort. I heard Doshah screaming. His grip tightened, and I felt ribs snap. I cried out and looked into the angry eye of the beast.

"Come on, fella," I said, trying to be calm. My vision was blurred by tears of pain. "Time to let me down. I know you're upset. Nobody's going to hurt you. Come on, big boy." I tried to stroke his skin with my left hand, but it didn't seem to do anything. For his elephant-sized stress, he'd need a lot more than my small hand to massage away his worries.

It seemed like time was going by so slowly. Every step he took made my ribs scream in pain. I felt like a rag doll caught in some giant, maniacal kid's hand. I kept trying to talk soothingly to him, but it didn't seem to be doing much. I tried to look around from where I was. All I could see were the tops of the lower buildings around me and the trees. Occasionally I could look down and see the people about twelve feet below me and a safe distance away. I prayed this would end quickly. Every couple of seconds, his trunk would tighten around me, making it harder to take a breath.

I briefly thought about yelling or screaming for help, but I was concerned that Dumbo Sr. would become more violent, and I didn't want to be his battering ram.

I heard voices below me. Something about shooting the beast that held me in his trunk. I heard a whine of some sort, like a laser blast. The beast shook me like a rag doll and screamed. I gasped in pain. My body jerked forward, and the animal threw me across the path. The last thing I remembered was hitting something solid.

—◦◦◦—

"Jackie." It was Kanir.

I tried to answer, but I was so tired.

"She's trying to wake up." A voice I didn't recognize.

Someone took my hand, kissed it. Had to be Kanir.

"Jackie, come on, my love. Wake up."

I opened my eyes and looked at Kanir. The concern was so different from what I was used to seeing on his face. He looked pale, his eyes full of concern. He almost smiled and kissed my forehead.

"How are you doing?" asked the nurse. She adjusted something on a panel next to the bed and then moved something I couldn't see that was next to me.

I opened my mouth to say something, nothing came out. My throat was so dry. I cleared my throat. "Please stop yelling."

She smiled. "Headache?"

"And a half," I answered. "I'm really thirsty."

Kanir had a cup with a straw for me in a few seconds.

"What else hurts?"

"Name it."

Everything ached. My right arm especially. I tried to lift it then looked down. I was in an interesting sort of splint from my shoulders down to my wrist. It was held across my middle by something that went around my waist. Every breath hurt. "Oh man. What happened?"

"You don't remember?" Kanir asked.

I tried to think about it. "I remember thinking I had to help someone. I think it was a mother and her kids. I don't remember after that." I searched Kanir's face. "Did I help them? Are they okay?"

"Yes, my love. You saved their lives. A Baash elephant had gotten loose somehow. The mother and child fell. You got them to their feet, and he grabbed you instead. When he threw you across the path, you hit the wall of one of the shops and went to the ground. You broke a number of bones, got some other injuries, and a nasty concussion as well."

"Wow. What happened to the elephant?"

"Shot and killed."

"So he's dead?"

Kanir nodded.

I looked around the room. Plain, like almost any other hospital room. At least, I was pretty sure it was a hospital room. You never know about these things 100 percent when you're on another planet. Equipment, some of which I recognized, some I didn't was in the room. There were a few odd things around that looked sort of like get-well cards, but with videos on the face of the cards. I was already starting to lose steam, or I would have taken the time to get a closer look at them.

"Where am I?"

"The city hospital."

I found out it had happened three days before. I had been kept sedated to keep still and let my body heal without moving around a whole lot. Kanir hadn't left my side since he'd gotten the call and made it to the hospital. I sort of remembered a bit of the experience.

"What were you thinking?" he asked.

"I wasn't," I answered. "They needed help. I had to help them."

I looked around the room. "Are Doshah and Remon okay?"

"They are fine, getting over the shock. Doshah hasn't stopped crying. Mother is very concerned for you."

"Really? I didn't think she liked me all that much."

"You need to give her time, Jackie." He said, "And besides, you're still her daughter-in-law, my wife. Of course she's concerned."

The effort to talk was exhausting. "Kanir?"

"Yes, Jackie."

"The next time you want to show me a planet"—I paused for a breath and took a sip of water; my mouth was so dry—"give me some pictures."

He smiled, a look of relief on his face. As he touched his forehead to mine, I could see the wetness in his eyes, tears he refused to let go.

I felt myself falling asleep again.

Several times I heard Kanir praying as he kept watch over me while I slept. It was always for my recovery. I never told him I heard him, but there was comfort in knowing that he was starting to develop a faith in God similar to mine, and that he recognized the need for it. He held my hand constantly, never letting me see that he was praying or believing the way I did. It was kind of a strange place to be, but I figured for now he needed that part of himself to be secret from me. I knew when he was ready he would share it with me. I just had to be patient.

———

I was being prepared to leave the hospital several days later. The doctor, an older man who seemed very cautious about everything he said and did, recommended a full-time nurse for the next week.

"I'd like that," I said.

"That won't be necessary," Kanir said.

"Kanir, Jackie needs that cream applied to the bruises and areas over broken bones twice a day," the doctor advised. "She can't move that easily. She's going to need help getting around, bathing, dressing, as well as other things."

"I can do all that," he replied, adding that he had his mother who would be of help.

"Kanir, I'd prefer a nurse," I said.

Kanir had been the one for the last two days to help me, simply taking cues from the nurses. I had tried to dissuade him, but he insisted that as my husband, he wanted to be the one to help and actively participate in my recovery. It had caused us to become a lot more intimate than I was ready for just yet, and at the same time, it seemed totally natural. I was scared as much as I was happy with where we were going.

"You are my wife. I'm capable of doing what you need. None of it is beyond what I can do. If I do get over my head, then we will consider a nurse."

"I suppose that will work," the doctor said. "I would like a nurse to visit once a day for the next week just to make sure things are going well, and then you two should be in good shape after that."

"I—"

"Thank you, Doctor," Kanir said, finalizing everything.

"I don't think it's a good idea," I insisted.

"You'll recover just as easily with or without a full-time nurse," the doctor said. "I think it's a good plan, and certainly the nurse will see pretty quickly if you need more help."

I took a deep breath and sighed.

We left for his parents' home a short time later. Kanir had completed the work he had come planet-side for, so he had time to stay close to me and make sure my needs were met.

The whole family treated me as if I were fragile and made sure I had everything I needed and wanted. I had never been so pampered and was not entirely comfortable with it now. Their love and acceptance of me as a new addition to their family was touching. If I'd had any doubts about how they felt about me before this, they were washed away as all of them went out of their way for me.

That evening, Kanir helped me wash up. He was gentle with the washcloth and warm water and then applying a special cream to the bruises, which seemed to cover a good portion of my body. His touch was warm and careful, afraid of hurting me. As he gently worked the cream into my skin, he looked at my eyes, obviously enjoying the contact with me. I thought he was enjoying it more than I was comfortable with.

"What?" he said quietly.

I shook my head no. "Please, don't."

Kanir nodded and took a deep breath. He finished spreading the cream, tucked me in, and I think he took a cold shower as I slept.

Getting up the next morning was painful. I was stiff and everything still hurt a lot. Kanir was trying to be helpful, but I was still trying to keep my distance from him. With him at my side, making sure I was comfortable, that was becoming more difficult. I needed someone to help me do almost everything. Kanir was that help and was better at it than I originally thought he might be.

The nurse who made brief daily visits for the first week was pleased with my progress and the care Kanir was giving me. She gave him a few suggestions for some of the meds and made sure Kanir was getting enough rest himself.

Kanir was the perfect spouse. He was caring, he could be funny, and he never forced himself on me. I needed this kind of care, and Kanir was more than happy to provide it. This drew us closer together than ever.

My personal prayer time was constantly asking God for strength to keep distance between Kanir and me. I wasn't ready to be with him as he wanted me, but the time we were spending together was drawing us closer, making the effort not to become intimate with him more and more difficult. I couldn't believe how hard it was to not give in to the feelings that were growing.

By the end of the week, it had gotten totally out of control. I was tired. It had been a busy day with visits to see the doctor to have my progress evaluated and get more treatment for the healing of the bones I had broken. There wasn't the time to rest that I'd had the past few days before and at the hospital, and I was exhausted. Kanir spread the cream on my bruises as gently as ever. He leaned over and kissed me gently. He was looking at my eyes again as he applied the cream.

I put my hand over his then brought his hand to my lips to kiss it then held it to my cheek. His warmth was comforting, the smell of him intoxicating as we kissed.

———⟨ᴑᴑᴑ⟩———

I awoke in the morning to the smell of coffee as Kanir brought it into the room. I sat up slowly. Mornings were so hard. I was stiff and sore, and it took a while to work out the kinks in my body. Once I was moving for a while, I was good for the day.

Kanir sat on the edge of the bed and handed me a cup of coffee. He kissed me gently.

"How are you doing this morning?" he asked.

"Sore, but better. Last night—" I began.

He put his finger on my lips.

We sipped the coffee quietly. Neither of us said anything. I realized I could feel Kanir within me, like a presence. I looked at his eyes. There was a knowing there that puzzled me.

We hadn't said anything to each other, but there seemed to be a wordless conversation going on that only we could hear as he helped me bathe and dress.

"What is that?" I finally asked as Kanir buttoned the shirt I had slipped into.

"What are you talking about?"

"I woke up this morning and I can…feel you in my head. Or feel your feelings. I guess almost the…the essence of you."

"That would be from the joining."

I had to think about this for a few seconds. I hadn't expected this. "So you can feel or sense me too?"

"Yes. It's a bit odd at first, but I am enjoying having you as part of me."

I smiled. I had tried so hard to keep my distance from this man, and overnight something had changed. I was overwhelmed with the love that I felt for him. It was a sweet, peaceful feeling. I tried to analyze what was going on, but it was just beyond what my mind could grasp.

"I like having you there too."

We shared another kiss.

"We need to get downstairs," he said quietly.

"I'm starving."

"Your hrova is lovely."

"My what?" And then I remembered. I looked a little closer at the area surrounding Kanir. I could see a slight coloring of light surrounding him of a light blue.

"Kanir, you have a hrova, too. I didn't know what to expect, but it makes you look wonderful. Healthier."

The love he felt for me was suddenly overwhelming. I could feel it so strongly I had to sit down for a moment.

"Are you all right?" he asked.

"Yes. I'm fine." I looked at his eyes. They had changed. When I had looked into his eyes the past several weeks, they had usually been dark and guarded as if he was working hard to keep something from breaking inside of himself. Now they were gentle; I could sense a peace about him that hadn't been there before, as if some great stress had been let go.

"I love you too," I said quietly.

"I know." He almost smiled.

The breakfast his mother made had filled the house with fragrances that had our mouths watering. We both gave her a hug, and then she held me by my hands and stood back for a moment, looking. Then she looked over at her son for a few seconds. Her smile was huge.

"Oh my goodness," she said just above a whisper. A few tears rolled down her cheeks, and she gave us each a hug.

—◦◦◦—

Doshah and Remon visited a few times. The first time Doshah saw me in the hospital, she cried and held my hand. At home, she was happy to sit and chat and be good company. She taught me a couple of card games, and we found out that we were both pretty competitive.

I only wanted to rest and sleep a lot. I read as much as I could, watched their version of television, and played a few card games. I was supposed to be taking pain medication, but I was trying desperately to take as little as possible. I didn't like the way it made me sleep a lot more.

We had two more days with his family when Kanir and I were watching their version of news. There was a follow-up story on the elephant attack. The woman and her children were trying to find me. Kanir had kept as much information from the public as he could. My name was not even released. But he couldn't stop the video that had been filmed of me running to the aid of the people about to be hurt by the huge animal and then being attacked myself. Whoever had shot the video had gotten a number of close-ups of me. Since I was so easily picked out of a crowd here, there was no mistaking me for anyone else. I was stunned, not realizing how horrible a sight it had been. I could feel Kanir stiffen next to me on the couch. His mother gasped. Kanir got up and left the room. I was surprised at how it seemed to affect him.

The next day, he was finalizing things with the doctor and anyone else he needed to finish things up with. Watching him, I sensed something else was going on that I couldn't figure out. I finally asked him what was going on.

"Nothing. We're just tying up any loose ends before we have to leave tomorrow."

"Kanir. I've never seen you move so fast. What's wrong, really?"

He stopped and considered me for a moment. "I'm sorry. I didn't mean for any of this to upset you."

"I'm not upset, just…I don't know. You're not like this normally."

"I'm just preoccupied with getting back on schedule, I suppose."

"The video on the news…that's it, isn't it?"

He nodded and didn't say anything for a few long seconds. "Someone will recognize you and come for you. We have to be gone."

"Kanir, how long are you going to run and keep me hidden away?"

He regarded me for a moment and then smoothed my hair. "For as long as I need to. I'm not letting you go."

"The Usians are likely to be looking for me."

"You're my wife now. This is where you belong." His voice seemed to have gotten dangerously low. His hrova actually darkened slightly for a few seconds.

His mother made a wonderful meal for us the last evening. Doshah and Remon shared the meal with us, and it was a good evening. Doshah and his mother made me sit and chat while they cleaned the kitchen.

The next morning, we had a good time of visiting with everyone again over another great breakfast. The kitchen was cleaned up, and we were ready to leave, taking our time with good-byes. Aside from the attack and my injuries, it had been a great visit.

When we had first arrived, I felt like these people were Kanir's family. Now I knew they were my family too. I had been accepted, grafted in.

Things had changed dramatically between Kanir and me. There was no desire to be distant from him anymore. I knew I was supposed to be where I was. At the same time, there was always, still, just a whisper that I was supposed to be someplace else. It was almost like a brainwashing that wasn't quite complete.

We were about to walk out the door to leave when his mother took a small box from her pocket. "What do you think, Karch?" She asked her husband.

He took the box from his wife and handed it to Kanir. "Give this to Jackie."

"Now?" Kanir asked.

"Of course."

Kanir made me sit down on a sofa in the living room. He opened the box and took out a ring. The three stones in the setting were like diamonds, only more brilliant, similar to the stones in the ring Kanir had bought for me earlier during our visit. He took it from the box and slipped it on the ring finger of my other hand. The swelling had gone down enough that it fit nicely.

"Are you two sure you—" I began.

"Of course we are," his mother said. "That has been in the family for a few generations. It always goes to the bride of the eldest son. I never passed it on to those others of his because they were more affiliates than family. And I never had a chance to meet them. You, my dear, are part of our family now."

"Thank you, Mother." I gave her a hug.

25

We were back on the ship, heading for another ship building location. Kanir had four plants spread out around the area. Each one specialized in two to three different ships. He traveled between the four of them, wanting to keep his finger on the pulse of his business.

Kanir had someone meet us in the shuttle bay to help get our luggage to our rooms.

He kissed my head and was about to leave our rooms.

"Hey, what am I supposed to do now?" I asked.

"Do you feel up to going to the office with me?"

"For a short time, at least."

He nodded. "Come with me. I don't know what I can have you do, but I imagine we can find something. Make sure you let me know when you need to rest. Especially if I'm too wrapped up in what needs to be done today."

"I can do that," I said.

Throughout the morning, I could sense him relaxing, content to be back on his ship, in his traveling office, on his way to his next appointments, in his element.

There were two short meetings followed by lunch, and then time in the office, going over other details. Different parts of what he was working on involved what I helped him with. I organized meals and tours and other activities with clients. There were a few things on the schedule over the next couple of weeks that I was able to work with, in between working directly with him on his projects. He had somebody else work with me from time to time to go over the cultural differences of different planets.

I had overdone it, walking and visiting more than I should have while still trying to recover from my injuries. I had fallen asleep on the couch that was against the wall in the office. Kanir woke me and walked me back to our rooms. He tucked me in bed, kissed me, and left.

My body had healed enough within a week of being back on the ship that I could start back to some light strength training again. Even with the last of the bandages gone, Kanir was concerned for the longest time about how he should handle me. He was still concerned he might hurt me, thinking that I was breakable.

Despite the direction our relationship had gone, Kanir felt more comfortable assigning a guard to me. Then I found out it was common for business leaders of Kanir's reputation to have guards for their families. The threat against them was often very real. Employees, business associates, and others were not always trustworthy. One more thing that was galactic—greed and the desire for power, often at any cost.

There were two guards who were assigned to me. I had them on alternating days. They were both females. Tenuah was smaller than me, but strong. She took no nonsense from me. Swess was my height, just as no-nonsense, but a bit more fun. We had a great friendship between the three of us. I finally felt that I had as good a friend in these two as I had had in Karen on Earth.

It wasn't unusual for Swess or Tenuah to catch the last few minutes of the time Kanir and I had in prayer and study. It seemed that they were showing up earlier and earlier to try to catch more of our discussion and prayer time.

"Why don't you just come and spend that time with us?" Kanir invited Tenuah one morning.

She looked at me for confirmation. "I think it would be a great idea," I said.

I told her how to find the Bible on her computer and suggested some reading. Both she and Swess began showing up every morning to enjoy our sessions. Within a few days, Swess decided it wasn't for her, and we didn't see her again for that part of the day. But Tenuah had a lot of questions. She enjoyed the sense of peace she had, spending time with us in prayer and study.

"I've been talking to a friend in engineering, sir," Tenuah said as we finished our study one morning. "Would it be all right to invite him? He's having some problems, and I think he might be able to find help here."

Kanir looked to me. "What do you say?" he asked.

"What if we make this accessible to everyone?" I asked him.

I could feel Kanir's concerns over a number of different issues. "You and I will discuss that. For right now, you may invite your friend, Tenuah. However, I think it would be simpler and wiser to do this someplace else." Kanir paused for a moment, considering where to go. "There's a meeting room on level 5. It hasn't been used in quite a while. It's across from the traveler."

"I know the one you mean," Tenuah stated and gave the room number.

———∽∾∿———

When Tenuah had gone, Kanir was lost in thought for a while. "I just can't afford to have it conflict with anybody's work schedule."

"That's reasonable. What if we kept this morning session, started an evening one, and did a once-a-week big session similar to the ones I attended on Earth." All at once, I knew I had bitten off more than I could chew.

"Won't you need time to prepare and study?" he asked.

I paused. I had stepped into something huge here and was suddenly concerned about how I would do this. Billy Graham I was not. I wasn't a pastor or a missionary. I was just leading people toward something I loved and believed in with my entire being. I didn't know if I could put this together, and yet there was this drive within me to get it going. It was a knowing that I wouldn't be on my own. Spiritually, I knew I was not alone. God was with me, guiding me. It wouldn't be long before others would be trained up to come alongside me, even advance ahead of me, as they should.

The ideas I was presenting were so foreign to everyone, and yet they were being embraced. That blew me away, made me careful about what I did and said.

"I want you to draw up a plan and a schedule for me as to what you want to do. We will post it, and I want you to lead it. We have a small event room where we can start this,"

"Kanir isn't that kind of big?" I asked.

"I don't think this is going to be small," he replied. Kanir got up and poured another cup of what I called coffee. He called it something else that I couldn't pronounce. Coffee was close enough and kept me from spraining my tongue. Somehow I had become a coffee snob, trying to find one close to what I had been familiar with on Earth. Every place we stopped, I was anxious to find some of the brew. None of them had been fatal, but some of them I regretted trying. There were a couple I thought might melt my fillings, and another couple I thought might have been glorified dishwater. Finding just the right blend turned out to be a chore I took seriously and made Kanir watch with amused fascination. He enjoyed trying the samples I felt were worthy of being called coffee.

"So you like what this is doing for you," I commented

"Actually, I'm still trying to figure it out," he admitted. Kanir seemed to be considering what he wanted to share. "I like that it is bringing us together. I'm enjoying finding out about the things that are important to you. Whether or not it is or ever becomes important to me—I'm still waiting. But I see what it has done for Tenuah. And how she sees what it can do for others. I think this is likely to be bigger than we imagine."

It kind of surprised me that Kanir was able to express how he felt about my faith and that he was still on the fence. If it was meant to be, all I could do was just share and be the example of what I believed. There wasn't much else I could do besides that and pray.

"You know, when I was in the hospital, after that attack," I spoke slowly, quietly, "I heard you praying for me a few times."

He took a short time to think about this. "I did." He admitted, "And I still pray. It brings me peace."

"If I'm out of line here, let me know. I'm trying really hard not to push things. But you have grown so much in our study time. I see the strength in your spirit. It's like you're on the edge of it all, just not ready to really jump in and let it be all it can be for you. Would you like to pray with me, to give your heart to God?"

Another pause. The man was the prince of pauses. "I'll let you know when I'm ready."

By the time we left for the office, we decided to keep it to the meeting room until our meetings outgrew the twenty seats there.

It shouldn't have surprised me, but within two weeks, twelve of the twenty seats were filled, and not always by the same people. There were questions that taxed what I knew, kept me humble, and on my toes. I was spending more time in prayer and study to stay ahead, to the point where Kanir made that my new position within his organization.

We were seeing changes in the people who attended the meetings. There was a peace that was falling over these people that hadn't been there before.

Kanir cared about his people. Those who had problems who became part of our group seemed to be handling their circumstances a lot better. There were only a few of those, but they began bringing friends who saw the changes and wanted something similar for themselves.

The peace had an underlying sense of excitement to it. I was having more fun doing this than I ever thought could be possible. It was fulfilling and joyful. Kanir stayed with me in all of this, wanting to be part of it, yet still questioning.

Along with my new duties, I began taking very physically demanding classes in self-defense from one of the trainers in the fitness department. It wasn't unusual for me to leave the class with a sprain or one or two significant bruises. This seemed to concern Kanir, so he started taking them with me. It gave us something else to do that was productive and a life skill and drew us that much closer together. Kanir was about ten years older than me, yet he was in very good shape. Aside from making us both that much more fit, we were equipping ourselves with something practical.

Life had been going well for nearly six weeks. The last of my injuries were pretty much history, except for the memories. I had become a trusted partner with Kanir. We discussed business dealings before anything was done, to the benefit of his company. News of what I was sharing was making those people even more productive, making the business more successful than ever, with even more ships being ordered than ever.

I had my own office next to Kanir's. I attended meetings with him, and he seemed to value my input. If someone questioned what I was doing at a meeting or inspection or other business, he was quick to let the others know I was his partner and therefore, part of whatever needed discussing.

I was enjoying this far more than I ever thought I might. I had never been that interested in business, yet Kanir made it fascinating. I especially enjoyed the people part of the whole operation.

If nothing else, I still caused a lot of conversation. I had been out here for some time and still hadn't seen another "Earther," as I was called. Where I was from still wasn't discussed with others. I was still getting used to being seen as an anomaly.

We had been married for nearly four months. Kanir and I had just finished dinner when he told me he had arranged for me to have a physical.

"What for?" I asked. I tried not to make it sound quite so defensive, but that's the way it came out. I truly appreciated what the doctors had done to treat my injuries after the elephant attack. I had spent a lot of time in their care, and I really didn't think I needed a physical so soon after that experience.

"We have a new ship's physician. He wants to be familiar with the people he's treating."

Okay, that made sense, but... "I don't need a physical."

"Jackie, don't make me have one of your security carry you there."

"Oh please," I began, just a bit annoyed. "Six weeks ago, I had all I wanted to do with doctors. I don't want to see another one for a long time, unless it's absolutely necessary, and even then, it will likely be under duress."

Kanir took a deep breath and got very quiet. I could sense his frustration.

"What the heck," I said, shaking my head. "What time tomorrow?"

—◦◦◦—

Tenuah walked me to the office and let me go in on my own. She had other things to tend to and would be back before the physical was completed. I walked into the medical office and did a double take.

J'Neer stood by one of the counters, studying some of the equipment before him. He looked up at me. He actually looked relieved to see me. He hadn't changed since I had seen him last; if anything, he looked like he had taken some time to put on some muscle.

We regarded each other for a short time.

I looked around the room. I didn't know if the room had any kind of surveillance equipment. Kanir didn't ordinarily have that kind of equipment installed, but you never know. If he had reports of something happening that could be of concern, he just might.

J'Neer figured out my concern and said, "No 'bugs,' as you call them. I told him I would not work like that, his people need privacy when it comes to their health. He agreed. And I check the room regularly. He hasn't had any installed."

"So you stopped in for a cup of coffee and decided to stay on as ship's doctor?"

J'Neer smiled. "Not really."

"What are you doing here? Did you get traded again?" I asked.

J'Neer almost snorted. "Nice to see you too, Jackie."

"I'm sorry," I said. "You caught me totally off guard. Are you okay?"

"I'm fine."

"So were you...were you traded again?"

He didn't smile. "No. I escaped on a shuttle. Timed it just right and offered my services to Kanir. He's in need of a medical man on his ship. Most ships out here are without one. It's a big deal to have your own ship's physician."

"What's going on?" I asked guardedly. Something was wrong with this story. Something about all this told me there was more to this than he was sharing, and I wasn't sure how I felt about him being here.

"Nothing. But I'm really happy I finally found you. I've been looking for you since I left Ronnok's ship some time ago."

"If you're the cavalry, you're too late."

"The what?"

I shook my head. "Never mind. Ronnok's not looking for you? He's rather possessive." I looked at him sideways. "How did you really get away?"

"Ronnok's not an issue any more."

"Really." I was almost afraid to ask what had happened to him, but… "Are they alive?"

J'Neer consulted what I thought was a watch on his wrist for a couple of seconds, then looked at me. "No."

I blinked, did a double take, swallowed. I had to wonder if I was going to get a straight answer any time soon. "What… how?"

He took a resigned breath and said, "I was trusted probably more than I should have been. I knew the ship. I released a gas into the air system that rendered them all unconscious, set course for a black hole, and left."

I was more than a little shocked. "That's pretty cold-blooded."

J'Neer regarded me curiously. "The man auctioned you off to the highest bidder, Jackie. He dealt in slavery of the worst sort. Don't tell me that's not cold. The man was a pig. The only reason he kept you alive and in halfway decent shape was to reap a profit. The sale and trade of exotic females is extremely lucrative."

I had never considered myself exotic. Out here, I suppose I was. J'Neer had done the universe a favor by eliminating Ronnok and his crew, for sure. For every leader like Ronnok in this vast empty space, there were likely a dozen more just like him. Taking him out wasn't much more than taking a drop out of a full bucket of water. And despite how debased Ronnok was, there was some part of it that still unnerved me a bit.

"I don't get it. So then you made a beeline for here? Why are you here? You could be anywhere else, and you—" I stopped and considered this man again. "Does Kanir know what happened to Ronnok and his ship?"

"I thought you'd be pleased to see me. I was your only advocate on Ronnok's ship."

"Yeah, I'm glad you're alive, but that doesn't explain why you're here."

"I'm here to help you."

"To help me escape?"

"Yes. You know I wanted to help you when we were on Ronnok's ship, and even before then when we were on D'Nar's ship. You're still needed on Usia."

I was torn. I was married, joined to Kanir. My life had gone in such a different direction from where it was supposed to go when I was first taken from Earth. Gosh, even before that. But I knew I was supposed to be on Usia. I didn't know what to say, what to do.

And then the light went on, a new revelation. "You're going to sell me to someone else!"

"Wha…no! Jackie, wait a minute."

"I'm not going with you anywhere. I'm not going through all that again. Some—"

"Have you two joined?"

Now I was angry. "What? You have no…I'm out of here." I turned to leave.

"Jackie, stop. You need to let me help you." He ran to me, tried to grab my arm, but I pulled away.

"I don't have to do anything," I said angrily.

Kanir would not be happy. Probably send this man out the closest portal into the empty darkness. Part of me was happy at the prospect of being rid of him, part of me was surprised at my reaction…

"Let me explain." He pressed. "Look, I handled that badly. I'm sorry. Just hear me out. This is important."

I shook my head. What was I thinking? "I'll give you a minute."

"Have you kissed him? Have you two had—"

"You are really crude, you know that? That's none of your business."

"Jackie, calm down and let me explain."

I took a deep breath, pushed my hands through my hair, and sighed. "What the heck."

J'Neer paused a moment, looking me over. "You clean up well."

"J'Neer, get on with it."

He took a breath, looked around the room, then at me. "I'm a mercenary, an operative, hired by Usia. My cover is that I'm a doctor. We are placed all over, from planets, to ships, everywhere in the galaxy. It's been necessary. And we're not alone.

"Every other planet, race, whatever, has its own operatives out there, spying, collecting information, helping their people when they find them in danger."

"Why didn't you tell me this then?"

"I wasn't given the assignment until just after you were auctioned off and sold to Kanir. In fact, Ronnok wouldn't release the information of who you were sold to. Conveniently lost the information. There was no mention of you in any of his ship's computers, no transaction trails, nothing. There was no time to move on what I had, so I eliminated them and came looking for you. I did a thorough search of Ronnok's records before I left his ship. He swore everyone to secrecy. It was like you had never been on the ship. Nobody would even acknowledge that you were ever even there. Then I happened to see the video of you being tossed by a Baash elephant. I tracked you from there, and here I am."

Now I had full understanding of why Kanir had been so concerned about the incident when we saw the news that evening weeks before. He knew this was coming. Suddenly the universe, as huge as it was, didn't seem quite so vast. Weird feeling. Who knew one planet in a whole universe of planets would send out that video, only to have J'Neer be the one to see it and act on it?

I was surprised to hear this. "So why haven't you just contacted the planet and called for reinforcements?"

"It's not that simple. We're hundreds of light-years from Usia. There are no military ships out here. Communication from this distance isn't quite impossible, just time-consuming. It takes a couple of days, sometimes more for contact to get from point A to point B, especially when you have to be on the move."

"And they send you out unarmed?"

"I'm a doctor. I have no need to be armed, unless I'm told to be armed by whoever I happen to be working for at the time." He paused. "I do keep a stash of personal weapons that cannot be detected."

"Kanir didn't meet you on Ronnok's ship?"

"Never made contact with him."

I paused, taking this all in. "So what's next?"

J'Neer took a deep breath. I could see him preparing for a bit of a confrontation here. "Have you been intimate with Kanir?"

It seemed I was pausing a lot. "We're married. Of course we're intimate."

J'Neer just stared at me for a moment and slowly shook his head.

"What? Look, I tried hard to keep from even liking him a little bit. He had the ship's captain marry us the second day I was here. I wasn't allowed to protest or anything. We…joined about two months ago. J'Neer, I can't keep this from him. By now, he already knows that something's wrong."

J'Neer seemed to be considering something he wasn't willing to share just yet.

"What?" I asked. "Look, let's come up with a plan that's workable—"

"It's not that easy now."

"Why not?"

"Jackie. He's a Matakian. The males have a hormone in their sperm that sort of rewrites some of the female's DNA. It goes after mostly the emotional receptors of the brain and binds the two together. When the male has sex with a female, they are joined for life."

It was one of the weirdest things I had ever heard, but my life had been far from normal for several months now. It just seemed to fit the whole scheme of things. "Okay, so we'll figure something out that works for all of us."

"Listen to me!" J'Neer said angrily and then caught himself. I could see his frustration now. He was shaking his head. Something was wrong, and I was missing it. "If you leave him, you both die. You are joined for life. You can't leave him, and he can't leave you. Separation for an extended period of time is fatal. It's one of the deepest binding relationships in the galaxy."

I felt like someone had slapped me. I was stunned. Now it made sense. The closeness I felt toward Kanir was so intense that it sometimes took my breath away. Since the first time we had joined, the desire to leave, go where I was supposed to go, or back to Earth had waned. It still whispered to me in quiet moments when I had too much free time, sometimes when I was overly stressed. But it was not nearly as strong as when I had first been taken from my home on Earth. Joining had done more than solidify the bond of marriage; it had literally joined us on deeper levels. It was at once satisfying and terrifying.

"Oh, Lord," I whispered. I sat in a chair that happened to be close by. I took a moment to collect my thoughts. I couldn't believe Kanir hadn't told me about that part of our relationship, but I suppose he didn't think it was important. Or that maybe I'd figure it out, or—who knows what the man was thinking. "I guess that cuts down on divorce, huh?"

"There is no divorce between Matakians."

"Wait a minute. What if one or the other dies of natural causes, or an accident or something?"

"It depends on a lot of things like age, health, how close they were in all aspects of their joining, the will to live without that contact. Mostly, family members ease the remaining partner through it. Occasionally it works. The bond of—I guess, love—is so strong, that when it's severed by either one, it's not unusual for it to be fatal." J'Neer picked up a piece of equipment and started pressing some buttons on it.

"He wants me to give you a physical. Make sure you're healthy enough to get pregnant. And he wants to make sure that the blending of the two races will not be damaging to anyone."

Pregnant? Another slap.

"What? I don't want to get pregnant yet." This was another conflict going on inside my head. Like most other red-blooded Earther women, my biological clock was ticking, and the part of me that loved Kanir was excited by the prospect of having his children. There was that small, tiny, whispered voice that occasionally mentioned being somewhere else that encouraged me to wait.

"You might not have a choice. I told him not to be concerned. Your body probably just isn't ready yet, you're probably stressed by something. And sometimes it takes a while—"

"Don't encourage him, J'Neer!"

"What was I supposed to tell him? I'm the ship's doctor, I'm supposed to have the answers to most of these questions, and he expects me to give them to him."

We were both quiet for what seemed a long time. It was taking a while for me to process all this information. I was so torn in so many ways. I didn't know what to do or say, and I was confused on a number of fronts.

"What can I do to keep from getting pregnant? Surely you have something that is the equivalent of the pill here? Some kind of birth control?"

"Foolish. He'd figure it out. He's not stupid. Kanir is very intelligent actually. And he knows you better than you think."

We were quiet again for another minute.

"This is taking too long," J'Neer stated, moving toward the center of the room. "Let's get this exam started. I'm assuming nothing has changed since I examined you last time."

"I'm fine."

He stopped again and looked at me. "I need to talk to the two of you together this evening. It's important."

"That shouldn't be a problem. What is it about?"

"I'd rather wait and talk to the two of you together."

I nodded. I told him the time we usually finished dinner and where to find us.

J'Neer was in the middle of running the physical when he stopped and asked, "Do you love him?"

There was no hesitation. "Yes. You have no idea how hard I tried not to." I told him about our relationship—or lack thereof—when I first came aboard this ship. How I fought to keep my distance, and then the change of heart I'd had. I told him about our trip to Matakia, the attack at the zoo, my recovery, our joining. "I love this man with all my being, but there's still this little tug to be somewhere else. The desire is fading slowly, but it's still there. I still think about Usia, and home. I desperately want to be back with my family. I feel such a pull to be there. He knows my heart. He knows where I want to be, what I want to do. But I know this is where I'm supposed to be. For the most part, I'm actually at peace with all of this finally.

"Listen, we'll get you out of this."

"I don't want to get out of this, J'Neer. I belong here, and I love this man." I shook my head slowly, looking at him again. "I guess I want my cake and I want to eat it too."

"What?"

"Nothing, just an Earth saying. I want it all, but I'm not sure I can have it all."

Something suddenly occurred to me. "How are things on Usia?"

"Not good. She died, and civil war is imminent. You're needed there very desperately. Alive."

"I don't know what good I would be, anyway. I'm not 'ruler of the world' material, I don't think."

"Having you there would make a difference you cannot understand. Just the presence of the leader they expect would bring peace."

"I don't get it."

J'Neer spent the next hour giving me a physical, running tests, asking questions.

I got up, adjusting my shirt. "So what do your tests say?"

"You're perfectly healthy, no reason why you can't conceive. Some people just take longer than others."

"I'm sure that will make my husband very happy."

"Not as happy as the day you can tell him you're with child."

I offered a crooked smile. "Thanks, J'Neer. I'm glad you're here. And I'll see you later."

26

THE FINAL DATE to have Jackie Laughlin installed as our leader was coming upon us quickly. Patience was wearing thin as the date approached. Those members of the council who were less than pleasant to deal with were becoming increasingly difficult. Their petty differences were more frequent, and a couple of them were barely civil to those they had to work with. I was more than ready to hand over the position to our new leader. At the same time, I pitied her the job she had ahead of her to keep these people in their places and working together.

I sat across from Mohorja Tarr, head of council security. He had been working with other security in the city to determine who had leaked the information of our new leader. The report he was giving me was a disappointment.

"Still nothing?" I asked, somewhat incredulous.

"I'm sorry, Corrett. I've chased down leads, checked all their backgrounds, where they were at the time of the taking, but nothing is adding up. I'm still nowhere. Whoever gave out that information, if they paid someone to take her, it's not showing up in any of their financial reports. Interviews have lead to nothing."

I sighed, not knowing what to do next. This was not what I was hoping for.

"Any word from your operatives?" Tarr asked.

"Not yet. They've been very good about keeping me informed about what they are doing to locate her—so far, nothing. It's not good, Tarr. If she's been killed, it's going to be another six months before we can replace her. Likely I will need replacing long before then. Surely the council will need to be replaced, or a good number of them anyway, if I have to continue dealing with them. My nephews and nieces are easier to deal with on their worst days."

"They are a temperamental bunch, this council, aren't they?"

"Childish. Lady Minkas even said so a number of times. Thankfully they're only in office another year, and then most will be replaced. Nyast is due to be replaced especially, and that will be a relief to many."

"He is rather full of himself, isn't he?" Tarr commented.

"Yes, he is. Comes very close to needing to be replaced ahead of schedule, but that's not likely to happen."

There was a pause in our conversation.

"That information should not have left that council," I insisted.

"Would you approve me looking into the backgrounds of those who work with the council?"

I considered this for a moment. How far did we have to go to find out who was responsible for putting our leader in jeopardy? We needed to know who it was who was less than trustworthy.

"Go ahead, Tarr," I said. "Take it as far as you need, just keep me informed as to who you are working with and what you're doing."

"Of course."

I paused a moment before leaving the room. "Tarr, has the room been checked for listening devices?"

"It is a requirement before each council meeting. Nothing has ever been found."

"It might be worth while to check on those who have maintained and examined that room as well."

Tarr considered this for several seconds. "I will follow up on that."

I had returned to my suite of offices, where my secretary Norim greeted me with alarm.

"You are needed in Councilman Perr's office. He was just discovered by his secretary. He has been killed."

This was startling news that stunned me to my core. "How?"

"They wouldn't say, sir."

"I have two meetings this afternoon. Please contact those two people and reschedule them. I will be in touch with you when I have more information that you might need."

I paused. My assistant, Yazz, would be back from some other business shortly. I gave Norim instructions to have him meet me at the councilman's office.

She nodded and began contacting those individuals as I left the office.

A short time later, I arrived at Perr's offices. Vehicles from the local protectors' offices were pulled up in front of the office. There were several protectors in the offices as I entered. I was stopped, and my information taken before I was allowed to ask questions, but I was not permitted into Perr's office itself. His secretary, Masyah, stood sobbing by her desk. When she saw me, she came to me. I held her for a few minutes.

"Masyah, are you well enough to help out here for a while? I know the other council members will be checking in shortly. We really need somebody to help us out here for the rest of the day."

"Of course, sir. There were some things he needed done—"

"Don't do anything you don't feel up to right now, except anything that absolutely needs your attention. Other things can wait."

She nodded.

"Just one thing," I said to her. "Who was his last appointment?"

"He didn't have any," Masyah replied. "He was taking the day to go over some proposals for his continent. And he had a number of contacts he was returning."

I considered this for a moment.

"I was at lunch. When I returned, I just found him there," she said, and the tears started again.

"I will make sure you get home safely when your day is finished. I don't want you transporting by yourself today."

"I will have my husband come for me."

"If he can't do that, let me know. We can make arrangements."

"Thank you, sir."

Perr was well liked by most of the council, as well as most of his constituency. He was one who frequently sided with Nyast. This was not going to be an easy time for anyone. Within a short time, most of the other councilors were calling the offices, asking for details, some offering help.

Nyast arrived quite a bit later and was primed to be difficult. He began ranting shortly after arriving, complaining about the ineptness of security, the lack of orderliness, and the inability of staffing to hire adequate employees.

"That's enough," I finally interrupted. "Nyast, I believe you need to leave."

"You have no spine for this, I understand," Nyast said. "I say you let me take control of this council and lead it where it needs to go so that our planet—"

"I think not," Kenbar responded, having walked into the room to hear Nyast. "Dolm Corrett is doing better than an acceptable job. It would be fruitless to turn this over to you."

"You want this assistant—"

"He is not an assistant, he is our interim leader. I think maybe we all need to take a closer look at what Nyast has to gain if he is made emperor," Kenbar stated to the few council members present.

The argument began, loud and angry. Accusations were lobbed back and forth, mostly from Nyast to Kenbar and me.

I left the room when one of the protectors asked me to join him in the quietness of Perr's office. His body had been removed from the room.

"What do you need?" I asked as soon as the door was closed.

"I'm not sure at this time, Emp—"

"Please, you may refer to me as Corrett."

"Thank you, sir. I've had a number of my investigators examine the blast that killed Perr. It is their professional opinion that the blast came from a military weapon not available to the public."

"You can tell that how?"

"The depth of the wound, the amount of burn at the edges. It also leaves a specific signature on the flesh."

"So this is from someone within the military?"

"Or somebody who was able to purchase a weapon himself."

My mind raced. Which of the council had a military background or had access to military weaponry? Who wanted Perr dead and why?

"What do you recommend we do?" I asked.

"His assistant has already given me a list of those he works with, as well as those he had problems with."

"He had very few problems with most of the council. He was actually well liked. I can't imagine who would want to hurt him." I pondered this further. "We actually do have a couple on the council who are frequently hard to deal with, but I can't see them doing something like this."

"Who would that be, Corrett?"

I took a deep breath. This whole thing was going to have such huge ramifications. It was going to make tempers flare, bring out a side of some of this council none wanted to see, and make most of them question everyone else on the council.

"You know the council as well as anybody, if you keep up with the politics," I said and gave him three names. Those three were good men but hard to get along with. I truly didn't think they would do something like this, but there's no telling what men will do sometimes.

"Thank you, sir. I will be talking to all the other councilmen, of course."

"I understand. I will try to find out who his last contacts were."

"I've already done that, sir. His assistant told me he saw nobody today. We'll be checking for travelers into the room, as well as those who may have come in while his assistant was at lunch."

"You know we're trying to get the empress brought here."

"I don't think there's anybody who doesn't know that."

"Yes, well…I have to wonder if this is connected with her disappearance somehow."

"I've already made notes to that end, sir."

I nodded. This was going to be a rough time.

27

I WAS HUGELY concerned for J'Neer. I knew there was no keeping this information from Kanir. I was sure that he already felt a disturbance within him from what was going through my mind. We couldn't read each other's thoughts, but there was a sense of the emotions of whatever the other was going through.

When Swess had left for the evening and we were having dinner, I could tell he knew something was wrong. His dark eyes seemed on guard, concerned. What didn't help was that I had no appetite and just picked at the food in front of me. Kanir always came back to our rooms ready for dinner. As far as he was concerned, if nobody was dying, it could wait until he was done with his meal.

Once he was done, he got up, took my hand, and led me to the living room.

"What has had you so concerned all day?" he asked.

"I had my physical," I replied. "Everything is good there." I looked at the wall for a moment and then, "Kanir, I know the physician you hired."

"Really. How do you know him?"

"He was the doctor on D'Nar's ship, and then on Ronnok's ship."

Kanir considered this for a moment, and he nodded. "I'll have him dismissed."

"No, Kanir. He helped me, probably saved my life. He wants to meet with us after dinner, should be here shortly."

"For what purpose?"

"He didn't want to say at the time."

I could tell Kanir was a bit concerned. He arranged for Tolf to be with us when the doctor arrived.

———∽∾∽———

"My wife tells me you know her," Kanir said as we all sat around the table. He was studying a vid card J'Neer had given him shortly after coming to our rooms.

"Yes, sir."

"Why didn't you tell me this when I hired you?"

"Here's the deal. Kanir. I've been looking for her for some time now. I wasn't 100 percent sure I'd actually found her until she showed up for her physical earlier today."

Kanir handed the vid card to Tolf with the instructions to make contact with whoever was listed on the card. He wanted some proof of who J'Neer was and what he was saying.

"Why have you been looking for her?"

J'Neer looked as if he'd been about to snort. He looked down, shook his head, and then looked up at Kanir. "I don't need to tell you that. You know who she is. She is supposed to be the empress of Usia. She was taken from Earth, and through a series of events, she wound up in your…care. I just happened to be on D'Nar's ship when she showed up. I tried to help her escape. I didn't know who she was at the time. For whatever reason, D'Nar chose not to have me killed but sold me to the same person he sold her to. I had no opportunity to help her there, and then you"—J'Neer searched for a word for two seconds—"you purchased her. I was actually given the assignment to look for her about a week after you took her from Ronnok. I got off the other ship when I was finally able to and came looking for her." J'Neer paused, looking at both of us. "There's a new wrinkle on this now—D'Nar's been ordered to find Jackie and kill her."

Kanir's eyes darkened, while I felt like I had just been slammed up against a wall.

"What?" I said, astounded. "Why?"

Kanir held up his hand to silence me. "Don't do that," I protested. "This involves me as much—"

"Quiet." The voice was stern. He turned to J'Neer. "What proof do you have?"

Tolf came back into the room. "He's correct, Kanir. I just spoke with his supervisor. He has orders to take Jackie into custody and take her to Usia. And D'Nar was seen on Eduinne two days ago."

J'Neer took a deep breath while I felt Kanir stiffen next to me. "How far away is that?" I asked.

"Eduinne is two days from here," J'Neer said. "He could be here already. He probably found similar clues to the ones I had to find you."

"Or he could have followed you."

J'Neer nodded. "It's possible. No matter how he got this close, we need to get out of here as soon as possible." He turned to Kanir. "You get to go too. You joined with her, and you can't be separated, so you two go together."

Kanir sat there quietly, considering what he had just been told.

"And, Kanir," J'Neer continued, "it's in your best interest for her to go there. I've had to keep everyone informed, and they know you have her. If she's not there in what they consider a reasonable amount of time, you risk starting a major inter-planetary incident between Matakia and Usia. Matakia will not stand behind you. In fact"—J'Neer pressed some buttons on an electronic board he had with him and much like similar equipment Kanir had in his offices, documents hung suspended just above the board—"these are the signed documents from the Matakian high council for me to take Jackie to Usia. And like I said, you're now in the mix as well."

I closed my eyes. Kanir covered my hand with his. He had gambled that I wouldn't be found, and he'd lost. Things had turned sour so fast I was amazed at how calm he was. Ever reserved, his eyes still betrayed nothing, but I could feel what was going through him. He was frustrated, angry. There was also a great deal of satisfaction that we would not be separated. I had to admit I was comforted that he would be with me.

My mind was racing. I was trying to comprehend what was about to happen. I would be taken to Usia with my husband. I would be made the new leader, the empress. The title did nothing for me, actually sounding pretty hokey. I was concerned for Kanir; he had a business with thousands of people depending on him. It wasn't like he could just take off and leave it there. This was a lifetime appointment.

Kanir nodded, looking at J'Neer. "How soon do we need to leave?"

"Tomorrow at noon. There's a galaxy-class battle cruiser three days out, the trip from there should take another two weeks."

"That would be fine." He turned to Tolf. "Contact the group of eight immediately, schedule a meeting first thing tomorrow morning."

We decided the story we would give was that we were leaving on a honeymoon. Nobody would ever describe Kanir as being impulsive, so it was decided that the whole plan was my idea, which was fine. Kanir had nothing going on that needed his attention right now, so this seemed as plausible a story as we could drum up. We quickly made reservations on a planet about two days away. It was supposed to be an incredible place to spend time vacationing. I looked forward to actually checking it out someday.

"What can we take with us?" I asked.

"A small traveling case each. Perhaps some finances," J'Neer suggested.

"I have to go to my offices and put some things together for the meeting tomorrow morning," Kanir said to me. "I'm going to let you pack for both of us. Make sure they are practical things, we don't know what we'll need."

"Of course," I said.

Kanir glanced at J'Neer, took my hand, and led me into the living room.

"Are you all right?" he asked quietly.

I nodded. "A bit shocked. Overwhelmed. A lot of things that I'm still processing. My brain is overloaded with everything I've found out today."

He looked directly into my eyes. "I'm sorry."

"I'm fine, Kanir. Everything will be okay." I reached up to kiss him. "I'm glad you're with me for this."

Almost a smile. He leaned into me and whispered, "I love you."

I looked at those eyes again. I could feel the uncertainty of what was going on and how it was affecting him. He was concerned for both of us. It was a huge thing for him to use "sorry" and "I love you" statements in the same conversation.

"I love you too, Kanir. We're going to be all right."

"Yes, we will. I need to go now. I don't know how soon I'll be back. Don't wait up for me." He kissed me quickly and left with Tolf.

I stood there for a moment, just taking a moment to let the whirlwind of confusion settle around me.

"He really loves you," J'Neer commented.

"Yes, he does. Are you surprised?"

He shrugged. "I wasn't sure if you were an acquisition or a wife." J'Neer paused thoughtfully. "You're definitely a wife."

28

I AWOKE THE next morning without Kanir next to me in bed. I could feel his fatigue. By the time I'd gotten up, showered and dressed, he was back. He looked exhausted.

"What can I get for you?" I asked, going to him.

"Nothing. Give me a short time, and we can be out of here."

J'Neer arrived at our rooms as Kanir finished dressing. The tension surrounding him was palpable. Something had changed that wasn't good. I knew he'd get around to telling us what it was, even though I wasn't sure I really wanted to know. Wasn't there enough on that plate already?

"We have to leave now," J'Neer said hastily.

"We're ready," Kanir said.

"You said we had until noon, why the hurry?" I asked. It was midmorning now. Bags were packed, and we were showered, dressed, and ready.

I knew something was up, but J'Neer wasn't keen on sharing it. It almost seemed like I could see what was going on in his head. This man who faced realities I didn't want to think about was trying to avoid sharing something with us, with the idea that if he didn't tell us, maybe whatever it was wouldn't actually be true.

The only reason I knew this was because I had tried that a few times in the past myself. It almost makes sense; if you don't put words to a situation you don't want to acknowledge as being real, maybe it will just go away. It didn't work for me, and all the adults in the room knew it wouldn't work for J'Neer either. Reality was reality. There was no skewing it to look like something else or hope it would just go away.

"Your guard, Swess, was just found in her rooms with her throat slit. Let's move."

Definitely one I would have loved to have skewed somehow...

Another blow. "Oh, God!" I whispered.

Kanir took my hand. "Let's go, Jackie."

Tolf was waiting for us in the shuttle bay. There were several shuttles ready to leave; all but one would be distractions for our getaway. Tolf gave us both a hug, wished us well, and we were on our way.

We were all on edge, not knowing if our shuttle would be a target for D'Nar. After nothing happened within the first couple of hours, Kanir fell asleep next to me, his head on my shoulder, his hand on my leg.

We had a false sense of security, since nothing happened the first day and a half. J'Neer was a good pilot and kept us informed; he even taught me how to pilot the shuttle. Kanir was also very good at flying the machine, and between the two of them, I became pretty good at navigating it. I was a good driver on Earth, but this was a very different sort of vehicle. The challenge was a great diversion from what we were facing, and I had a great time being able to do something so outside the box of what I had normally been doing over the last couple of months. J'Neer was happy for either of us to take control of the vessel so that he could get some rest.

We heard the second day that the shuttle headed for the resort planet had been destroyed, as well as one headed for Matakia. We had all expected that at least one of the shuttles would be taken out, but to hear that two were gone was startling. The shuttles acting as decoys had all been unmanned, but with false life signs emanating from them, it was nearly impossible for anyone to know if they were occupied or not. It had been a good plan, and now we just hoped that our shuttle was no longer in danger. There was just no way to be sure until we actually got to the battle cruiser.

It was our second day out, and we had just finished lunch. I was mesmerized by the view out the side portals, as well as the forward screen. The colors of planets passing by faster than Kanir's large office ship were so brilliant. I couldn't get enough of what was out there. It was a pleasant distraction from the reading I was doing, trying to make myself more prepared for what I was expected to do on Usia.

Kanir had brought along a lot of work to keep up with. It would be sent back as needed to the offices for follow-up or whatever needed to be done with it. I could feel the pressure he was under. He was leaving his livelihood; like any other male, it was what defined him. It was what he seemed to live and breathe, almost bringing me along for the ride. I managed to separate it out from other activities and interests. But now I could feel the stress he was dealing with. There would be a lot of decisions that would have to be made that were definitely going to change not only the business, but a lot of lives as well.

"Kanir, I have an idea."

"Yes, my love." He looked up from a report he had been studying.

"What if you moved your operations to Usia and the surrounding quadrant?"

He considered this for a moment. "I don't know, Jackie. It's a huge move, and most of my people will not want to leave their families and friends."

"Then bring part of it out there. Why does it all have to be back near Matakia?"

"Whether it's part of the business or the whole thing, it will be a huge undertaking that could last years."

"You ever hear of the elephant plan?" I asked him, looking at him almost sideways.

Confusion crossed his eyes for just a second.

If nothing else, over the last couple of months, I had become a source of amusement, sometimes confusion for Kanir, and whoever else happened to be nearby. Whenever I made some comment that was an Earth analogy or a saying that obviously made sense only to me but made no sense to the people around me, it usually at least got a snicker—once in a while, a belly laugh. Kanir would merely smile, the master of banality that he was, and ask for an explanation. Sometimes I explained, sometimes I let him think about it. I usually ended up explaining.

"The what?"

I took a deep breath. "How do you eat an elephant?"

"What does an Earth delicacy have to do with this?"

I laughed. "Kanir!" I couldn't stop laughing for a minute. He smiled, enjoying watching me laugh, even if it was at his expense.

"It's an analogy, sort of," I was finally able to explain. "Okay, you would eat a piece of bread one bite at a time, right?"

"Of course."

"If you were to eat an elephant, something so big and impossible to do quickly, you would break it down step by step or bite by bite. It makes the situation look more doable. You would eat the elephant one bite at a time. You could move your operations, or some part of it, one piece at a time."

Kanir nodded. "I considered it briefly when all this started but dismissed the idea because of the difficulty. I will consider it again and look at it more seriously." He stared at me for a few seconds. "I know I don't say a lot, but I think I need to tell you that you have become a valuable asset in my life."

"I know," I smiled.

Looking at his eyes, I suddenly realized how they continued to change. I remembered those eyes being dark and hard. The effort had been to keep me here, keep me quiet, figure out a way to get me to want to stay, make me love him. Without much effort on his part, I had become content to be here with this man, and I did love him. It had softened his eyes, softened the man. I saw him almost smiling more and more, especially as we spent more time together.

The metamorphosis was just beginning. He was loosening up, even though he still maintained a rigid exterior.

The hardness that had been there when we first met was melting, becoming less hard, more pliable, lighter.

Certainly less frightening than he had been when I'd first met the man.

"Hey, you two. Come up here," J'Neer called. We went to where he was at the front of the ship.

"What's up?" I asked.

"I'm not sure. I'm getting some readings in the area from another ship, but I can't see it. Might be cloaked, which could mean D'Nar."

I sat in the chair next to him and flipped the switches and dials as he directed me to. He was right. I didn't know as much about the systems as I wanted to yet, but there was something out there.

"I'm changing course for Detuv," he announced. "I don't like this. If we need to do something radical, we can do it there."

"Where's Detuv?" I asked.

"About an hour away from here," he said, finishing the maneuver on the board.

We had been on this new course for a short time when an alarm sounded.

J'Neer swore quietly. He did something on the board to make us gain some speed. We could hear the engines roar quietly as the speed picked up quickly.

Our shuttle suddenly shook violently. Kanir was sitting on a jump seat behind me, looking at what J'Neer was doing. We all grabbed for something to hang onto, startled by the attack.

"Get buckled in, if you're not already!" J'Neer shouted above the alarm.

He pressed a couple of buttons, and the outer cameras finally gave us a look at what was attacking us.

"It's a pirate freighter," J'Neer announced.

He did some more things on the panel before him, and beams of light, the lasers, leapt from our vehicle, striking the other ship. Our little shuttle picked up speed, as J'Neer directed us closer to Detuv.

He was doing some things to try to keep us from being hit, as well as trying to strike back; he was actually somewhat successful.

Kanir lifted me out of my seat and took the seat himself. I hadn't even noticed him unbuckle my harness. I buckled his harness and then my own as I watched his hands dance across the panel, occasionally going over to the panel in front of J'Neer. The ship settled and leapt ahead even faster. I could feel it moving side to side as if in some sort of weird dance to keep from being hit.

"Not bad, Kanir," J'Neer commented.

We were close to the planet's atmosphere when the other ship fired on us again, spinning the shuttle out of control as it broke into the atmosphere around the planet. Things that hadn't been secured inside flew around, bouncing off walls and other stationary things. J'Neer pressed a button and a force field appeared in the middle of the ship, keeping most of the stuff at the back of the ship contained.

In seconds, we were in the sky above the clouds. They were dark and roiling, lightning leaping frequently from them, some of it uncomfortably close to our little ship. The shuttle was still falling fast, out of control, and broke through the cloud cover.

The area of the planet where we had come in was in the middle of a storm that would put the daily Florida monsoon to shame. Lightning strikes seemed to come every few seconds, and had it been under any other circumstances, they would have been spectacular to watch. Rumbling, often piercing thunder seemed to be never ending, and the roiling masses of clouds unleashed torrents of rain that, partnered with wind, probably left little standing below.

"We've lost the primary engines," Kanir stated. "I can't get enough power to keep us airborne."

"I'm sending a message to the ship we're supposed to meet," J'Neer said, hands flying across the communications portion of the panel before him. "Maybe they can get here faster and lend us some assistance."

I could see J'Neer reaching for things on the board, but he kept being jerked away by the force of what was happening to us. Kanir seemed to be able to reach the controls better and was able to at least level off our flight as we descended rapidly from the sky. The tops of trees were coming up to us fast, and within a few seconds, we were clipping the tops of them. I wasn't sure, but I thought I saw plumes of smoke rising from some parts of the forest below us. Another shuttle came out of nowhere and flew above us, as if trying to see who we were. When the ship that had been chasing us took a shot at us, the other one fired on it. The ship erupted in a huge ball of fire and fell into the forest behind us.

"That ship is trying to hail us," J'Neer said, flipping a couple of switches.

"Identify yourselves," came the order.

"Greetings from Matakia," J'Neer responded. "We were on our way to meet up with a freighter when we were attacked. We thank you for eliminating our attackers. Right now, we're in bad shape." He gave them our situation.

There was a gap in the trees a short distance from us. Kanir steered us into it. It turned out to be a shallow canyon. Lightning reflected off the wet walls that seemed to turn at sharp angles.

A few seconds later, the lights went out, followed by the whine of the engines powering down. Kanir said something in another language I hadn't heard before, but I was pretty sure it was a swear word. We were now no more than a glorified falling rock that happened to stay airborne for just a while longer. The two men at the board were working furiously to find someplace to land gently enough to keep us alive. They were working together to level out the ship and keep it from landing badly, but it was obvious that no matter how hard they worked this was going to be messy. The canyon took a hard right, and despite their best efforts, the ship made only a slight correction, crashing into a rocky wall with a glancing blow. Everything lurched forward and to the side as the ship went from the face of the rock wall to the floor of the canyon below us, landing almost on its side among some huge boulders, close to a fast moving river.

It seemed to take a few seconds for everything to settle in the shuttle and then it was totally quiet, except for a beeping noise coming from the panel in front of Kanir, and the storm outside that was rapidly moving away.

The shuttle had landed slightly on one side. The front window was smashed, held in place like the windshield of a car on Earth would have. From where I sat, I could see that the shuttle was now a twisted wreck that was done flying. Cold rain and wind were blowing into the shuttle, making it instantly chilly from the rear door that had been breached. The smell of ozone from the storm as well as the river just outside the shuttle made for an earthy, intoxicating fragrance, making the air feel alive and wild.

There was something eerie about the way the cabin felt. It wasn't silent with the storm going full throttle outside, but it had something to do with this ship that had just been flying so valiantly now totally still and not by our hand. I looked around for a second, trying to get my bearings. I did a brief assessment of myself and decided nothing was broken.

"Jackie?" Kanir asked.

"I'm all right. You?"

"I'm fine. J'Neer?"

"Yeah, I'm okay. I think I have a cut on my face."

We all unbuckled and went to the rear of the shuttle. Kanir found a flashlight and shone it on J'Neer's face. There was a long gash just under his right eye, bleeding heavily through his fingers.

We had obviously landed toward the end of the storm. It seemed to be traveling quickly away from this area, but every minute or so, there was still a good gust of wind that brought more cold rain into the shuttle. Lightning still crackled around us from time to time, and we could hear the thunder starting to rumble and fade off in the distance.

The cabinets at the rear of the ship had opened at the force of the attack and then the crash landing. The contents were spilled all over the floor and up the wall. I picked up a cloth and handed it to J'Neer and had him sit in the seat I'd been using. Kanir looked around for the medical kit. It took him about a minute, and then he removed a couple of interesting things: first there was a pencil-size laser that he began playing back and forth across the cut as he held it together with his fingers. Within minutes, the gash was looking sealed, the scar tissue pink against his tan skin. Kanir then sprayed it with something, played the laser across it for a few more minutes, and the cut was almost nonexistent.

"I'm impressed," I commented. "I've never seen anything like that."

Kanir stood beside me, regarding J'Neer.

"J'Neer, are you able to travel? Kanir asked.

"Yeah, I'm okay." He stood up and nearly fell over again. Kanir caught him, easing him back onto the bench. The loss of blood and likely the shock were more than he realized.

"We need to get out of here as soon as possible," Kanir said.

"Why?" I asked.

"If we get caught by whoever is in that shuttle, there's no telling what they might do. When the battle between our two planets was over, things were still not settled. I don't know if I will be recognized or not. The biggest concern is their twisted memory of what happened during that time. The natives are just as much a concern. If they get here first, it will definitely go badly."

"Define badly."

"They take prisoners and then extort money for their release. The longer it takes, the less likely the prisoner is to live. If you survive long enough, you become a slave."

"Is this a reputation or you know this from personal experience, or what?"

"I fought here. I know the people," Kanir said.

"You fought here?" I couldn't hide my surprise. Every now and then, Kanir came out with something that showed me just how much I didn't know him. So now I'm finding out he's a former soldier.

"Kanir was a high-ranking military man," J'Neer supplied. "He was a major in charge of forces and frequently went on missions himself. Looked up to and admired by all the men who worked and fought with him. Decorated a number of times."

Kanir was looking away. He had talked about having been wounded during a war but hadn't offer any more information. At the time, I was trying hard not to get any more involved with this man than I needed to and didn't follow up on what we had talked about so briefly. Kanir was happy to leave the past where it was, giving no more information.

"It sounds like we're screwed either way," I commented.

Kanir regarded me for a moment, puzzled by what I said.

"I mean, either way, we're probably in a lot of trouble."

He nodded.

J'Neer and Kanir were both looking through the piles of stuff on the floor of the ship. They were collecting things and putting them aside.

"What can I do to help?" I asked.

J'Neer pointed to one of the cabinets that hadn't been jarred open. "There should be some carriers in there. Get out three and start packing them with the things we're putting aside."

I found several backpacks—pretty good-sized ones at that. Black, heavy canvas with several compartments each. I began carefully packing them with the things the two men were putting in piles. Medical kits, food items, blankets, tools, and other things.

"No weapons?" I asked.

"Not for you," Kanir replied.

"You have some trust issues, husband."

"Perhaps. When the time comes, you'll have one."

"I think the time is now, if—"

"You don't even know how to shoot these weapons," Kanir argued.

"I made marksman in my department. I was better than most of the guys I worked with. Show me how to fire one, and we're good."

"Not now."

"He's right," J'Neer said. "These are much different from what you carried on Earth. Once we're out of danger, I can give you some quick lessons in handling these."

"I can teach my wife, J'Neer," Kanir said matter-of-factly.

J'Neer was quiet.

Alpha male vs. alpha male. Here we go.

"When's the last time you qualified?" J'Neer asked, still going through the jumble of supplies on the floor.

"I stay current on all weapons."

"What?" I looked at Kanir, now just a bit angry. "When have you qualified? I had no idea. There's a range or something?"

"Range?" J'Neer asked. "What's a range?"

"Someplace to shoot weapons safely. Indoor or outdoor."

"I take time at least once every couple of weeks to go to the 'range,' as you call it, to stay sharp," Kanir said.

"I had no idea!" I said. "I would have asked to go, to learn. I haven't shot since I was taken. I could have been part of this whole security thing on the ship—"

"I couldn't risk it."

"Risk what?" I asked, slamming something resembling an MRE into the bag I was packing.

Kanir just looked at me for a moment. He hadn't seen me angry like this before.

And then I knew. Apparently there was some part of our joining that wasn't complete, or the man had trust issues even our joining couldn't contain.

"You still think I'll leave. However I can figure out."

He looked away.

"Kanir, I'm not going anywhere. Ever." I shrugged gave him a loopy smile. "I can't. Remember? It's a sealed deal."

He nodded, unable to say anything.

We just stood and looked at each other for a moment. His eyes betrayed the—was it shame—he was trying so hard to rise above, but I could sense it. I could sense his love for me above all else. His strong desire to not have us separated.

And there was likely some male control issue in there as well that just wasn't worth the time to evaluate.

He was just a man, like any other man in the universe…
okay, maybe not like any other man.

"Listen, you two," J'Neer interrupted. "We don't have time
for this. Have your little quarrel later, when we're safe and out
of danger and so I don't have to be in the middle of it. Let's
concentrate on what we need to do now and get out of here."

I had the backpacks loaded up. The storm had moved on,
and now it was just raining lightly. It was dusky outside, and
the rain had left the air chilly and damp. I was shivering until
Kanir put a dark jacket over my shoulders. I slipped into it
and then slipped into the supports of the backpack. It was
heavy, but nothing I couldn't handle.

J'Neer had a handheld locator. It seemed to have the ability
to bring up a sort of map of the area, pretty much like a GPS
would; the clarity and detail were far better than anything
I had ever seen on Earth. Kanir was studying it with him,
and they were discussing possible routes out of the canyon.
We could hear the shuttle somewhere in the distance getting
closer, probably with reinforcements.

"There is a small cabin out this way." Kanir was pointing
to an area on the locator. "It was owned by an old woman who
helped us twenty years ago. She might be there still, unless
she's moved on."

"Or died," J'Neer supplied.

"Doubtful. She is an android. It would take a lot to kill her."

We all looked outside the door and into the sky.

"Let's get out of here," J'Neer said.

We left the shuttle and began walking along side the river, toward where Kanir had directed.

"Where's the shuttle that shot down the other one?" I asked. "Why haven't they shown up?"

"For one thing, there's no room here for another shuttle to land," J'Neer answered, "and for another, considering the natives, they might not be too concerned about us."

"That's not encouraging."

We walked for several minutes. As we rounded a bend in the canyon, we could see where the other shuttle had landed. About a dozen men were doing some preparation for reconnaissance. It was uncomfortably close to where we were, and we quickly took cover in some tall grass. J'Neer had some kind of foreign version of night-vision binoculars.

From what Kanir and I could see, there were several two-man shuttles going up. These things looked like something out of a cartoon. They seemed to accommodate the men who rode them just up past their waist. It sort of looked like the vehicle was wrapped around them, and probably had a control panel or something in front of them to pilot these flying cars. They lifted easily into the air and over the canyon wall, the pilots taking their time looking for us.

The three of us headed back in the direction we had come and ducked into a scrawny stand of trees just before the air cars passed over us. I was amazed and grateful they hadn't spotted us, but I knew it wouldn't be long before they did. There was no place for us to go. I looked back from where we had come. In the sand and mud, it wouldn't be hard to miss our tracks. I took a few deep breaths to stifle the panic that wanted to rise up inside. Kanir sensed my concern and took my hand.

"Jackie, we'll be all right," he whispered.

I started wishing for something in my hand to help defend us. I'd even be grateful for the handgun, even the shotgun I owned, up against the lasers used out here.

I nodded. The three of us tried to hide in the densest part of the stand of trees, which wasn't easy; there wasn't much there. We watched as two of the small vehicles came from where our shuttle had landed. One slowed, the other landed briefly. There was a brief conversation between the men in the two cars, and then the second one went airborne again, landing on the other side of the trees where we were hidden. They were obviously following our tracks.

Kanir and J'Neer readied their weapons. A quiet, short beep let us know they were powered up and ready.

"Jackie, when they call, you go out to them. We'll take them out," J'Neer said to me.

"What?" I looked to Kanir.

He nodded. "Just go," he said. "They don't know if there are two or three of us. If they ask you about any others, tell them there's one more injured in here. And then drop down. We'll take them out."

"Just don't kill them," I said.

J'Neer looked at me like I had grown a third eye in my forehead. "What do you mean don't kill them? If they take us—"

"I'm not doing it if you're going to kill them. Can't you set those things to stun?"

"Yes, but—"

"If we have to deal with them later, it will go better for us if we don't kill their men."

J'Neer and Kanir looked at each other.

"Is she like this a lot?" J'Neer asked.

"Stubborn, yes," Kanir responded. "Full of spirit. It's one of the reasons I wanted her."

J'Neer took a deep breath and shook his head. "Okay," J'Neer said, not quite sure he understood that statement.

They took a few seconds to adjust the settings on their weapons for stun, and we waited.

Nothing in my experience as a cop had prepared me for this. The closest I had ever come to something like this was going into a building as point. We didn't know who was in the building, if they were armed, where they were. Aside from not being armed myself, it wasn't that far removed from this, but it was no less unnerving. I was scared out of my skin, but there seemed to be no other way to do this. I took another deep breath. Time to suck it up and just do it. I nodded. I could do this. I had to do this. I turned back to the four men nearing our hiding place. They were approaching with their weapons drawn.

"Come on out of there," one of them called.

I hesitated a moment. Kanir gave me a gentle push, and I went forward, my hands raised and open. Lord, I hoped this was the absolute universal sign of being unarmed and wanting to appear cooperative. Please, please, please…

"I'm alone," I said, keeping my voice steady, "I'm not armed."

"Take the jacket off," one of them said then called past me. "Get out here, you two."

"There's only one. He's injured and needs medical attention," I said, taking off my jacket. Two of them had come to either side of me. I didn't have to fall to the ground; they threw me down into the sand and muck where I stayed. I heard several long whining sounds, obviously the lasers. The leader tried to radio for help but was quickly taken out by a laser from Kanir or J'Neer.

"Jackie, get up." Kanir was next to me faster than I thought he would be. I got to my feet, grabbed, and slipped into the jacket. We ran past the fallen bodies to the air cars. J'Neer got in one, Kanir and I got in the other, and we took off up over the wall of the canyon and across fields, toward a forest. I kept looking behind me to see if we had company. It wasn't long before several of the air cars were coming our way from behind. We had the advantage of having a couple minutes lead on them, but they knew the terrain a lot better.

I looked at the panel in front of Kanir and me. There was a screen similar to the one J'Neer had on his GPS gizmo. It showed the forest coming up in front of us, and I could see several swirls of smoke rising from different points above the trees. From where we were, there was no telling if any of them were from fires purposely set or from lightning strikes. J'Neer and Kanir both steered the cars to the edge of the woods and landed. We got out and ran into the woods with Kanir leading us now. The forest was dense and dark, wet with the recent rain. In seconds, we were climbing over dead trees, fallen limbs, around the occasional huge bush that insisted on growing there. The moonlight barely made it into the dense overgrowth, making it hard to get around for the first minute or two. Once our eyes adjusted, it became a little easier, but not by much.

There was a small clearing with a huge overgrown bush in the middle, reaching out to the trees. We dove into the middle and sat, trying to catch our breaths as quietly as we could. Kanir was next to me. He took out a canteen of water and gave it to me. I took a quick sip and handed it back. He and J'Neer took a drink, and we waited. And waited.

29

A MOMENT LATER, it sounded like someone was taking a stroll past our hiding spot. We all looked at each other. And then we heard what sounded like a bunch of people running toward where we were.

"Tox," said a voice.

"Good to see you, Nomrah." This voice sounded like it came from a woman.

"And you." The voice had a bit of sarcasm to it. "Have you seen three people here in the last few minutes?"

"I just got out here, Nomrah. Haven't even seen a Gidku."

"Old woman, if you're hiding them or we find you've had anything to do with them, you'll answer to the Chomrek."

"Oh, please. He's the least of my concerns," the woman said.

The first voice gave some commands to his officers, and we heard them leaving.

We continued to sit quietly, just waiting.

"You can come out now, they're gone," the woman called to us.

We all looked at each other again. Kanir had that almost smile going on again.

"Who is it?" I asked him. I got the impression he knew who was out there.

"Come and find out," he answered.

We crawled out from under the bushes and stood up. She was an elderly lady and almost made me laugh. She looked like Mama from the Addams family, except she wore a dark pants outfit in a dark print with a long duster over it. When she saw Kanir, her face lit up.

"Kanir!" she said. The two of them embraced.

"Tell me about these two you are with…wait. This is your bride, I see her hrova. Ah, she's an Earther. Kanir, she's—"

She paused, looking intently at me. "You are supposed to be somewhere else, aren't you, my dear? You've had some adventures, some not very nice, no, not at all. And you're here because of where you're supposed to be." She paused, continuing to study Kanir and me. "Oh my." It was said with a touch of awe that had me concerned about what she seemed to know, or thought she knew. Very strange lady.

"Who are you?" I asked.

"I am Tox," she said with a bow. "Dweller of these woods. I took care of Kanir when this planet was at war with his planet many years ago. He was shot and separated from his men. He held off a squad of men so that his men could get away. I got him into my home just in time. He had lost a lot of blood and those that wanted him dead were not far behind us. I had to hide him for six days and keep them out of my hidden cellar all while trying to collect herbs I needed to treat him and keep him from dying."

I looked at Kanir. He wasn't enjoying being reminded of those days. I had an idea there was a lot of pain that he was pleased to leave in the past where it was.

"This is J'Neer," Kanir supplied. "He's why we are now on our way to Usia. If not for him, Jackie and I could be home with life going on as normal."

"Oh, Kanir," Tox said. "Normal is so highly overrated." She went to J'Neer.

"Hmm. Very interesting." She looked between the three of us and said to J'Neer, "I admire your restraint."

"What does that mean?" J'Neer asked, watching her closely, almost defensively.

Kanir said, "Those men are probably going to be back before long, if for no other reason than to get back to their ship. We'd better be gone when they pass through."

"Oh, you're so right," Tox said. "What am I thinking? Come with me. My home is only a short distance away."

There was just enough light to see where we were going, to avoid that branch, see where to climb over that tree, step around that huge rock in the path. Tox was a knowledgeable guide as she led the way. We could hear the nightlife now; it wasn't the high-pitched chirp of crickets, but something deeper in tone that seemed to surround us and lull us a bit as we walked.

"I would like to know how they didn't find us," J'Neer said as we started off toward Tox's home. "I know they had to have handheld locators."

"It's Tox," Kanir said. "Her very body blocks the effects of a lot of different equipment."

"I'm an advanced android," Tox explained. "I was a bit surprised I was able to keep my damping field over you for as long as I did. My powers are starting to wan with my age and lack of proper maintenance."

"I'm sure," I said. "How long have you been here?"

"Here, about fifty years, on your Earth another twenty-five. I liked your Earth. The people there are so…predictable, but in an interesting way. Interesting personalities, some of them. It's no wonder Usia values the leadership of your people. Especially those with a strong moral compass, as you like to call it."

I hadn't seen it like that. Politicians were notoriously dishonest, very few of them had any kind of moral streak. It made me think about the kind of leader I wanted to be. I wanted to make sure I did things for the right reasons, looked out for others before myself, and did things correctly.

"Tox, why don't you come with us?" Kanir suggested.

"Wait a minute," J'Neer protested. "We can't be collecting people to take along on this mission. This is not a pleasure cruise."

"Tox could prove valuable to us," Kanir argued. "She knows, senses things about people and situations."

"I don't think it's a good idea."

"I do," I said. "Lord knows when we get to Usia, I can use all the help I can get. It would be a great benefit to have her help me see some things from a different perspective. If there's something she senses about someone or something, it would be valuable. Not just to me, but to Usia as well."

"It's one more person to account for, look after," J'Neer argued.

"Look at what she did to help us back there," I said. "She protected us."

"She just admitted her powers are growing weak. How long is it going to be before she's totally without those abilities? Five minutes after we get to Usia? Come on, you two."

"She needs some proper maintenance and she'll be in good working order." Kanir said, "What do you say, Tox?"

"My, my. I don't remember the last time I was fought over like this." She took a deep breath. "Oh, dear." Tox had stopped. We all stopped and looked.

Just ahead in the woods was a small shack of a hovel of a hut. The large flashlights the soldiers held as they went around and inside the house let us see it just a bit better than the moonlight. It looked like it was about to fall down. The walls of the building were buckling, and the roof looked like it had patches on patches. The chimney, which was on the other side away from us, seemed to be leaning way too far away from the house. The soldiers had forced open the door, which hung by just barely a hinge. We could see the tracing beams of their lights inside the home.

"I found it!" we heard from where they worked. Several of them went into the structure.

"They found my cellar." Tox sighed, resigned to what was going on in her home.

"Is there anything in there that might be dange—" I was interrupted by a huge explosion. The whole house was an instant inferno, the remains of it having been blown in every direction. We all automatically went to the ground for cover from debris flying everywhere.

Kanir was grinning. It took total destruction to get a full smile from the man. It just figured…

"Oh crap," I whispered. J'Neer looked at me. "Half an epithet," I explained.

There had been about four or five men outside the house who had all been blown back by the force of the explosion. Only two now got to their feet. They stumbled around in shock for a few minutes, and then we could see them relating the incident via their radios. They checked the others who hadn't gotten up; it didn't look good for them.

"We have to get out of here," J'Neer said.

"Ya think?" I said. I looked at Tox. "They are not going to be happy with you."

She smiled. "Well, I haven't been happy with that bunch in a very long time myself."

"So where do we go now? Your place is gone," J'Neer said.

"You don't live on a planet like this and not have another place to go," Kanir said.

Tox had already started off down a trail that was barely visible in the darkness that now enveloped the forest. Moonlight, periodically obscured by passing clouds, constantly blocked by the tree branches overhead, barely lit the way.

"Are there any kinds of critters we need to be concerned about this time of night?" I asked.

"Mostly no," Tox said. "There are a few nocturnal animals that are less than friendly, but they tend to shy away from people."

We had barely started out when we saw the two-man air cars in the sky with large floodlights illuminating the forest below them. We quickly took cover.

"They're going to have equipment to locate us," J'Neer said. "We need to find someplace to go where we can't be detected or we're done."

"There's another place a distance away. We'll go there," Tox said, picking up the pace.

"We'll be discovered," J'Neer argued.

"J'Neer, please humor an old android. My damping is operating enough to keep us hidden from them for a short time. Probably long enough to get away from them. So we either go now and get there or stay here, let my field die, and be discovered. What would you prefer?"

J'Neer nodded resignedly. It was our only chance. It was eerie to be moving about with what was going on above us, even though we knew we were covered by Tox's damping field, when we weren't under the thick cover of trees. After a time, we seemed to have walked out of the area they were searching, but every now and then, one or more sky craft went overhead, making us duck for cover. The wetness of the storm still hung on everything, and as nighttime went on, it got colder. Walking as fast as we could kept us from getting overwhelmed by the temperature. We'd been walking for over an hour, and I was starting to feel pretty tired. I could sense the others were tired as well, with the possible exception of our android friend.

"How much further is this place, Tox?" J'Neer asked.

"About another two miles."

"I vote we stop for a break and eat something," I said. "My feet hurt and I'm starving."

"It will help us finish the trip," Kanir said.

"I think we'll be all right to do that," Tox said.

We found a clearing with a couple of fallen trees that we could sit on and rest. Kanir, J'Neer, and I snacked on jerky, dried fruit, and water for about five minutes. We were quiet for most of the time, until Tox asked me about Earth.

"I lived in Florida, in North America," I said.

"Really, what did you do there?"

"She was a protector," J'Neer provided.

"Otherwise known as a police officer or law enforcement officer," I added.

I could barely see Tox's smile. "Did you enjoy what you did?"

"I did," I answered. "I worked with some great people, and sometimes I felt like I made a difference."

"You must miss your family."

"I do," I admitted. "I was close to my parents. I loved holidays with them and—" I had to stop. That quickly, I had memories rushing in. I took a few deep breaths and bit my lower lip, trying hard to keep back the flood of emotion. I had been so busy doing things and now running for my life, I hadn't had time to think about all I'd left behind in some time.

Kanir was next to me. He moved closer and put his arm around me. Nobody said anything for several minutes. I was relieved none of them could see me. I didn't want an audience to my feelings.

"What was that?" J'Neer asked.

I could sense a change in the air. Something was different. Barely discernable, but there.

"My damping field has expired," Tox said. "We'd better move on."

We quickly packed up our things and started out again. A couple of air cars zoomed overhead. One circled back, looking closely at the area, panning a large floodlight. We all dove for cover under wet bushes, hoping the added coolness of the plants would hide us.

"I want you to keep moving in the direction we were going when I walk away," Tox said.

"What?" I think we all asked at the same time.

"As soon as I have left this area, keep walking. Kanir knows where to go. I will meet you there if I am able."

I looked up. Tox was still walking, but in a different direction. Had her circuits gone out with the damping field?

"Kanir, what is she doing?" I asked. He was about ten feet away from me, under a different bush.

"I suppose she's distracting them from us, but I'm sure they want her for what she left for them in her cabin."

We watched as she continued to walk. The air car above the trees had located her easily and was joined by a second one. Tox continued to walk calmly, seemingly oblivious to what was going on above her.

"Come on, let's go." J'Neer was on his feet. Kanir and I got up and ran with J'Neer. Kanir took the lead, leading us in the way Tox had been taking us earlier. I had never been a runner, even when I was a police officer on Earth, but adrenaline will keep you going for a long time under the right circumstances. Even in a dark forest, at night, after a crash landing followed by running from the enemy. I was thinking that any more adrenaline rushes, and we would all be on overload.

I was hoping we would see Tox again. She brought back endearing, grandmotherly things I missed in my own grandmother, with just a bit of a quirky twist thrown in for some odd good measure. But considering that she had given herself over to be discovered by our bad guys, her continued existence was kind of a toss-up.

I looked back for a moment and stopped. "Wait!" I yelled to Kanir and J'Neer.

They stopped and we watched Tox. She had stopped under the trees. We could hear and see the occasional glint of the steel of the air cars through the trees. Tox raised her arms straight in the air, aimed at the air cars. All we could hear was the loud hum of the vehicles, as they tried to lock in on what was below them. A few seconds passed and then a flash from one of the air cars split through the trees, striking Tox's arm. The discharge seemed to go through her body for a mere second then exited her other arm, striking the other air car above her. The explosion was great enough that it pulled the other car into the explosion, and they both were raining down over the trees. Tox stood for a few seconds and then toppled backward.

I took a few steps to go to her, when Kanir stopped me.

"We have to help her!" I yelled.

"Jackie, we need to go."

"She's a friend, she helped us," I argued.

"She sacrificed herself so we could get away. We're wasting the opportunity she gave us."

"Their friends are going to be here any minute," J'Neer added. "They had to have seen what happened, and they're going to be all over this place in a few minutes, if not seconds."

I looked over at where Tox was. I thought I could see some movement.

"Look!" I said.

They both looked at where Tox lay. It was a distance away and dark, but we could make out her arms and legs seeming to bounce up and down.

"She's an android," Kanir explained. "She could have some kind of regeneration ability. She will catch up to us if she can. And if she hears that we delayed for her benefit, she will not be happy. Let's go."

We took one last look at her and took off in the direction Tox had been taking us. We seemed to run for quite a while, when we stopped on the outskirts of a small clearing. The clearing was about fifteen feet of tall grass that ended against a tall rock wall. It seemed to go on for a good distance on each side. Some parts of it seemed to allow for climbing, but not for any real distance up, unless someone was an experienced rock or mountain climber. It felt like a dead end.

"This isn't good," I said. I fought the urge to panic.

"No, this is where we want to be," Kanir said. "Keep a look out for the air cars."

Kanir crossed the grass to the wall and began examining it with his flashlight.

"Kanir, what are you looking for?" I asked.

"A lever. Just pay attention to anything in the air, Jackie."

"Let us help you," I said. "Tell us what to look for."

"Sorry, love, but it's rather difficult to describe," he half muttered as he concentrated on searching the edifice. "I'll know it when I see it."

J'Neer and I kept watch on what was going on overhead. So far it was a listening game. The air cars seemed to be slowly drifting our way. They were obviously taking great pains to be thorough in their efforts to locate us.

"I'm surprised they don't have something more advanced to find us," I commented.

"They do. I don't know why it's not working. We should have been spotted long ago."

"You're a fount of optimism."

"I just happen to know the enemy to some degree, but Kanir knows them much better than I do."

"It's a part of his life he hasn't shared with me yet," I commented. "How do you know so much about him?"

"As soon as I found out he had you, I did some research."

I nodded. "Out of everything that has happened in the last several months, that's one of the few things that makes sense."

"Jackie, it's going to get better. Just give it time."

"Actually, things were a constant nightmare until Kanir. Well, even after I came to be with him, it was still insane. I guess after we—you know, joined—things settled down some. At least that's the way it seems. I've been content for the most part, but there's still been a small whisper, a knowing, that there's something else I'm supposed to be doing." I paused, watching Kanir still examining the rock wall. "A lot of it probably comes down to purpose. Even though I love this man and I want to be with him and share my life with him, I still know that my purpose is not being fulfilled. And I know I'm supposed to be on Usia, even though my heart still aches for Earth."

"You have a lot going on inside of you."

"I guess so."

We heard an air car come much closer than any had so far. Even Kanir looked up from what he was doing to see how close it was then went back to his task. This was getting tedious and a bit scary.

We had followed Kanir as he moved down a good portion of the wall. The rocks were becoming more brush covered; the grasses and small bushes were growing out of the cracks in the face of the wall.

Kanir was examining a portion of the wall that was a good deal more of a patchwork of dark, earthy color than the rest from what we could barely make out in the darkness. It had graduated to this and was covered in a lot more grass tucked into lines that seemed to be recessed into the wall. He was feeling along the wall with his hands as well as peering closely at what was before him when he stopped and stepped back. He stepped back to the wall again, and I watched as he traced his fingers through the maze of cracks before him, clearing grass and dirt from the crevices. His fingers stopped at several points for a few brief seconds each before moving on. As his fingers left those points and formed closed shapes, the shapes took on a darker color than the rest of the rock surrounding it. Having found what he'd been searching for, he went faster. The design that was taking shape was nothing I had seen before, made up of shapes and colors that seemed random to me. Kanir stepped back after a moment and looked at what he had constructed on the wall before him. He looked down and started clearing some of the sand and dirt with his feet in several different places at the base of the rock wall. It was a puzzle to be sure, and now he seemed to be looking for something that would complete it. I was hoping that the completion of this would do something to make us invisible to the people looking for us. I was thinking a cave or another damping field. I didn't care which it was, or even if it was something else. Anything would beat being out here with no place to go, waiting to be picked off.

Another air car went over head, skirting the edge of the trees. They couldn't see J'Neer and me, but I was certain they saw Kanir and I felt myself panicking.

"Kanir, I think they spotted you," I called.

"I know. Just one moment."

"I don't think we have a moment!"

"Jackie, be quiet, I can't concentrate."

I took a deep breath.

Kanir positioned himself against the wall. He placed his feet in two of the spaces he had cleared at he base of the wall. Then he placed his hands on the wall at specific points, flattening himself against it. The wall seemed to glow around him, and then the different spaces started glowing individually one at a time in some kind of random pattern that was hard to follow. If the men in the air cars hadn't seen Kanir before, the light from the wall was going to bring them here for sure. The light show stopped, and Kanir stepped back as the wall disintegrated, revealing the entrance to a cave.

"Let's go!" Kanir called.

30

J'NEER AND I left where we had been in the trees and raced into the cave with Kanir immediately behind us. He played his flashlight along the interior walls, found a panel, and pressed some buttons. The wall closed over, and it was extremely dark, except for the flashlight still illuminating the interior. Kanir was pressing more buttons on the panel; light filled the cave, hurting our eyes, after having been in the dark for some time now.

"That's better," Kanir commented. I could feel his stress starting to diminish now; he'd found the entrance to Tox's other location and had gotten us to safety.

J'Neer and I were looking around. It was a small room. The wall to the left had benches for sitting and storage shelves above. The shelves seemed to be storage for some kind of weapons. The wall in front of us had counter space and more shelves with other things I couldn't identify, and to our right was a corridor.

J'Neer sat on a bench. Kanir and I sat on another one.

"So what is this?" J'Neer asked.

"Tox told me she constructed this shortly after she arrived. There's a labyrinth of corridors for a couple of miles in different directions, with a number of entrances. One of them goes into what used to be her home. The explosion was supposed to be enough to keep this from being discovered."

"A little paranoid?"

"Hardly. The people on this planet are not always hospitable. She knew she needed to be able to disappear quickly if they suddenly became irritable about something they came after her for. This was it."

"She showed you how to access it all in the short time you were with her?" I asked.

Kanir nodded. His arm was around my waist. I leaned against him. The outpouring of adrenaline to get here and stay hidden from the bad guys while my husband worked on getting us in here was starting to dissipate, and I was feeling worn out.

Kanir kissed the top of my head then got up, taking my hand to pull me to my feet. "We're all tired. There are some rooms further in here where we can rest comfortably."

The lights in the corridor came up as we walked into the different areas, going back down as we left those areas. The corridors were impressive in their size and the consistency of texture. The first room was a short walk down the first corridor. It was a small bedroom. Across the hall was a larger bedroom.

"J'Neer, I would advise that you stay in that room until we're ready to move on. Tox built in some traps just in case this place was discovered by her pursuers, some of them deadly."

"I hope she survived," I said quietly.

"I know," Kanir said. "We'll probably know by morning if she did or not."

"How do you know that?"

"If she survived, she'll be coming here to finish any regeneration she might need."

"Good night, you two," J'Neer said and went into the small bedroom. A door of sorts closed after him.

Kanir and I went into the other room. It was very basic. There was a plain double bed against the far wall with a brown blanket and a few pillows in brown cases. A couch was in the room on another wall, and in the corner was a small closet that turned out to be a very small bathroom. Kanir took a quick shower and came out wrapped in a towel. I went to the bathroom immediately after him and got showered and cleaned up. Our extra clothing had to be left in the shuttle, so we were left with what we had been wearing. I rinsed out my undergarments and hung them to dry then went into the bedroom wrapped in a towel. Despite the excitement of the recent events, we were exhausted and fell asleep pretty easily.

The lights were dim when I awoke the next morning. Kanir was next to me, just beginning to wake up as well. He put his arm across me and moved closer.

"Sleep well?" I asked

"Hmm. And you?"

"After the running around and all the stress, I'm surprised I slept as well as I did. We should probably get going, huh?"

"We have time."

I had questions I had wanted to ask since my conversation with J'Neer. There hadn't been a chance to talk to Kanir alone from the time we realized we needed to be on our way to Usia. It didn't seem like the ideal time or place, but I wasn't sure I'd see either one any time soon.

"Why didn't you tell me about the outcome of our joining?" I asked. "That it made us inseparable."

Kanir studied my face for a moment. "J'Neer told you."

"Yes, why didn't you?" I wasn't angry; this was a fact-finding mission now.

"I didn't think it was important, I suppose." He considered me for a moment and then asked, "Is this a problem for you?"

I wasn't sure what to say, what to ask. I wasn't sure how important this was to our relationship. It didn't make me love him any less. I tried to figure out how that fit together. He was in my head, in my thoughts. I knew what was going on in him at any given moment. Because of our joining, there were no secrets. There was a forced trust, one that I could tell he didn't want to take for granted.

"Promise me there's nothing else I need to find out like this again."

"I will make sure we have nothing that would cause separation of a different sort."

I nodded. "I appreciate that. I don't want to not trust you."

"I never want to hurt you, Jackie. But I must tell you, for a while you were making me a bit crazy. When a Matakian male has set his heart on the female he has desired to join with, there's no turning back. There are no long engagements. The couple is married within a very short time so that they may join. If joining does not occur within the first couple of weeks of marriage, the male especially starts to decline in health. I only made it that long by taking special supplements and working far more than normal." Kanir paused. "Truly, I meant no harm to you. My only excuse, and I hate to use that term, is that in the heat of what was going on between us, revealing to you the results of our joining was not high on my list of priorities. And really, would it have changed anything, if you had known about that beforehand?"

I shook my head. "No. I would still have joined with you."

This was very unlike my husband; unless it was business-related, he wasn't one to say a whole lot all at once, and I was genuinely surprised by what he was sharing. As much as I was enjoying this side of him that I saw all too seldom, I knew we had to get going soon. But I was anxious to hear what was actually going on in his head rather than just going on what he was sort of feeling at any given time.

"The first time I kissed you, in our rooms on the ship, it was a huge effort not to take it further then. I don't know what came over me when I kissed you in front of my sister and her husband. But it was all I could do not to lose control, tell everyone to leave and join with you right there. Just having my arm around you was intoxicating. When you got hurt"—his voice broke, and he stopped talking for a moment, actually looking away—"and I was able to help you dress and bathe…" Kanir stopped, unable to finish his thought. He took a breath, blew it out. "I've never had to care for somebody like that. It was uncomfortable to see you so hurt and yet it helped me so much to be able to help you."

Kanir looked at his hands then back at me. "I know my family was not very accepting of you at first. Seeing us working together as they did had a huge impact. They might not say it, but by the time we left, they had grafted you into their hearts."

He went on to tell me that his family had some initial doubts about us, mostly because we had been "married" for such a long time without joining. And having chosen an "Earther" didn't help much. Not much was known about us. There was some concern that I wouldn't acclimate to being where I was, that I might never become Kanir's wife as a wife should be. It wasn't a typical marital choice, but then Kanir wasn't a typical Matakian in some ways. And they weren't fooled; they knew something was going on that was not normal, but Kanir had seen that I had begun to turn to him by a small degree. He knew what his kisses were doing to me. The kisses had a similar but less potent effect than joining. And the fact that I had come around to wanting to be his wife was huge to him.

"You know what Tox meant about J'Neer's restraint, don't you?"

"I don't even want to go there." I stifled an embarrassed laugh.

Kanir nodded. "I understand. He finds you attractive. You might as well know that no matter where you are out here, an Earth female is very desirable."

"I'm sorry, Kanir, but I don't understand that. On Earth, I'm not that special. I'm not unsightly, but I'm not considered a beauty either."

"Out here, you are stunning. In many ways."

I didn't know what to say; staying quiet seemed the best way to go.

"When I saw you, I knew I had to have you," Kanir said. "I saw the fire in your eyes when Ronnok displayed you. I knew that no matter what happened, you would make my life interesting. I was willing to wait for a long time for you to come around to me, but I had no idea it would take so long."

I looked away, smiling.

"You're proud of that, aren't you?"

"Yeah, I guess I am."

"You see, it's things like that that make you so endearing." He made me uncomfortable just looking at me for what seemed like a long time. "I love you, Jackie. I don't say it very often, I know. But I would do anything for you. Including go to Usia to help you with what has to be done there."

"I love you too, Kanir."

When we were dressed, we went into the corridor. J'Neer was in his room with the door open, waiting for us. We could smell something cooking somewhere in the vast network of corridors.

"It's about time, you two," J'Neer commented.

"Good morning to you too," I said then looked at Kanir. "Did she make it back?" I asked.

"I don't know. There's a kitchen out this way and somebody's using it. Let's go see."

We started down the corridor, the lights again leading the way, shutting down as we left the last space. The smell grew deliciously stronger as we progressed forward. It smelled like something baking, and maybe some kind of meat cooking as well. It made my mouth water in anticipation. I thought there was also the comforting fragrance of good coffee brewing. So far, what passed for coffee out in the great expanse of space left much to be desired. If the aroma I smelled was any indication, this coffee might not be disappointing. Kanir lead us into a large kitchen where Tox was busy cooking over a woodstove.

"Tox!" I yelled.

31

SHE TURNED AROUND, eyes bright, like nothing had happened the night before. The outfit she'd had on the night before was gone. Now she wore a dress that fell to her ankles in a subdued gray.

"I wondered if you three would ever get up," she commented. "We have some things that need to be taken care of today before you can leave." She carried a pan of some kind of meat to a large kitchen table that was already set for the four of us. She already had out some kind of breakfast cake.

"Ah, gidku," Kanir said, taking a piece of meat from the platter and taking a bite. "It's been a while." He handed the morsel to me. "It's commonly used as a breakfast meat here." I sniffed it and took a bite. It was almost similar to bacon, just a bit chewier and spicier, not very different from a good jerky.

We all sat down at the table after Tox brought what I figured was their answer to coffee. She poured some of the dark liquid into each cup. I added a bit of the brown-colored sugar on the table, as well as some cream, took a sip, and closed my eyes.

"Good?" Tox asked.

"Better than good. We need ten pounds of this before we leave. I'm impressed that despite the technology out here, a good cup of coffee is so hard to find."

When had I become a coffee snob?

I put a piece of cake on my plate. "So what happened to you last night?" I asked.

"Well, first of all, I'm very glad you three took off and left me. I knew I could handle what would happen. I set my circuits to keep that charge from doing any permanent damage. And when the charge left my body, it was accompanied by a bit of radiation that kept them from locating you right away. It hung in the air for nearly an hour. Nothing dangerous, of course. Just something to keep you hidden for the time I figured it would take you to get a good distance away. It also hid me, and I was able to regenerate what I needed to get back here. And once I got here, I did some repairs, and here we are."

We were filling our plates and eating as she told us how she had handled the attack the night before. I looked at Kanir. He smiled as he chewed a piece of the cake.

"Do you have a ship we can use?" J'Neer asked.

"Yes, I do."

"Will you be coming with us?" Kanir asked.

"If the offer still stands, I will. I'm afraid I've overstayed my welcome, after last night."

"And a half," I added.

"Tell me about this ship," J'Neer said.

"Well, there's not much to tell, except that it's an older model."

"How old?" J'Neer asked suspiciously.

"It's pretty old but reliable. I take it out from time to time and keep it up. It's kind of a relic, a Hemuu Naagen."

J'Neer was obviously impressed. "Does it run on trithal, or did you have it reconstructed to use drimice?"

It seemed men and vehicles were the same everywhere. They went on about the ship during the length of breakfast. By the time we had finished eating, I was full of food and information on this ship that would take all four of us to our next stop.

We collected the backpacks we had come with after taking care of the breakfast mess, and then Tox led us down a long corridor to a huge hangar. In the middle of it was a ship that was just a bit larger than the shuttle we had been in just the day before and obviously much older. It had some dents and scratches here and there, as well as a few scorch marks.

I looked at J'Neer. He had been transformed into a kid with a toy he was seeing for the first time. Tox opened a door, and we all stepped inside. It was cramped, but it would get us to where we needed to go.

J'Neer immediately helped himself to what I figured was the driver's seat. Tox sat beside him. Kanir and I sat in two seats behind them.

"Where's the garage door?" I asked.

Tox pressed some buttons on the panel in front of her, and the wall before us disintegrated much as the one had last night. A few more buttons and switches and the ship lifted off the ground and left the hangar. Tox took us immediately upward. It seemed mere moments and we were breaking through the atmosphere, back into space. By some miracle we weren't detected or followed. Tox commented a moment later that the damping field on the ship was still functioning.

Once we had left the planet's atmosphere, J'Neer got a message off to the battle cruiser that was supposed to be waiting for us. We were still at least a day away from where we were to meet it. It was humbling to think that a huge ship would be transporting us to Usia, it's primary concern getting me there safely. I prayed that I wouldn't let things like this go to my head and make me ineffective as a leader.

How did it happen that I had gone a few months ago from trying to get back to Earth with absolutely no interest in being a leader of some planet I had never even heard of, to where I was now, willing to do this to the point where I was reading as much as I could on topics of leadership, motivation, diplomacy, and other things pertinent to what I had to do. Had I settled for this, knowing there was no alternative? Was there really no alternative? Had I tried hard enough to get away and find a way back to Earth? Of course, now so much of it was moot; I was where I was. Kidnapped, traded, sold, married, and now being taken to what had been my original destination. I didn't feel trapped so much as I felt overwhelmed with everything.

Kanir put his hand over mine, where it rested on my leg. We were on the bench behind J'Neer and Tox.

"What?" he asked.

I shook my head.

"Jackie, you're going to be fine," he whispered.

I nodded. "I know. So much has happened. Keeps happening."

"That's life."

I smiled ruefully. "This isn't where my life was going four months ago. Four months ago, I wasn't being chased by some crazy person who wanted to kill me. I had never even thought about being out here in space. I wasn't considering getting married. My biggest concerns were keeping up my ticket quota and whether or not to get a dog. It's really tempting to go back and live a simple life there with you."

Kanir's eyes were serious. "Once things settle down and become a bit peaceful, maybe we can work on making life simple."

"How do you define simple out here?" I asked.

"I suppose whatever you want it to be."

I nodded. "Everything is relevant."

"You're right."

We just looked at each other for a moment. His eyes were mesmerizing; I still sometimes felt like I was falling into the warm darkness of them. He pulled me close and kissed me.

"This isn't good," J'Neer commented.

"I don't know about that," I said, resting my head on Kanir's shoulder.

I could just make out J'Neer's reflection in the forward window. "I'm sure," he said sarcastically and then, "The message we sent out just came back not received."

"Okay, what does that mean?" I asked, figuring it wasn't a good sign.

"It means," Kanir started, "the ship either isn't where it's supposed to be, or something has happened to it." He paused for a moment. "Or their communications are not functioning the way they should."

None of us said anything for a while. It was just quiet. I knew so little about all that was out here, I didn't know what to say or what to ask. I had a bad feeling that communications had little to do with the ship not receiving J'Neer's message. It was one more thing that added to the feeling of being overwhelmed by so much.

"We'll just keep going," Tox said matter-of-factly. "We'll know soon enough. J'Neer, keep sending that message, maybe it is just their communications. Even out here, equipment fails. No system is perfect, things break down."

I could see Kanir's almost smile. "I see you brought along your positive attitude, Tox."

"Negativity doesn't get anyone anywhere. On the chance there is a problem the cruiser can't overcome, we should have a plan."

"Hard to plan for," J'Neer said.

"Perhaps," Tox agreed. "If we find debris from the ship, what do you want to do?"

"Get to the nearest space station, contact Usia, and get started toward there again."

"And if the ship is disabled or under attack?"

Kanir said, "We can't afford to risk losing this ship. We're not armed the way we would need to be to assist in any attack. They would be on their own, and we would have to avoid the area as much as we could and continue on our way."

"Does D'Nar have a ship that can go up against a battle cruiser?" I asked.

"D'Nar has resources that are the envy of some galaxies," J'Neer said.

"Can one of you come up with some good news?" I asked.

"This is it," J'Neer replied. "We can come up with some contingency plans, just in case. That's good news."

I sighed. "I guess it beats the snot out of getting caught with your pants down," I remarked.

"What does getting caught with our pants down have to do with anything?" Kanir asked.

Tox regarded me curiously as I replied, "Just an Earth saying, means being unprepared."

32

"THIS IS IT," J'Neer stated.

The forward shield revealed just open space with stars and planets in the distance. None of us said anything for a short time. I didn't know what was going on, but it didn't feel right. J'Neer and Tox were working the panels in front of them, their fingers trying to ply some kind of answer from the ship. We all kept looking from the panels to the shield in front of us and back to the panels. I didn't know what exactly to look for, but the others did. I could feel the tension in the small space starting to grow. Something was obviously not right, but nobody was saying a whole lot.

I thought I saw something on the shield and pointed. "What was that?"

Kanir had seen it too and was trying to get a closer look at the panels in front of Tox and J'Neer. "Get us out of here!" Kanir shouted.

"What—" I began.

"Now!" Kanir shouted again.

The ship leapt forward.

"Tox, the damping—" Kanir started.

"Already on it, dear," she said calmly.

Two huge ships snapped into view. Their size was impressive one at a time; together they were impressively intimidating. Their massiveness dwarfed our little ship, making us feel insignificant. It was stunning to see them as they seemed to fill up every inch of space on the shield and get lost off the sides of it.

"Why aren't we moving?" Kanir asked.

J'Neer was struggling with the panel in front of him. "They had us in a tractor beam before we could do anything. I'm trying to break free, but nothing's working."

"Tox, what happened to the damping field?"

"I don't know. I think they may have been able to do a scatter field and got us that way."

"Break it!"

"I can't, Kanir. This ship isn't equipped for every contingency. It's just a small jump ship."

Our little craft was groaning in protest as J'Neer continued to try to do something to pull us away from where we were being taken.

"We need a plan. We can't break free," J'Neer said.

"Are they both D'Nar's ships?" I asked.

"No," Kanir answered. "The one furthest away is from Usia."

"It's the battle cruiser we were supposed to meet," J'Neer added.

"The other, closer one is D'Nar, or someone working for him."

"What do we do?" I asked, trying not to sound as panicked as I felt.

"This ship is from Minrokuh," J'Neer said, "D'Nar's from Xermanth. He might not even be on board."

"They want me dead! Someone has orders!" I said. Kanir took my hand.

"If he's not here, we'll be taken to him," J'Neer said. "He will want to be the one to take you out."

"Please tell me that's not supposed to make me feel better," I said.

"No, I'm saying that if he's not on this ship, we have time."

"J'Neer, they're not going to send us on a scavenger hunt to win our way out!" I argued.

"Jackie, he's saying we have time. We can get out of this."

I wiped at a tear that strayed from my eyes. I was terrified and didn't know what to do. The thought of having to go up against D'Nar again had me panicking. The man had orders to kill me! Something in my head said, "Roll film!" I was not ready to see the parade of my life pass before me on the screen of my mind.

Kanir grabbed me by the shoulders. "Jackie, you'll be all right. I won't let them hurt you."

"You can't guarantee that! He's—"

"Are you giving up?" he asked.

"No, of course not! I...I just remember what he was like last time. I don't want to go through that again. He's not going to give us a chance, Kanir. We'll all be killed. He won't think twice about it."

"Jackie, you're panicking. You can't think like this. Take a deep breath."

The breath I took shook me hard, but I took a couple more at his order. I wanted to fall into his arms, but he held me away from him at arm's length.

"Jackie. You're an officer. Get yourself together," he ordered tersely.

I nodded. I took a deep breath and held it for a moment then let it out slowly. I wiped at the tears that left my eyes and nodded. I forced my mouth not to tremble.

"Okay," I whispered. "What do we do?"

"All of you settle down," Tox ordered. I suddenly realized she had been trying to get our attention for the entire time I had gone into panic mode. What was that about anyway? I was not one to panic. I worked out the problems in my life as best I could. This was just one more.

The three of us looked to where Tox still sat at the helm.

"If you three will just stop, I can get some things going to help us. Sit down so I can get to the rear of the ship."

We sat as quickly as we could. Tox climbed over the seats to the rear of the shuttle and began opening the few cabinets that were back there. She was systematically pulling out different things and laying them out. It looked like there was three of everything.

"What are you putting together, Tox?" Kanir asked.

"Well, it's something I've sort of experimented with before. It works, but not for long. Give me a few minutes to assemble them…"

"So what are they?"

"Personal damping fields. They will make you three invisible for about an hour, each. It will be enough time for you to get out of here, onto the big ship, and find another way off."

"But they already know we're here," I argued.

"Do they?" Kanir said. "All the ships that were sent out all had life form readings on them, yet no life forms. They were also programmed to fight any kind of capture much as we have. We stand a very good chance of beating this."

Tox's hands were a blur as she set about putting together the small gizmos that would help us escape. I felt a bit better but was still uncertain. This ship we were a few minutes away from entering was huge enough to get lost in, which was not a comforting thought.

Tox handed us each a gray metal wristband with an odd attachment that looked like a cross between a watch face and the tiniest computer I had ever seen. She helped us secure them on our wrists.

"The small black button on the right is the power button. Once you are invisible, you will be the only one who can see them. The display will show you how much time you have left. It does its own countdown. You will not see each other clearly but as shadows. On my mark, push the black button. We'll be in the ship very shortly now."

We continued to watch our progression toward the ship. We were close enough to see some detail on the outside of the ship when Tox had us power up our fields. Instantly, I could make out J'Neer and Kanir as shadowy figures.

"Can you two hear me?" J'Neer asked.

"Yes," Kanir and I answered together.

It was a matter of about another three minutes and our small craft was swallowed into the ship. It was an immense hangar, with a few other craft on the sides. Straight ahead, we could see a control booth of sorts, several people behind glass observing our ship landing on the metal floor.

Tox flipped a switch on the panel. We heard a bit of static and then, "Welcome aboard the Toska. Be prepared to be boarded and taken into custody on behalf of D'Nar of Xermanth."

I felt a cold chill sweep through my body. I fought off the panic attack that threatened to return. I could do this. I had dealt with this man already. I had been kidnapped by him; I had killed, at his order, to stay alive and keep my family safe from him and his men. He had sold me to another man. He now had orders to kill me. I prayed the wristbands would be enough to get us out of this predicament and back on our way to Usia.

Kanir was at my side, and I could feel his comforting arm around my waist.

"We're going to be fine, Jackie," he repeated.

"I know," I answered.

I reminded myself in the quiet of the ship that nothing had yet happened that I hadn't been able to handle without help from the people God had sent my way. I marveled again for the millionth time in my life at how He always provided what was needed. Maybe not in my timing, but who was I to argue that with the creator of the universe? It was time to put on my big girl stuff again and fight like I meant it.

Kanir gave my hand a squeeze. "That's my girl," he said, sensing the change in my attitude.

Sirens blared a few times as other odd noises filled the hangar and our ship to some degree. The walls of the hangar were an odd shade of gray shot through with white flecks. Black lettering I didn't recognize was on different parts of the walls and floor. Within a few minutes, all the noise stopped, and we watched as a number of armed guards came from the control room. They came to the side door where Tox quickly admitted them. Kanir took my hand, and the three of us left the shuttle as soon as the last guard entered. We stood outside for just a few seconds.

"Where are the beings who were with you?" one of the guards asked Tox.

"I'm sorry sir. Beings? It's just me here."

"We picked up three life forms with you. Where are they?"

"Oh, those! Those would be the ones I always program into my computer to keep me company."

"You expect us to believe—"

"Just watch, sir." We could hear the responding beeps as Tox did some things at the forward panel, and then we heard our voices, talking, laughing. It was all conversations we had been having. We took a very short glance into the shuttle and saw three holographic images that were not us having the conversations we were hearing.

J'Neer grabbed my elbow, and we ran for a door. He seemed to know where he was going. The door opened and then closed again once we were through. We were in an empty room that had two doors on each side.

"Where are we?" I asked.

"A hallway into the ship," J'Neer answered. "We need to find someplace to get info on how to get off of this ship, and a ship to get us out of here."

"Do you know the layout of this one?" Kanir asked.

"Yes. The problem will be doing it under the radar so they don't see us." He reached out and made us flatten ourselves against the far wall. A second later, three uniformed guards walked from the side door on the left and out to the hangar. We took a peek out onto the hangar and could see through the shield on the ship that Tox was holding her own with the team that was in there with her. The three who went through the door were heading for her small craft.

"Come on," J'Neer said and took us through the other door.

As we passed different crewmen, we silently flattened ourselves on a wall and let them pass. It was the craziest, scariest thing I could imagine. I looked down at the timer on my wristband. I was impressed we had used so much time. It didn't seem as if we had used more than a few minutes, but the wristband indicated we had used more than that. J'Neer took us down hallways, up a couple flights of stairs, finally into another hangar. It faced the other ship, which we could see beyond the force shield that kept the crew working on the floor of the hangar safe and with plenty of fresh air. J'Neer ducked us into a room off the small hallway. There was equipment all over the place that seemed to be monitoring a number of things I couldn't even guess at.

J'Neer went to one of the monitors that seemed to be dormant, and after some initial difficulty, he was logged on. It took a few minutes, but he was able to find out that the ship out there was indeed from Usia and had been boarded by D'Nar's men. The battle was on for control of the ship. It had been identified as the ship that was to meet us. D'Nar was not far from us and would be on board shortly.

"We need to find uniforms," J'Neer said and began searching the ship through the computer to get us to someplace on board that kept the crews laundry.

"Let's go," J'Neer said, and we took off, us following him again through the maze of hallways and stairways for the next three minutes, dodging the crew more times than was comfortable. We had just reached the final hallway, when we physically ran into two guards coming from the other direction. I wasn't even sure how it had happened. One second we were passing them, and then next, they seemed to step out of the direction they were going, and were in our paths so quickly, there was no time to react. The two of them grunted, one of them falling flat on his back. The three of us fell against each other and the wall, still unable to be seen. We straightened up and hugged the wall.

"What was that?" The one who had fallen asked, as his partner gave him a hand to his feet.

"Don't know," the other replied.

They both began looking closely at the walls around them as we backed up. The first one went to a panel on the wall, punched in some information.

"There are other life forms here," he reported and detailed what he and his partner had just experienced. Once he was done reporting, he and his partner began looking around wildly for us.

We had already turned to run the other way. J'Neer took us down a couple of hallways and then into a room that turned out to be a closet. We sat on the floor for a moment, panting as much from the run as from fear. We switched off our bands to save what time we had left.

"We were in the corridor to the laundry in this area of the ship," J'Neer said finally. "It's going to be harder to get back there now."

"This isn't too different from the first time you tried to escape from me, is it?" Kanir commented, half smile in place.

I nodded. It seemed like forever ago when that happened. J'Neer looked at us questioningly, and we filled him in on the brief attempt I had made to try to leave within days of coming into his possession.

J'Neer smiled knowingly. "She can be scrappy when the need arises," he commented.

"There has to be more than one laundry on a ship this size, right?" I asked.

J'Neer nodded. "Yes, but the other one is on the other side of the ship, much harder to get to."

"I don't think we have a choice now," I said. "Let's just figure out where over there, how to get there and go."

"Not that easy, now that they know they're looking for more people."

"Then let's just take some of the crew out and use their uniforms and get the heck out of here."

"You make it sound so easy," Kanir half smiled again.

"Well, come on. We still have the element of surprise to some degree. Let's just do it."

J'Neer seemed to be contemplating what I was suggesting. "I don't know." He looked at me, shaking his head. "Too much of your planet's people watch too many movies."

"Please, life imitates art and the other way around all the time. Do you have a better plan?"

He shook his head. "No, I don't. What do you think, Kanir?"

"I think it's a good thing she's on our side."

"Thank you, Kanir," I said, genuinely touched.

"Before this melts into something else, let's get going," J'Neer said, standing.

Kanir and I also stood. We switched on the bands. We had another forty minutes of coverage left. J'Neer eased the door open, and we stepped into the hallway quickly. There was a lot of sporadic activity, but about twenty minutes later, three people were unconscious, bound with wire he had found in a cabinet. We were all dressed in the uniform of the day. We kept the communications devices to look official and know what was going on. And there was plenty of radio traffic to keep us up on what was going on. There was a lot to be said about knowing what was happening around us. We each had a side arm as well, and the two men gave me some direction on firing it. It was going to be as easy, or even easier, than the firearms I used in my previous life.

The area of the ship we had just left was swarming with activity, all in an effort to locate us, and that effort was spreading out to other areas of the ship. I heard someone inquiring about some kind of equipment that I was sure was meant to disable the power of our bands. We stood up straight and tall and walked through the corridors, past personnel who recognized the uniform and didn't question who was in it. J'Neer took us into another computer room where he set about finding another hangar with a shuttle or similar vehicle that could get us off this ship.

"We need to get below to this hangar." J'Neer pointed to a section of the ship. "We are here." He pointed to another section of the ship about six floors above where we had to go. "This is going to be hard to navigate. They're already all over the bay corridors. They know what we're trying to do. If we keep our heads and just do our best to blend in, we should be able to make it. It's going to be pretty intense. D'Nar's not a man anyone wants to cross, and he's already frustrated with his men for letting us slip through their fingers twice. If they fail a third time, he's likely to send them packing. Or worse."

"Ever the fount of positive vibes," I commented.

"He's right," Kanir said.

I sighed heavily and nodded. "Okay. So what do we do?"

"We'll do it this way: We're going to go take the same route, but spaced apart. I'll go first, Jackie's behind me by about twenty feet, and Kanir's behind you by the same distance. They may be expecting to see us together, so splitting us up like this might just work."

"If one of us gets caught?" I asked.

"The other two activate the wristbands and get back here. If this place is occupied, we should be together enough to get somewhere else."

I nodded, even less assured than I had been. I closed my eyes. I had such a bad feeling about this and was working on some positive self-talk inside my head. We could do this. We had to do this.

Kanir put his arm around my waist, and I rested my head on his shoulder. J'Neer looked at us for a moment, quietly just observing, then he shook his head.

"What?" I asked.

"The worst word in the world keeps going through my head. "If."

I considered what he said for a few seconds and nodded. I had my own list of "if" scenarios. J'Neer was right. It wasn't a good word; it kept us in the past. We needed to move on and make this happen.

I said a quiet prayer with my eyes closed. I felt Kanir take my hand; I could feel that he was doing the same. We took a few minutes to make sure we were all ready and started out as planned. We had a good twenty-minute hike through the ship to get to the hangar. I kept J'Neer in my sight ahead of me yet kept my eyes neutral around the wide corridors. We passed numerous small squads of armed personnel.

A couple of times I heard radio chatter, hearing something about the people they were looking for. It was unsettling to hear it and be right next to the ones looking for us, pass them, knowing we were the ones being sought. Forget unsettling; it was downright unnerving. It was so tempting to cut and run, get away. I kept the goal in my head. J'Neer turned a corner ahead of me. I turned it twenty feet later. I knew Kanir was right behind me. When it came time to get on one of the elevator cars, I got on following J'Neer and got off after him, briefly going down a different corridor, then doubling back to stay behind him. I heard the door whoosh open behind me a few seconds later and knew that Kanir wasn't far behind me. We were moving as fast as we could without attracting attention, and each time we turned a corner, it got scarier. At any time, one of the people we were passing could recognize us. We had been moving for a good seven minutes now. It was going so smoothly, it was almost scary.

I kept telling myself not to get cocky. Cocky always ends badly. Moving through the ship in the uniform of the day was definitely riskier than going through cloaked by our wristband gizmos. This way felt so incredibly vulnerable.

The brief conversations I had been hearing on the radio stopped abruptly. I tapped the earpiece a couple of times, but nothing happened. I didn't think it was a good sign.

I watched J'Neer ahead of me duck into a room. I followed him in, and a moment later, Kanir joined us. We were in a meeting room of some sort. There were maps and charts on one wall, a meeting table in the middle of the room surrounded by about eight chairs, and a viewing screen on another wall.

"Something's wrong," J'Neer announced.

"I hear it too," Kanir agreed.

"What is it?" I asked.

"I don't know. I was listening to conversations on the radio, and it sounds like they found the guards we left back there. And then the radio went dead."

Kanir and I both said something about the same thing happening to our radios.

"We need to get rid of the radios. Take them off now. There's too much of a chance that they have some kind of locator on them. I think D'Nar might be on board already.

We're going on invisibility from here. When we get closer, you two will hang back while I check out the hangar."

We had taken off the radio earpieces. The second we placed them on the table in the room, they disappeared, obviously traveled out of the room.

"Oh crap," I whispered. My two partners said something I believed was a swear word, likely not as mild as the one I used.

"We've got to get out of here and off this ship," Kanir said.

We turned on the wristbands and left the room. We were going down the corridors again. It was scarier than before. I knew that despite not being able to be seen, it was still likely that the person they had summoned with the equipment to locate us could be exactly where we were headed. We turned a corner, and there was D'Nar. I could feel my heart speed up and get louder at the same time. I prayed our invisibility was not an illusion to us. He was walking briskly in our direction, eyes focused ahead of us, yet scanning the area ahead of him at the same time, his face a study of quiet fury and determination. He was spitting out orders to the two men with him.

I felt Kanir take my hand and lead me along, past D'Nar and on down the corridor. I glanced back a couple of times to be sure he was still going in the opposite direction. This was not fun. I thought of the times I had to step out of my comfort zone when I had been a police officer. The times I had gone into a building or residence taking the point, working with the SWAT team. Handling shootouts, going into some of the low-income housing areas where young, fearless gangsters were not afraid to take out a cop and spend the next bunch of formative years in a prison cell. Some considered it a badge of honor in the crowds they moved in. The apprehension and fear I had felt at those times was usurped by the determination to get the job done quickly and go home safely. I had stuck it out, gotten through it, and grown.

This wasn't any different, as long as I got through it and lived to tell about it.

Please, please, please…

We kept moving toward the other hangar, walking quickly. We had another twenty minutes of time on the bands, and we were minutes away from getting there. I didn't understand the signs on the walls as passed them, but every now and then, Kanir would whisper in my ear what it was, as long as none of the crew was around to hear a disembodied voice. He kept me informed about how close we were to our destination.

We turned one more corner; Kanir whispered that the bay door was just ahead. J'Neer started to press a code into the panel beside the door.

"Wait," I said.

"What? We need to move now," J'Neer said.

"No, she's right," Kanir said. "This was too easy. There's nobody around here. They're waiting for us somewhere here. J'Neer, let me take it from here. I know these ships. I've built them. Follow me."

"Where?"

"We don't have time for me to explain. Just follow me." Kanir took my hand, and we took off in the direction we had been moving. I glanced back in time to see several armed crew members come from the room we had just contemplated entering.

One of them lifted a handheld instrument just as we turned a corner. Kanir led us down another corridor that ended abruptly. We could hear footsteps behind us.

"Great, now we're blocked in!" J'Neer commented.

Kanir stopped, studying the wall for about one second. He ran his hand down the wall then stopped just at hip level, striking it twice. The wall opened up, we stepped inside, and Kanir struck the space above the door, making it close again. We all took a deep breath. I leaned back against the wall behind me, mere feet from the wall in front of me that we had just come through.

We could hear voices on the other side of the wall. Something about the life signs having disappeared, no clue as to what had happened to them, and were they really there in the first place.

33

"FIND THEM!" D'NAR's angry voice was unmistakable through the wall, followed by retreating footsteps. There was no doubt that at least one person was left behind to see if we came out of hiding.

I could hear Kanir running his hand along another wall, and then lights came up dimly above us.

"What do we do now?" I asked.

"No need to whisper," Kanir said. "You would have to yell to be heard, as demonstrated by our friend out there."

"What is this place?" J'Neer asked.

"These were built into a lot of ships. All close to travelers and shuttle bays, just in case hiding was necessary. Out here, you never know what you might run into. Not too many owners know about these places. Ships get sold so many times, the owners forget to pass the information about these rooms to the new owners."

J'Neer nodded.

We all looked around the room we were in. It was small, just enough room for a handful of people. The walls were an unfinished dark gray, with darker patches here and there. There were no furnishings, but there were two video screens on opposite walls from each other, one next to the doorway we had come through, the other across from there. I figured there had to be another doorway next to it.

"Is there another way out?" J'Neer asked.

"Most times, yes. They're well hidden on both sides of the walls. Once we're out, we need to get to the engine room."

"We need to get off this thing, not steer it," J'Neer argued.

"I've let you run us around enough already. We go to the engine room and shut down some operations, prepare the ones we need, and get out of here."

"I don't think that's a good idea."

"J'Neer, I've kept my feelings about your plans to myself so far. You're a good officer in every way, but in this case, you're not doing too well, and I don't want to risk our lives any more tonight. You let me run this part of things for a while, or we just stay here."

I could feel the tension in the air. The testosterone was thick in the room, and watching the two men in front of me, I hoped they would settle this peacefully. J'Neer regarded Kanir quietly. I could just make out the flashing of his eyes. Pride was on the line here, and he wasn't happy about it.

"What do you think?" J'Neer asked me.

"I think he's right. D'Nar knows what we're trying to do, and no matter what shuttle hangar we go to, they will have someone waiting for us. If we can travel in these uniforms and use the damping field once we're in the engine room, I think we can make some things happen that will help us."

J'Neer wasn't happy about it, but he was outnumbered. "Okay, so what's your plan to get there, Kanir?"

Kanir crossed to the screen on the opposite wall we had come through and began pressing buttons on a panel below it. He brought up a map of the immediate area then scaled it down, bringing up a map of where we were to where the engine room was located.

"That's not far at all," I commented.

"No, it's not. We leave this room and go straight down the hall to the transport, down one level, and at the end of that corridor. We have seventeen minutes of damping left, we probably will need less than five to get there. You two will wait in this access room here." He showed us a room down the corridor from engineering. "I'll slip into engineering and program a few things to help us get out of here."

"Such as?" J'Neer asked.

"I can orchestrate a couple of emergencies. Power and life support outages, which we can make happen over half the ship, then start a self-destruct countdown. Once that's in place, we're in one of the hundreds of escape pods that get off the ship."

"Can you do a self-destruct without being one of the ship's command crew?" I asked.

"My…our company put it all in place. There are ways to override whatever commands they have initiated and start an SD countdown. Shouldn't take more than a few minutes."

"How far do we have to go to get to an escape shuttle?" J'Neer asked, newly intrigued.

"They're actually all over the outside of the ship at strategic points. There are a large number there between all the personnel in engineering and the other departments in that area. We won't have a problem getting near that area and into one."

Kanir took a moment to show us via the map the close proximity from engineering to the emergency shuttles. It wouldn't take long at all. Even if the bands failed at this point, there would be so much confusion and chaos we would easily blend into what was going on around us. Even if somebody recognized us, the desire to live another day would outweigh the desire to gain points with D'Nar and capture us.

We hoped…

"What about Tox?" I asked. "Shouldn't we find a way to get her off here too?"

"I'm sorry, Jackie," Kanir said, "there's no way to do that. Knowing Tox, I wouldn't be too concerned. I fully expect to see her again, probably sooner than later. She hasn't gotten to be as old as she is and not be extremely resourceful."

I nodded, but I wasn't happy about this. The woman… machine—whatever—had gotten us out of a couple of jams while we took off, saving our own skins. There was just something wrong about not doing something to help her. But time was a huge issue right now, and realistically, there was no time to look for her. There was no reasonable way to figure out where they had taken her, or if they had launched her into space. That was a scary thought and made me shiver.

—◈—

The corridors were active with personnel still looking for us. Somehow, we managed to avoid colliding with many of them. Just because we couldn't be seen didn't mean we weren't there physically.

We ducked into the closet down the corridor from engineering.

"Wait here," Kanir said.

"How long will you be?" I asked.

Kanir kissed the top of my head. "Not long, my love. Ten minutes at the most and then we leave." He gave my mouth a quick kiss, eyed J'Neer briefly, and left.

"Show-off," J'Neer commented quietly.

"What's your problem?"

He shook his head. "Nothing. Just some of those 'if's' coming up again."

"I know you don't like how things have worked out. I mean about Kanir and me being married."

"No, I don't like it. It has made a difficult situation harder to navigate."

"I'm sure. But I'm glad he's with me for what's going to be expected of me once we get to Usia. He's been a business leader and respected employer, and he's worked closely with the leaders of his planet to build his business. He's a man of integrity—"

"Integrity?" J'Neer quietly snorted. "If he is a man of integrity, why did he marry you? Why weren't you taken to where you were supposed to go, or at least back to Earth? Your *man of integrity* has done everything he can to keep you with him, to avoid having you taken from him when he got caught. I don't see integrity. I see a man who took advantage of a situation for himself."

"I understand what you're saying. But he's going to bring so many things into this position that I am going to depend on, J'Neer. He may have taken advantage of a situation, but I'm going to be taking advantage of his knowledge and experience."

J'Neer shook his head. "I guess we'll just have to see."

"He's the first person who didn't want to make a profit on me since I was taken from my home. Didn't want to humiliate me or hurt me. Up until Kanir stepped into this picture, my life was in total chaos. I know this is not an ideal situation. I have D'Nar to worry about again, and Lord knows who else is out there who might take his place, but it's still a whole lot better than what it was." I paused. "If it wasn't Kanir we're dealing with, it could be somebody considerably worse."

"At least I'd be able to get you out of whatever that situation would have been. I can't even separate you two, or you both die. Jackie, don't be fooled by him. He's a smart man. He's got some of the warrior in him. He knows what to do to manipulate a situation. And don't depend solely on him once you're on Usia and running the show. I don't trust him, and you shouldn't either."

"I don't think any leader should depend on one source for counsel."

"Just remember that," he said pointedly.

We were quiet for a moment.

"J'Neer, what are you going to do once you get us to Usia?"

"I have no idea. Find someplace to work until my next assignment, probably."

"I'd like you to stay there. Head up security or something. I'm sure there's a position there somewhere that would fit you."

J'Neer half smiled. "I don't think so, Jackie. I'm not meant to be in one place for long. I get bored and cranky. I need to be doing exactly what I'm doing here. Being a bit of a mercenary, fighting off the bad guys on foreign ground."

"How much are you being paid?" I asked.

J'Neer laughed quietly, looking at me. "Why? Are you going to try to buy me?"

"No, I'm wondering how much I'm worth, I suppose."

"It's none of your business," he replied. "I can tell you it's some of the biggest money I've ever made. They want you there desperately. You're needed. But if you really want to know, ask your staff when you get to Usia."

"Would you just check in with me from time to time?"

"What for?"

"I don't know. You've kind of grown on me, I suppose. You've rescued me from a couple of situations, and I guess there's a part of me that wants you around."

"What about your husband?"

"I'm not talking about some kind of liaison, J'Neer," I retorted. I took a deep breath. "I'm just thinking you might be someone to seek out for counsel once in a while. But you're probably right. I don't need to complicate matters any more than they already are."

"If you ever need counsel, I'll make sure you have a way to reach me before I leave. And I'll check in on you from time to time."

"I would appreciate that."

We lapsed into silence for a few minutes, waiting for Kanir to return. I felt anxious about the whole thing. I was sure J'Neer was concerned about Kanir and this plan as well.

I thought about what J'Neer had said about Kanir. I understood his concerns. Kanir had set himself up pretty nicely, pairing up with me. As much as I didn't like how he had manipulated the situation, I could honestly say that I had accepted it for what it was. We were married, and the consummation of the marriage had set it in stone. There was no getting out of it. I hadn't considered not trusting the man, but I could see what J'Neer was talking about.

I wished desperately again that my life was my own and not complicated. As much as I was willing to go to Usia and be the leader, I still really wanted to return to Earth. Married to Kanir, that would be almost impossible now. Nothing was easy anywhere, I suppose. Everywhere I turned, there was another wrinkle in the story of my life as it was happening. I wasn't certain my life would ever feel as if it wasn't couched in chaos. Just that thought alone was tiring. I didn't want to be fighting some battle on some front all the time for my entire life. I wanted peace. I wanted normalcy, whatever that was. I just wanted things to be the way they were before I ever opened the envelope that introduced me to what was going on now.

I sighed and leaned back against the wall behind me.

"What?" J'Neer said.

"Nothing," I replied. "My life is such a crazy collection of weirdness."

"Yes, it is. But rest assured, so is everyone else's."

"J'Neer, that's not comforting."

"Not supposed to be. When you get to Usia, it'll probably get weirder still, for a while. Once you get things settled and in place, your life might quiet down for a bit. But then you'll get tired of the same old thing all the time and want a bit of chaos to liven it up. That will be exactly when the planet falls off its axis long enough to send everyone into a panic, and once it's righted, you'll be back to the same old things again. That's just the way life goes. There's an uncanny rhythm to it. Probably a different rhythm from what you had on Earth. But you'll find it and you'll be all right."

I paused, thinking about what he'd just shared. "That's deeply prophetic, J'Neer."

He shrugged. "Don't expect that from me all the time."

I nodded.

It was just a few more minutes before Kanir returned. He slipped into the room, and J'Neer and I got to our feet.

"How'd it go?" I asked.

"Fine. Things should start to happen in the next two minutes."

"Like what?" J'Neer asked.

"Major core breach of the engines, followed by a wall breach of the entire port side of the ship, which will cause a massive explosion when the atmosphere is gone. We need to go. We need to be in place by the escape pods when this starts to break apart."

"Will they be able to stop any of this?" J'Neer asked.

"Not in time," Kanir replied. "Turn on your bands and let's go."

We slipped invisibly into the corridor and made our way through several more corridors. We arrived at a long hallway that was obviously different. There was door after door along one wall, each with some kind of writing on them that I was sure designated the pod number, possibly even a letter. Half a minute later, the ship shuddered, knocking us off our feet. There were two crewmen in the corridor with us who also fell to the floor. Alarms sounded instantly, and half a minute later, the ship shook again with such force, we nearly fell to the floor again. A siren began wailing, followed by an announcement that the ship was heavily damaged, and all should proceed to the escape pods. Kanir went to one of doors. He pressed a code into the panel beside the door. The door whooshed open, and we stepped inside.

There were other people doing the same thing at other doors. It was obvious that they were waiting for other people, trying to make sure that each pod did not leave the ship with fewer men than it could hold.

Kanir was at the control panel, fingers flying across the board. J'Neer and I sat in other seats.

"What are you waiting for?" I asked.

"Not a good idea to be the first one to leave the party," J'Neer offered. Kanir nodded.

That made sense. I could hear and feel slight power thrusts that I realized were some of the pods around us leaving their ports. After a moment of them leaving, the noise stopped. I knew there were many more pods, but nothing was happening. The sirens for the alert still blared, the ship still shuddered from time to time, but that was it. A couple of times, we heard a pod leave, which was followed by the sound of a muffled explosion.

The door to the pod opened. We turned as one to see who was about to discover us, at the same time that we each brought up our weapons. Tox poked her head around the corner. We all just stared for about three seconds.

"At least a greeting please, Jackie," she said.

I sighed. Smiled. Felt relieved. "I didn't know if I'd ever see you again," I said.

"Almost impossible to take me out," she said, smiling. "I just monitor the situation until it seems right to jump back in."

"Monitor. Very good," I said.

"Hello, Tox," Kanir said over his shoulder. "Good to see you made an escape."

"Good to see that you three are so resourceful. You know, D'Nar's not far behind. He's given the order to stop the pods from leaving. Any that leave from here on out will be destroyed. He knows you're in one of these things. They'll be searching the pods within the next few minutes."

Kanir and J'Neer looked at each other.

"Suggestions?" Kanir said.

"Can you do another dampening field?" J'Neer asked.

"It won't help here," Tox replied. "I can't override their monitoring. They'll know we left, and no matter how I dampen this, it won't be enough."

Another challenge to rise above, trying to get away from D'Nar to get to Usia. I could see the gears turning in the men's heads. I had no solution. This was beyond what I could fathom. It wasn't a burglary in progress or anything else I could navigate.

"If it helps," Tox offered, "I am logged into the ship's systems. I can tell you what's going on in almost any part of the ship."

"Let's go get him," I said.

"What?" J'Neer looked like I had grown a third eye in the middle of my forehead.

"I'm tired of running. I'm tired of being pursued. I'm ready to pursue. Let's go get him, take him out, and get out of here."

Kanir regarded me with raised eyebrows while J'Neer looked as if he was seriously considering it.

"We have an element of surprise," I said, trying to argue for my plan, such as it was. "They won't expect us to go after them. Or him."

"Jackie, have you ever killed a man?" J'Neer asked. "Other than the one D'Nar had you execute."

"No," I admitted. "But I was trained to do it if I had to when I was a police officer. Sometimes it has to be done. It will probably have to be done here."

"I don't like it," Kanir said. "I don't want my wife having to—"

"You don't have a choice," I argued. "Look at where we are. We are wasting time. If D'Nar gets to us before we get to him, we're done."

"She's right," Tox said.

We were all quiet as the two men considered my idea.

I was scared out of my skin. What had I just suggested? I was going to have to get some help for the seriously running off at the mouth I seemed to do from time to time. At the same time, I didn't know if there were any other options.

I could feel Kanir in my head. I could feel his concern—fear—for me.

It was times like this that I wished we didn't have this connection. I didn't want him to know what I was feeling, and I didn't know how to keep that from Kanir. Yeah, I was afraid, but I was also afraid that if we didn't do something very quickly—and this was definitely a something—we would be gone with this ship.

Not much of an option, really…

"Okay," J'Neer finally said. "Keep your weapons drawn, down at your side. We stay close to the walls, walk quickly and quietly while we still have damping."

"Damping is gone," Tox supplied. "They have disabled it. You are totally out there."

"Good thing we don't kill the messenger," J'Neer muttered.

"So where do we go to get to D'Nar?" I asked.

"He's actively looking for you," Tox said. "He's two decks below us, heading to this side of the ship where many of the pods are."

"How long do we have before the ship explodes?" I asked.

"Until that wall breach, we have about thirty minutes."

"I don't get it," I said. "Is he willing to go down with his ship?"

"As I understand it, if he does not eliminate you, he will be eliminated. He has nothing to lose," J'Neer supplied.

Heck of a motivator…

"Who's he working for?" I asked.

"I don't know," J'Neer replied. "Someone not aligned with Usia obviously, but beyond that, I don't have a clue. And that doesn't matter now. We need to get out of here."

We took a minute to look at each other.

We all nodded. I looked at the weapon I carried.

"As we take out some of these men, take their weapon if you can," Kanir said. "We're going to need them."

He came to my side and looked down at me. "Are you sure you're ready for this?"

"I'll be all right," I answered quickly to hide my own concerns and fears. Which was silly, since he was so dialed in to me.

Kanir nodded, looking grim. He knew. He kissed me quickly. "You tell me if you can't do this," he said quietly.

"I will. I can do this, Kanir."

He nodded, still searching my eyes.

"If you two are ready?" J'Neer said impatiently.

Tox said, "D'Nar is now on the deck below us. They have begun checking the pods on that deck."

"Let's go. I'm on point," J'Neer said. "I want Kanir behind me followed by Jackie, and Tox can take up the rear."

The ship continued to shudder and shake every few minutes as it continued to deteriorate. Every now and then, the ship seemed to buck strongly enough for us to almost lose our footing. The siren continued to wail on, warning of the impending explosion that would destroy the ship. I kept wondering if we actually had thirty minutes. Given how much and how often the ship seemed to be rattling, I was concerned it could be considerably less.

Not a comforting thought. I didn't want us to be here when the vessel heaved its final death rattle.

We left the room. Several soldiers were on each side of the pod we left, but they were tending to the pods, making sure they were full, as well as keeping watch. Two recognized us and raised their weapons. Before they could fire, the three of us fired on them, beams of destructive light leaping from our weapons, taking all of them out. Their bodies lay on the deck of the ship, lifeless. Those around them paused only briefly then returned to getting the pods loaded.

Rats fleeing a sinking ship…

I allowed myself a brief second to feel nauseous. I could feel the color leave my face. Kanir took my hand, but I pulled away. "I'm okay," I said, turning away back toward where we needed to go. I blinked away tears and bit my lip. *Okay, girl,* I said to myself, *I have to do this. I can do this. Please, God, help me do this.* And then I wondered if it was okay to pray to be able to kill people.

We approached the bodies. Kanir and J'Neer went to two of them to remove weapons. I started toward a third but was motioned by Kanir to stay back. He brought the weapon to me.

"Don't do that again," I said. "I can do this."

He nodded but didn't look happy about it. I figured we could work on happy once we got out of this current situation.

"The next door on your right goes into a stairwell," Tox advised. "It will take us to the lower deck where D'Nar is."

Just before opening the door, three men came from around the corner ahead. I heard J'Neer and Kanir's weapons fire. Tox picked me up and turned me to where two men were approaching at a full run, weapons drawn and about to fire. I fired my weapon, and somehow dropped them both. There was an odd shock wave that went through my body from killing the men. Tox grabbed my hand and pulled me into the stairwell access.

"Jackie?" Kanir said.

"I'm fine." I lied, looking directly at him. I was shaking, and pretty sure my eyes were as big as saucers. This was harder than I thought it would be.

"Let's go," J'Neer said.

Kanir was about to say something. I shook my head "no" and pushed past him to follow J'Neer. We took the stairs to the lower deck, stopping at the door.

"On three," J'Neer said.

I nodded. Kanir pulled me back behind him. J'Neer finished the count and opened the door. We ran into the corridor, shooting, keeping low. Instantly, the world around me was sizzling with laser beams meant for death. When two opposing beams crossed; there was a whine that hurt my ears.

When they met one of the metal walls, there was a pinging sort of sound followed by a sizzle. When a beam struck a body, a whirring sound could be heard almost at the same time that the person struck yelled in startled pain. There was a lot of shouting, thankfully not from us. Tox had stepped behind me, had her arms around me, her hands on my weapon. We turned as one as she guided my weapon from target to target at alarming speed; I just kept firing. I knew it was less than a minute, but it seemed much longer than that.

We stopped and looked around. There had to be over a dozen bodies on the floor. I had no idea how many I was responsible for, and I didn't want to know.

"Did we get him?" I asked. I thought my voice seemed amazingly calm.

"I don't know," J'neer said. We moved around the carnage, looking specifically for D'Nar, keeping watch for any more men. It was horrible being so close to the death that I had taken part in. The worst part of it was that D'Nar wasn't there. We all looked at Tox.

She seemed to be consulting something in her head. "He's in one of the pods, I can't get an accurate read on which one."

Several of the pods left the ship.

"He's still here, and those pods have been destroyed," Tox said.

J'Neer motioned us to follow him. He went to the first pod. He and Kanir took positions on either side of the door to the pod. J'Neer did a finger count to three, Kanir opened the door, and they prepared to blast whoever was in there. While J'Neer and Kanir were on either side of each door, Tox and I stood behind them watching their backs. Our other weapons had long ago ran out of power, now we had weapons confiscated from those we had killed. Every few seconds, a number of more men came from around the corner or from somewhere down the corridor. Tox and I continued to shoot them as J'Neer and Kanir kept working on getting into the pods, looking for D'Nar. As scary as it was to be in the middle of an ongoing battle, there was an odd sort of comfort in doing something toward getting rid of him. Even if he managed to get away from us, and we left this ship without eliminating him, it would be worth it just having done something toward that end.

"Stop, not that one!" Tox ordered the men. "It's set to explode upon being tampered with." She paused for about two seconds. "D'Nar's not in there. He's—"

I didn't know where to look first. A dozen men came from both directions at the same time that D'Nar came from a pod two doors down. More troops traveled in, appearing just feet from us. There were more weapons aimed at us than I could count. I didn't recognize most of them. We were so outnumbered, there was nothing to do. There was silence for a moment.

"Drop your weapons," D'Nar ordered. All of us placed them on the floor.

I looked around. Kanir stepped in front of me. I tried to push him aside, but he wouldn't budge.

Sure, like having my husband stand in front of me would make me invisible...

"So...where is the cause of all this chaos?" D'Nar asked.

I could hear footsteps coming closer to where I stood behind Kanir. He was forced aside by one of D'Nar's men. D'Nar stood looking at me. "You have no idea how much trouble you have caused me the last several days."

"Get used to it, D'Nar, because it's not over," I said. My hands were balled at my sides. I was sure I was shaking from anger and fear.

He slapped my face, knocking me into the wall. Kanir stepped in to attack D'Nar and was held back by several of D'Nar's men.

D'Nar looked Kanir up and down. "She doesn't need your help." D'Nar suddenly made the connection and almost smiled. "Ah, the husband. I heard that she was married off. This should increase my profits quite a bit."

Something over by where J'Neer stood caught my eye. His hand moved to the controls of the pod he and Kanir had been about to open. He pushed a button and moved out of the way almost imperceptivity. Two seconds later, the pod exploded outward. Most of D'Nar's men had been standing directly in front of or close to it. Bodies and parts flew everywhere. J'Neer was pushed toward where D'Nar was, knocking him to the ground. Kanir, Tox, J'Neer, and I grabbed up the weapons we had placed on the floor and began shooting. I turned my weapon on D'Nar. He was rising from the floor, looking at me.

He raised his weapon to fire on me as he raced away down a corridor. I followed him, shooting. It was hard to get an accurate shot off with the ship shuddering more frequently and with more strength. Neither one of us seemed to be able to run and shoot with any accuracy at the same time, which wasn't terribly unexpected.

Note to self: this would have to be included in some training later on.

I thought I heard Kanir behind me, but I wasn't sure.

D'Nar was getting close to turning a corner. I stopped, aimed, and shot. I got his shoulder, and he fell to the floor. I started to walk toward him as he got up and turned around to face me. His shoulder was ripped open, wires and metal exposed.

I was confused for a moment, trying to wrap my mind around what I was looking at. It took a few seconds to realize this wasn't D'Nar, but what? A copy, a clone, something else? I was stunned for a moment, not knowing what to do. I wasn't expecting to see a robotic copy of the man who had sent my life into an out-of-control tailspin. I shook my head, trying to clear it. I had to force myself to take a look at what was going on and what I had to do.

D'Nar had managed to hold onto his weapon and pulled it up to shoot. As he did so, the ship bucked again, sending us both to the floor.

"Jackie!" Kanir called.

I had fallen on my back, holding my weapon. I turned over on my stomach and looked up to see D'Nar already on his feet. His eyes were cold, flat, no life in them. There were occasional sparks coming from his shoulder, and I could see a dark liquid starting to spread around and down the front of his jacket. He yelled something at me that, if it had been true, would have brought shame to my family. I raised my weapon, took aim again, and shot him in the chest. The blast sent him back against the wall behind him, and he fell to the floor, lifeless. The equipment in his chest was now exposed. A few wisps of smoke rose from the wreckage that used to be this facsimile of D'Nar as sparks slowed and stopped.

I got up and went to where he lay. His eyes stared lifelessly ahead.

34

I LOOKED AROUND. The fighting had stopped. I looked at D'Nar again. Kanir stepped over to me and pulled me away.

"Jackie."

I heard Kanir but couldn't respond. The ship shook violently again, reminding us that we needed to get off this vessel quickly.

"Jackie."

"It's not him," I whispered, unable to take my eyes off the carnage that used to be D'Nar.

"You don't know that."

"This is a robot or android or something else. It's not a living thing."

"We don't have time to figure out what this is."

"I have to know!" I argued. "If this is just a copy, if this isn't D'Nar, the real D'Nar could still be after me. I can't leave like this."

"We have to leave, Jackie. This ship is going to explode within minutes."

"What?" It suddenly dawned on me what he was saying.

Somehow, the need to eliminate this enemy of mine had made the other looming disaster either disappear from my mind, or I just blanked on it in the heat of the moment.

Heck of a time to have a blond moment.

"We have to go now. Come on." He took my hand and led me back to where the others were.

Tox had taken out the last couple of bad guys as we came into the corridor of pods. I was pretty sure the only reason there were no others coming was because the ones left were trying to find a way off the ship.

That had to be our priority now too.

Tox had stayed close to J'Neer to protect him. He was crumpled on the floor, semiconscious, blood staining his side.

"Oh my God!" I said and ran to him. Kanir was right behind me.

"J'Neer," I said, crouching down next to where he lay.

"I'll be okay," he said, face contorted in pain. "I just caught some shrapnel in my side."

"We need to go," Tox said. She pulled J'Neer up then steadied him. "We can't use the pods. They still have orders to destroy them. I know where D'Nar's personal shuttle is. It's not far. I believe we can make it."

Kanir and I followed J'Neer and Tox as she supported him. J'Neer's face grew even more pale from being moved. Tox took us to a stairwell. We went down two flights, down a corridor, and into a hangar. A huge shuttle sat on the deck, gleaming silver in the room. Nobody was around. The ship shuddered again. We heard a loud explosion, followed by shaking that threw us to the deck. We got up and ran to the shuttle. Tox got it open, and we stumbled in as the ship continued to shake and heave.

Tox dropped J'Neer in a seat and went directly to the helm. She began punching orders into the instrument panel, and the bay doors at the end of the hangar slowly opened. We could see the other ship slowly making its way away from where we were. Our shuttle rose into the air and left the hangar. Kanir had joined Tox at the control panel and began trying to hail the departing ship.

Within a few minutes, we were outside the ship, following the departing vessel. Tox called back for us all to be strapped in. An instant later, the ship rocketed ahead at an alarming speed, quickly catching up to the huge ship ahead of us. Tox split the screen. On one half was the ship we were pursuing. The other half showed D'Nar's ship. Within seconds, the screen filled with light and fire for an instant before the whole explosion seemed to fall in on itself, as if being contracted in. A split second later, it went huge and dramatic as the explosion expanded beyond the limits of the screen, then slowly faded to nothing.

J'Neer grabbed my hand. "How are you doing, Empress?" he asked.

I did a double take. "What?"

"That ship ahead of us is your flagship. You are about to 'take your throne,' as I believe it is referred to."

I closed my eyes. I was supposed to have been taken there months ago. I had spent the last three days trying to get there. It was finally within reach, about to become reality. I was suddenly very nervous, almost afraid. Running from and then taking out D'Nar seemed easier, almost preferable to taking on this huge position.

And I was tired. Running from, then running after, D'Nar for the last few days seemed to have depleted all my energy. I had killed people. I had killed D'Nar—or at least a facsimile of the man. I had always known as a police officer that I might be called upon to take a life; it never occurred to me that I would have to take more than one. All in the same day. Under these circumstances.

I was so tired in so many ways, I was ready to sit down in a corner and cry.

"Are you all right?"

I paused. "I don't know."

I couldn't get D'Nar out of my mind. I didn't know if he was alive or dead. I didn't know if he was an android or a living being. I didn't know if I could let my guard down and not be concerned about where he might be, if he was still an issue in my life.

"It's been a rough week." One side of his mouth went up a fraction.

I closed my eyes for a moment, nodding.

So tired, so emotionally raw...

J'Neer listened as I told him about what happened when I shot and destroyed what I thought had been D'Nar.

"I can tell you for certain that the D'Nar I know is not an android. I treated him a couple of times for minor things."

I took a deep breath. I didn't want to dwell on this too much.

Kanir had come to where I was sitting with J'Neer. He took my hand and steered me to a bench at the side of the ship.

"You're having some problems handling what happened earlier."

I nodded. I could feel his concern. He felt helpless to do anything to get me past the events of the day. He kissed the top of my head. "That's why I didn't want you to have to participate in that."

"There was no other way."

Kanir nodded. Tears rolled down my cheeks. Kanir wiped them away gently then kissed my mouth.

"We'll get through this," he said.

"I know."

"What's the first thing you want to do when we get there?"

"Take a long shower, have a drink, something to eat, and take a nap."

Kanir nodded. "That would be reasonable."

"They are ready for us," Tox called. She had finished doing what she could for J'Neer and was at the helm again.

I wiped my eyes. Kanir kissed me again. I smiled at him.

Tox stood by the door, ready to open it. "This is your destiny," she said quietly.

"I don't understand how a girl from Earth could have her destiny clear across the galaxy."

"You don't have to understand it. You just have to accept it."

"And if I don't?"

She paused for a moment. "The alternative is not acceptable. You have no choice."

So tired, so raw, so conflicted…

Kanir and I lifted J'Neer between us and went to the door as Tox opened it. We stepped forward and looked out at two men standing on either side of the door, looking expectantly into the shuttle. There was about half a minute where we just looked at each other. I imagine the sight of us was not what they were expecting. We still wore the uniforms we had taken from the soldiers on the other ship. We were filthy. My hair looked like it hadn't seen a brush or comb in several…days, maybe. We probably didn't smell very good either.

We were definitely not the leader and her entourage they were expecting.

Some part of me hoped that would work in our favor. I could picture the conversation that would happen between these two men and their co-workers later on.

"I can't believe what we have in a new leader. You should have seen her. Them. Filthy. Smelly."

"Her entourage—really. That's what Dolm Corrett has gone out of his way to secure for our planet?"

Would that be enough to make them want to consider another victim for leadership of their planet?

Fat chance…

The taller of the two men cleared his throat and took a step forward, offering his help to relieve us of J'Neer. There were a number of other people close by. Obviously Kanir had called for medical assistance; a few people I figured were doctors and/or nurses helped get J'Neer off the shuttle and onto an air gurney. I was transfixed by the piece of equipment. They still were a fascination to me.

"Empress," somebody said quietly. I suddenly realized somebody had said that several times. It sounded so foreign to me.

"I…I'm sorry. I didn't mean to ignore you. I'm Jackie," I said and extended my hand to shake.

"We cannot allow such familiarity" was the reply.

Had I just been rebuked? Granted, I wasn't crazy about being their leader, but did this man just put leadership in its place? What was leadership's place anyway?

I looked at this man sideways and went to where J'Neer lay, about be carted off.

"Please let me know how he is."

"He will be taken care of immediately and should be able to leave here within the next day or two," said the doctor.

I looked at J'Neer. Kanir had come to my side and had his arm around my waist as I took J'Neer's hand.

"Please see me before you leave."

J'Neer hesitated, looking at Kanir and me. "Not a problem, Empress."

"Jackie," I corrected.

J'Neer shook his head. "Empress," he said firmly. There was no hint of a smile on his face.

35

"EMPRESS, I AM Yxaad Juum. I am your personal assistant," said the man waiting patiently for me to finish with J'Neer. And then he bowed to me.

I started to bow in return, but Kanir held my hand close to my side, keeping me from bending forward. I looked at him, and he did a very discreet shake of the head. I nodded. Leaders don't bow to their constituency. I got it. This leadership thing was going to be very interesting. Confusing.

"Pleased to meet you, Mr. Juum," I said. "Were you the personal assistant to the former empress?"

"No, Empress. That would be Dolm Corrett. He is back on Usia, acting as Emperor Pro Tem. Can I take you and"—he regarded Kanir for a moment—"your husband to your rooms? I imagine you would like a chance to freshen up and rest for a short time. And then I could show you around the ship."

I wasn't sure, but the "freshen up" part of his suggestion seemed to be very important to him. I knew it was to me.

I looked at my clothing. The confiscated outfit was torn and filthy, had blood on it from J'Neer, and I'm sure I smelled bad. Kanir was in much the same condition.

"Jackie," Tox appeared behind Juum, a guard at each side.

"Oh, Tox. Please make sure she gets a lot of attention. She will be staying here on this ship and accompanying us to Usia."

"Jackie, I can't stay there with you."

"Well, let their people get you the maintenance you need. We can supply you with a ship."

"Empress," Juum interrupted.

"Yes?"

"I don't think we can do—"

"This woman saved our lives more than once. Her shuttle was on D'Nar's ship when it was destroyed a short time ago. We will take very good care of her, Mr. Juum."

He bowed, understanding now. "Yes, Empress. I didn't realize who she was to you." He turned to Tox. "Forgive me, I will make sure you are well treated." He called over another person who took over taking care of Tox. I made it clear I wanted to see her before she left.

A few minutes later, Juum let us into a suite of rooms. We entered what was a living room. It was a good size with comfortable furnishings and colors. A doorway off the wall on the right led into the bedroom. Somebody came into the room carrying clean uniforms for us.

Juum took a few minutes to give us a brief tour of our quarters. We were shown how to get a hold of him and told we would both have communicators before long. Juum left saying he'd return at our request via the computer.

I sat down on the bed feeling exhausted. I had been pulled to a lot of limits in so many ways the last several days. I was almost numb from the running, killing, escaping.

I wanted a month-long vacation. I would start with a week at home, just relaxing and enjoying my home. Gardening, shopping, cooking—I might even get in some target practice, just for fun. A few movies, dinner with friends and family. And then I would take a cruise in the Bahamas. Allow myself to be pampered. Go home for another two weeks and get back to work.

If only…

Kanir sat on the bed next to me, put his arm around my waist. This was my life now. I couldn't believe I was accepting what someone else had suggested some time ago. There would be no dinners with friends or family. At least not the ones I had left back on Earth. No movies or cruises. My life now would consist of keeping the peace a planet that apparently didn't know how to get along without an outsider telling them how to do it. Almost seemed like a bit of sibling rivalry, if you sat and thought about it long enough, put things in that order. Rivalry on a pretty big scale actually.

And somehow incorporating God into everything I did to bring Him into the lives of the people on Usia, maybe even beyond that planet.

Kanir kissed the top of my head. Who was this stranger I was permanently attached to anyway? There was so much I didn't know about him. I could feel…sense his love for me. I knew his mind and his thinking better than I would ever know anyone else. And yet there was so much I didn't know about him.

"Jackie, we're all right now," he said quietly.

I nodded. "I'm going to get a shower," I said and got up. He grabbed my hand and pulled me into his lap for a kiss then looked into my eyes, holding me there for a long time.

"You're going to be all right," he said reassuringly. "Just give it time. So much has happened the last several days. You're raw inside from what we had to do. Talk to me. Talk to others you trust. You'll get past this. You're strong."

I nodded. I could feel tears pressing to come but held back. I didn't want to cry and be a mess. I wanted to be strong. I took a deep breath, held it for a moment, and let it out shakily, slowly.

"It's all right to cry, my love."

I nodded. "I'm going to get showered," I whispered hoarsely and went into the bathroom.

EPILOGUE

I WAS ON my way to Usia—at least for now. No telling what was going to happen between now and actually getting there.

I made sure Tox was taken care of appropriately. Juum was a bit concerned I was going above and beyond what was necessary, but that was my prerogative. I was willing to push the envelope here and make a few people uncomfortable to take care of those who had gotten me here. Lord knows, Tox deserved that and more, as far as I was concerned. So I made sure she got to leave with the vessel that we had taken from D'Nar's ship. We first made sure it was fit for travel and that any kind of technology and any kind of information stored on the computers was downloaded to our ship's computers. Tox was also treated to an android's equivalent of a day at the spa. She was completely overhauled, physically and technologically. This took about twenty-five years off her appearance, which I was sure could possibly make her very attractive to a number of the serve-droids on any ship.

I was going to leave that thought right where it was...

Before she left, Tox left me with a gizmo that, when placed in my hand, brought her to me in miniature to actually commiserate with her face-to-face. She also assured me she would come to assist if I was really in need of her help. I offered her our services in return, should she need us. It was a huge comfort knowing we would be there for each other.

J'Neer, who also had no ship, was outfitted with one from a neighboring planet, approved of by Kanir. Of course, J'Neer's approval of this vehicle was uppermost in my mind. I made sure our people outfitted it with whatever he needed. We laid in a generous amount of food and supplies. J'Neer, too, left me with the equivalent of the bat phone, something I could use to contact him at a moment's notice. He was not adverse to this at all.

I was going to miss them both tremendously.

D'Nar was still out there somewhere, under orders to find me and eliminate me. There was a handful of staff dedicated to finding him and removing him from the universe, but he, like so many people out here, had the means to disappear and stay hidden until he decided he was in a position to do something. Nobody had a clue yet about who he was working for, so until this was cleared up, Kanir and I were under constant protective surveillance. Not the way we wanted to live our lives, but there wasn't much choice.

So Tox and J'Neer left to do what they knew they had to do, as Kanir and I began our trip to Usia. I was naturally more than a bit concerned about what I was going to face once I got there, but it couldn't possibly be any worse than what I had gone through out here in space.

Yeah, right...

Seriously...